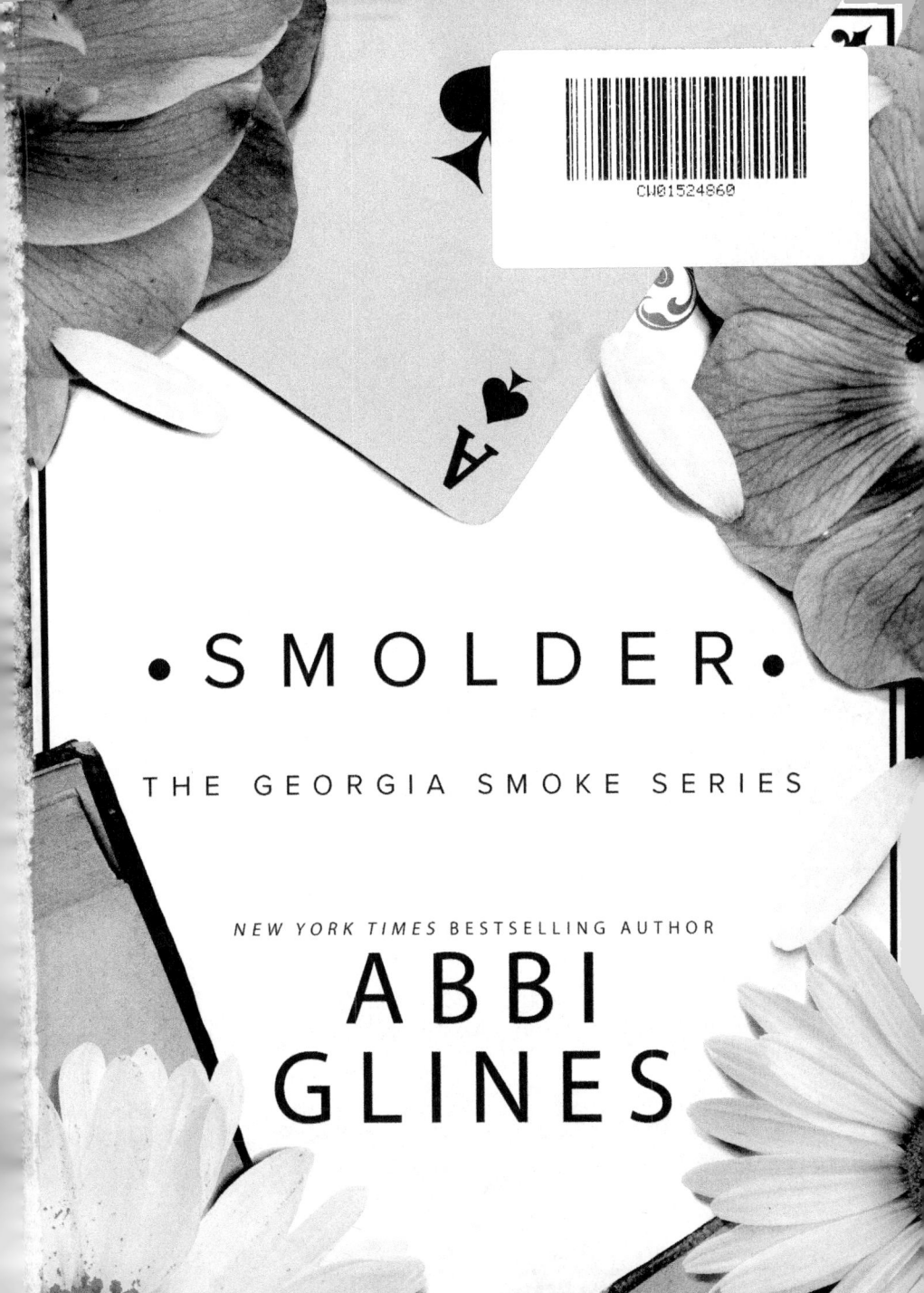

Smolder
The Georgia Smoke Series
Copyright © 2024 by Abbi Glines
All rights reserved.
Visit my website at https://abbiglinesbooks.com

Cover Designer: Sarah Sentz, Enchanting Romance Designs
Editor: Jovana Shirley, Unforeseen Editing
www.unforeseenediting.com
Formatting: Melissa Stevens, The Illustrated Author
www.theillustratedauthor.com

No part of this book may be reproduced or transmitted in any form or by any means, electronic or mechanical, including photocopying, recording, or by any information storage and retrieval system without the written permission of the author, except for the use of brief quotations in a book review.

This book is a work of fiction. Names, characters, places, and incidents either are products of the author's imagination or are used fictitiously. Any resemblance to actual persons, living or dead, events, or locales is entirely coincidental.

• THE FAMILY •

started by Jediah Hughes. It began with horse racing, moonshine, and illegal arms in the early 1900s

Jediah Hughes
├── **Eustis**
│   └── **Feldman**
│   └── **Tipper**
│   ├── **Garrett**
│   └── **Gregory** (died at three years old in a house fire)
└── **Elmer** (died from Typhoid at ten years old)

• THE HUGHES •
Hughes Farm

Garrett Hughes (BOSS in books 1-9)
Wife: **Fawn Parker Hughes** → *SCORCH*

Blaise Hughes (Current BOSS/oldest son)
Wife: **Madeline Walsh Hughes**
(parents Etta Marks/dead and Liam
Walsh/President of Judgment MC)

Cree Elias Hughes →
SMOKESHOW and
FIREBALL

Trev Hughes
Fiancée: **Gypsi Parker** (also stepsister) →
FIRECRACKER

• THE SHEPHARDS •
Oldest family inside the southern mafia other than the Hughes

Charles Livingston Shephard
Best friend of Jediah Hughes

- **Gerald**
- **Joseph** (became a priest)
- **Jeffrey** (died from Spanish influenza at fifteen years old)

Gerald's children:
- **Charles II**
- **Darwin** (died from gunshot at twenty-four)

Charles II's children:
- **Charles III** (drowned in childhood)
- **Joshua** (became a missionary)
- **Lincoln**

Lincoln's children:
- **Lincoln II (Linc)**
- **Stellan**

Mississippi Branch

Linc Shephard
(left Florida to run Mississippi Branch when **Levi** was twenty-two)

Florida Branch

Levi Shephard
Wife: **Aspen Chance Shephard** → *WHISKEY SMOKE*

Georgia Branch
Shephard Ranch

Stellan Shephard
Wife: **Mandilyn Shephard**

Thatcher
→ *DEMONS*

Sebastian
→ *SMOLDER*

• THE KINGSTONS •
Mars Kingston joined the family in 1921

Mars Kingston
Childhood friend of Jediah Hughes

Hollis

Son (died in childhood) — **Atticus** — **Son** (died in childhood)

Rollin — **Raul**

Creed — **Barrett**

Florida Branch

Creed Kingston (dead)
Wife: **Abigail Kingston** (dead)

Huck
Wife: **Trinity Bennett Kingston**
→ *SMOKE BOMB*

Hayes (dead)
engaged to **Trinity**
at his death

Georgia Branch

Barrett Kingston
Wife: **Annette Kingston**

Storm
→ *SIZZLING*
and *STORM*

Lela
Book coming in 2025

Nailyah
Book coming in 2025

• THE HOUSTONS •
Joined the family through horse racing in 1938

Kenneth Houston Wife: **Melanie Houston**
Moses Mile Ranch

|

Saxon Houston
Wife: **Haisley Slate Houston** →
SMOKIN' HOT

|

Winter Noel Houston

• THE LEVINES •
Joined the family in 1977

Alister Levine

|

Mississippi Branch

Luther Levine
Ex-Wife: **Chloe Wall**
(Moved from Florida when **Kye** was nineteen)

|

Florida Branch

Kye Levine
Wife: **Genesis Stoll Levine** → *BURN*

|

Jagger Henley Levine

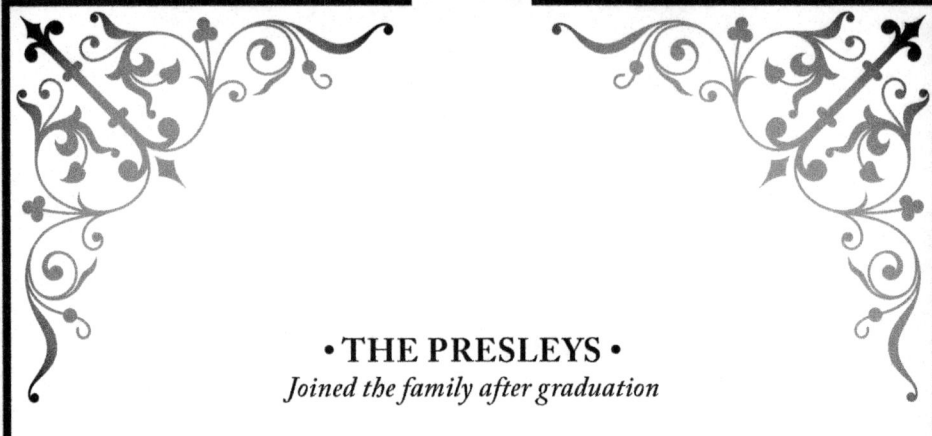

• THE PRESLEYS •
Joined the family after graduation

Gage Presley
Best friend of Blaise Hughes in high school
Wife: **Shiloh Carmichael Presley** → *STRAIGHT FIRE*

• THE SALAZARS •
Joined the family through horse racing in 1958

Georgia Branch only

Efrain Salazar

Gabriel Salazar (dead)
Wife: **Maeme Salazar**

Ronan Salazar
Wife: **Jupiter Salazar**

King Salazar
→ *SLAY* and *SLAY KING*

Birdie
w/Ex Wife: **Estela Salazar**

· THE JONES ·
Joined the family through joined real-estate in 1966

Georgia Branch only

Hoyt Jones

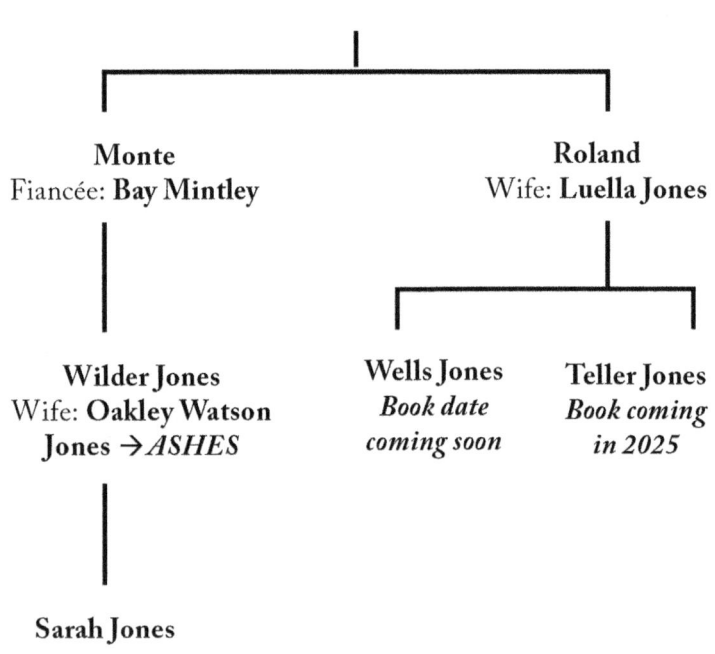

Monte
Fiancée: **Bay Mintley**

Roland
Wife: **Luella Jones**

Wilder Jones
Wife: **Oakley Watson Jones** →*ASHES*

Wells Jones
Book date coming soon

Teller Jones
Book coming in 2025

Sarah Jones

• THE RICES •

Oldest family in Mississippi Branch. Hiram Rice left Ocala in 1912 to move to Madison, Mississippi and run a speakeasies in Jackson and one on Madison both Jediah Hughes had purchased. Illegal gambling as well as moonshine was sold inside the bars.

Mississippi Branch

Hiram Rice

Whitmill   **Frances**

Junior

Hart

Gannon (former head of Mississippi Branch. His Parkinson's progressed until he had to step down 12 years ago. Linc Shepherd was moved there to become head over Mississippi Branch)
Wife: **Edy Rice**

Fia Rice Castron   **Saylor**
(married to a member
of Louisiana Branch)

• THE CARVERS •

Awbrey Carver joined the family in 1928 through bootlegging and running illegal gambling rings.

Mississippi Branch only

Awbrey Carver
|
Robert
|
Hale
Wife: **Lethia Carver** (dead)

Ransom Opal Than

• THE CASHES •
The Cash Ranch

Mississippi Branch only

Hawkins Cash
Joined the family in 1922 through horse racing

Samuel
(shot and killed at 20 years old)

William

Fender
Wife: **Grissele Cash**

Bane
→ *TORE UP*

Crosby
(dies in prologue of TORE UP)

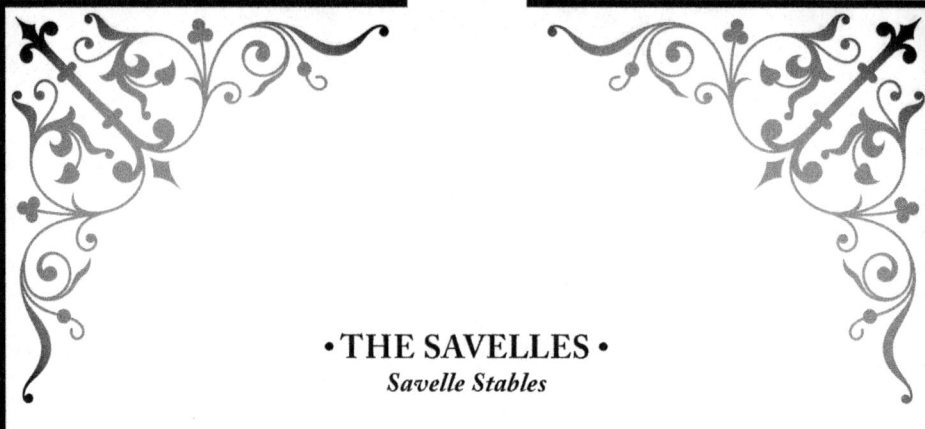

• THE SAVELLES •
Savelle Stables

Mississippi Branch
Oz Savelle
joined the Family in 1967 through horse racing

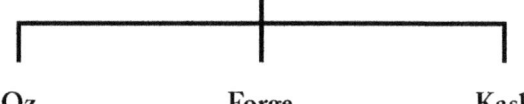

Jonas
Wife: **Ellender Savelle**

Oz   **Forge**   **Kash**

Alabama Branch
Kash Savelle
moved to Alabama Branch when he turned 21

• THE BOWENS •
Lewis Bowen joined the family in 1975

Mississippi Branch

Lewis Bowen
Oz Savelle's best friend since childhood

Malbrough 'Mal'
Ex-Wife: **Celeste**

Locke **Gathe**

• PLAYLIST •

Royals
Lorde

Blue Ain't Your Color
Keith Urban

You Say
Lauren Daigle

You're Beautiful
James Blunt

Stolen Dance
Milky Chance

Grenade
Bruno Mars

Body Like a Back Road
Sam Hunt

Set Fire to the Rain
Adele

Grace
Lewis Capaldi

I Wanna Be Yours
Arctic Monkeys

Best of You
Foo Fighters

Only You Can Love Me This Way
Keith Urban

· ACKNOWLEDGMENTS ·

To the people who suffered, stood in the gap, and worked magic to make this story happen:

Britt is always the first I mention because without him, our house might literally fall apart.

Emerson, for surviving without me. I would say she didn't complain, but that would be a lie. There is always a lot of standing at my office door and scowling at me.

My older children, who live in other states—They called and texted and were also ignored. I felt bad, but I replied, "Writing deadline. Will call when finished." And they didn't mind, but they also didn't stop calling and texting, so … anyway.

My editor, Jovana Shirley at Unforeseen Editing, who was understanding about me missing not just the first deadline, but the second one too. She worked with my tight schedule, and I would be screwed without her. She's a godsend. (This seems to be happening monthly, so I might as well copy and paste this into each Acknowledgments section.)

My formatter, Melissa Stevens at The Illustrated Author. Who has never let me down. She always does a speedy turnaround for me—monthly, I might add. She makes my books beautiful inside. Her work is the best formatting I've ever had in my books. I am always excited to see what she does with each one. Each book seems to be better than the last!

Autumn Gantz at Wordsmith Publicity, for saving me from losing my mind and taking over all the things that I can't keep up with anymore. Her help allows me to write quickly. She reminds me of the things I need to do. I don't think I would have been able to keep up with this one-book-a-month schedule without her.

Beta readers, who come through every time, Jerilyn Martinez and Vicci Kaighan—I love y'all!

Sarah Sentz, Enchanting Romance Designs, for my book cover. Again, she nailed it. I have no visual creativity to give her any help in the matter. But she manages to create something I adore every time.

Abbi's Army, for being my support and cheering me on. I love y'all!

My readers, for allowing me to write books. Without you, this wouldn't be possible.

•

*To every reader who counts down the days
to my monthly release.
If it wasn't for your enthusiasm,
I don't think I could keep this up!
Knowing y'all are out there is why I sit down
at the computer every day.*

•

• ONE •

"I'm the reason you have food to eat and a roof over your head."

ROYAL

The brand-new box of cereal I had bought yesterday sat open on the kitchen counter, along with two unused glasses, a jar of peanut butter, and the carton of milk that had been left on the stove. The bright side was, Grams hadn't turned on the stove. Rubbing my face with both hands, I groaned. I shouldn't have slept past six. Never a good idea. Not with Grams on the loose.

"You woke up hungry, I see," I called out, then covered my yawn as I walked over to get the milk and tuck it back into the refrigerator before it went bad. Thankfully, it was still cold.

The sound of her shuffling feet coming from the living room to the kitchen was a relief. At least she hadn't gotten out of the house. The new child locks on the doorknobs were working. I added water to the coffeepot. I needed caffeine. This was my only day during the week that my first class didn't start until ten. Sleeping until seven had been my plan this semester, but if Grams was gonna start fixing her breakfast, that wasn't going to be an option. Six o'clock it would have to be.

"There's a man on the sofa," she whispered loudly behind me.

I closed my eyes and sighed, then scooped the coffee grounds into the machine before turning back to look at my eighty-two-year-old grandmother. It was going to be one of those days. The days where she didn't remember who her son—my dad—was. Sometimes, I wished I could forget him too.

"It's okay, Grams," I assured her. "That's just Dad. He's your son, Vin, remember?"

She frowned and glanced back while straightening her shoulders and lifting her chin. "That is not my son. Vinson is a fine boy. That man in there," she said, pointing her arthritis-gnarled finger toward the door, "he stinks of liquor."

Yeah, Grams, he's always stunk of liquor.

Most nights, I managed to get him to the back bedroom so she wouldn't see him in the morning. Last night, he'd been too difficult, so I'd left him in the living room before he decided to take a swing at me.

"He was at Miller's Bar last night, Grams," I told her, not feeling like sugarcoating it today.

I had to get to class, and I couldn't do that if she was living in the past. Although I doubted my dad had ever been a fine boy.

"He drank until he got mean and started a fight," I continued. "Glenn called me to come get him."

The smell of the brewing coffee filled the small kitchen, and I inhaled deeply. I loved that smell. It reminded me of the past. The life I'd had growing up here when Grams's head was still clear.

"Hmph," she said, crossing her arms over her chest. "He did no such thing."

I motioned to the cereal. "What did you fix yourself to eat?" Might as well change the subject. Arguing with her was pointless. She'd forget about him in there soon enough.

She frowned at the mess she'd left behind. "I don't know."

I reached for a coffee cup and filled it to the top. "I'll get Dad up and have him go take a shower. Why don't you have a seat at the table? I'll fix you a nice cup of coffee and make you some toast just how you like it." Which was too much butter on a slice of almost-burned bread.

I didn't wait to see if she would do as told before heading toward the living room. The house was small, and I could easily hear her slippers as they slid across the linoleum floor toward the table.

The living room was a scattered mess. I had cleaned it up last night before I went to bed. Grams seemed to have been into many activities this morning. Including throwing things at Dad. There were several items surrounding him that didn't belong. Smirking, I hoped the spoon she'd tossed at him struck his head and left a lump.

I stared at my dad. One of his arms hung off the side of the faded sofa that had once been a flower-printed velvet. It was patched up with duct tape in several places now and still held the stench of cigarettes from when my dad used to smoke in the house.

A low snore came from his open mouth, and drool dribbled out the side onto the pillow he'd found to sleep on last night. I started toward him and glanced over to see a bowl full of oat cereal with no milk beside Grams's plastic covered green recliner that sat in the corner of the room. I hoped she hadn't done anything gross to the cereal. That was too much to waste. I'd just bought groceries yesterday.

I bent down to grab my father's arm and shake him.

"Wake up," I said firmly. "I have coffee."

He grumbled, then opened his eyes in a squint. "Why you waking me up so early?"

I continued to pull on his arm. "Because Grams thinks a drunken stranger is on our sofa, I have to get to class, and you need a shower. Now, drink."

He sat up and held out his hand for the cup. I gave it to him and made sure that he had it before letting go. I might want to slap him most of the time, but I didn't want to cause a third-degree burn. He wasn't the best dad—or even a good human really—but he was mine.

"What time is it?" he asked, then took a sip, wincing as it hit his tongue.

"Ten after seven. I'll get Grams something to eat, and then I have to go get dressed and leave. And I'm taking the Bug," I told him, already knowing he was going to bitch about that.

"Why can't Anya pick you up? I need the car," he immediately said.

"Because Anya doesn't go to college, Dad. You know this. And she's been at work for an hour already."

Anya was my best friend and had been my entire life. Her family lived two houses down, and although it was the same size as ours, her dad took pride in their home. The paint on it wasn't peeling, there wasn't plastic sheeting over any of their windows, and the front porch didn't have holes in it from rotten wood.

"You don't go to college either," he shot back at me with a scowl. "Going on like you do is a waste of time. Maybe if'n you got a job, then you could buy yer own car. Stop wasting time sitting in classes for nothing."

"I don't need a car. I have my Vespa," I informed him.

I'd bought it with my own hard-earned money two years ago. I loved my candy-apple-red wheels, but lately, it'd kept breaking down on me. Like now. It was back in the shop.

"No, ya don't. That piece of shit ain't here now, is it?"

I rolled my eyes. "I'm doing you a favor. If you get caught behind the wheel again, you're gonna be back behind bars. Suspended license means no driving," I replied, then spun around to go back to the kitchen. I'd left Grams alone long enough.

"You don't tell me what I can and can't do!" he shouted.

"I'd be easy on me, old man," I called back to him. "I'm the reason you have food to eat and a roof over your head."

I heard his muttered cursing and smirked. He didn't have a comeback for that one. Grams's monthly check from the government was spent at Miller's Bar, thanks to him. I'd given up on him getting and holding down a job years ago. I had learned early to be resourceful.

Grams was sitting at the table, staring out the window, with her hands in her lap. She had a lost expression on her face. It was never easy to see her like that.

I remembered her singing hymns in this kitchen while she cooked meals with the fresh vegetables from her garden. She was the only mother I had. The woman who had given birth to me split when I was six months old. Grams was the one steady, dependable parent I'd had—until her mind started going my senior year in high school. It was little things back then, but by the time I was nineteen, she'd forgotten how to cook or garden.

"Ready for that coffee?" I asked her.

She turned and looked at me. A sad smile touched her wrinkled face. "I suppose."

I took down her favorite mug and filled it. She didn't take sugar or cream in hers either. Her eyes followed me as I took it over and placed it in front of her.

"A strong cup of joe to get you going," I said brightly.

She patted my arm. "You're a good girl, Royal. Don't let him bring you down. You're better than him. You're better than both of 'em."

Seems her memory had been jogged, and she was remembering who Dad was again. I should be relieved, but with the memory came the disappointment.

I bent down and kissed her cheek. "I learned from the queen," I teased her. "You taught me everything I know."

A small chuckle came from her, and it eased the tightness in my chest.

"Now, don't be giving me the credit for all that you do," she said, patting me again. "I'm thankful for it. Good Lord knows, without you, I don't know where I'd be, but that savvy you got, it ain't from me."

I smiled, straightening back up. "Well, it ain't from Dad. It had to have come from somewhere."

I never mentioned the woman who'd given me life. None of us did.

"You pay my tab last night?" Dad asked.

I turned to see him standing inside the kitchen with his rumpled clothing, hair sticking up, scratching his beard. He had been forty when I was born. I'd seen pictures of him back then, and he'd still been handsome. Not so much anymore.

The life he lived had been a rough one. He had never married my mom, but he'd been married before her. Grams used to swear he was a good man back then. His wife had died young from a bad case of the flu. She'd had a weak lung already, and they hadn't caught it in time. They'd only been married two years when she died. Grams had said Dad wasn't good for much after losing her.

My mother had come along years later. He met her at a bar one night, and they got drunk, then had unprotected sex. She was significantly younger than him.

There was one photo of her in this house. Grams had kept it. She used to say I might want it one day. But I didn't, and I never would. It had been years since I'd looked at that photo, but it seemed the image of her smiling at the camera, holding me, was burned into my brain. I had her eyes, her mouth, and her hair color.

She hadn't wanted to live with an old man, Grams explained, but she tried for me. Dad wasn't easy to deal with. She hadn't put up with him for very long, but it was probably best she'd left when she did. That way, I had no memories of her and no attachment.

"Yeah," I told him. "Why don't you stay home tonight? I'll bring back dinner."

He looked at his mother, then back at me. "I'll go if and when I want to."

Which was every night.

"Fine. When I get a call to come get you, I'll ignore it. You can sleep on the floor of the bar—or behind bars. AND pay your own tab."

He scowled at me. "I thought you had to go to a fucking class. Why are you still here, jabbering on?"

"Good point," I replied, then looked down at Grams, who was staring out the window again. "I'll see you this evening. Maybe I can get some more of that chicken and dumplings you love, along with the collards and mac and cheese."

She nodded, but said nothing. Dad often put her in this mood. Maybe I should have just let her live in her memories this morning. The present upset her too much.

"I'll go get ready. Make her some toast since you're up and have nothing else to do," I said as I walked past him, heading toward the bedroom I shared with Grams.

"Thought you was gonna do that?" he barked at me, annoyed.

"I gotta get to class, remember?" I replied with a grin.

It was almost eight, and I needed to make a couple of stops before my Modern Literature class. Essays were due today, and Professor Brereton was too sharp. I didn't drop off any assignments on campus. Not with his class at least.

Opening the closet, I took down the box I kept on the top shelf. Keeping things out of Grams's reach was something I'd found was a necessity. She would move things around and misplace them. I took the lid off the box and counted out the three essays inside. Two of them would pull a solid A while one would be a mid B. I respected a guy who understood his limits. The B paper was smart. Professor Brereton would never believe Drace, a party focused frat guy, had written one of the A papers.

I closed the box and shoved it back up on the shelf, covering it with a pair of my folded jeans, then put the papers in my bag before getting dressed. I was enjoying this class. More than the others I was attending this quarter. Since I wasn't actually enrolled at Howison College, this was the next best thing. I got to do the essays and make money. I didn't always enjoy the classes or the papers that I had to write for others. But most of the time, I was thankful for the education.

The rich kids, whose parents could afford to send them to the private college, were more interested in Greek life, parties, social events. They didn't care for the actual work that went along with passing their courses. Lucky for them, there was me. I made sure America's future politicians, lawyers, CEOs and socialites at Howison graduated on schedule. It wasn't like the government and economy could get any worse.

• TWO •

"I even added a tip for such an entertaining performance.

SEBASTIAN

I picked up the beer the bartender had set in front of me without taking my eyes off the pool table. It was too damn entertaining.

I'd been annoyed that my dad had sent me here with King and Storm to handle something so simple. I was positive he could have sent my brother to do this alone. The fucker we were coming to collect from wasn't a big enough threat for all three of us.

But the complete stunner, who I was positive was hustling the two men she was playing a game of pool with, had me transfixed. I mean, I got how they'd be distracted by her looks, but, damn, they had to also be a touch stupid. She was really fucking good at this—I'd give her that. Batting her dark lashes and gazing at them with those ice-blue eyes, rimmed with slate outer rings, was powerful. My damn dick was affected way over here.

It could also be the pouty lips, which weren't painted, the color natural with a slight shimmer of gloss. My gaze kept zoning in on them—when I wasn't appreciating her above-average presentation. Seemed I must be the only one in here who was paying attention to this.

"You stare any harder, and you're gonna mess up her game," Storm drawled beside me.

I tore my eyes off her briefly to look at him. He was drinking from his glass of whiskey with a smirk on his face.

"You see it too then?" I asked him.

He shifted his eyes to me. "What? See the blonde who's taking those two morons to the cleaners? Yeah, I see it."

My gaze swung back to her as she bit her bottom lip and laughed. Fuck, that was a nice sound. There was a sultry lilt to it that made a man want to get closer and soak it up.

"She's about to turn it," Storm said with a low chuckle. "Briar would fucking love to watch this."

Briar was his fiancée, and if any woman respected a hustle, she did.

"OH!" the bigger of the two men said when she sank the ball.

Her eyes went wide and appeared to twinkle with excitement. Someone needed to get this girl an Oscar.

"You two done here? Because I want to get home to my girls," King said as his hand gripped my shoulder. His girls being his wife, Rumor, and their daughter, Cosette.

"Waiting on the fucker to show. I want to get home, too, but he's not here," Storm replied.

"You misunderstood what we're here for, but y'all are too busy watching the hot little blonde work that table like it's her job," King whispered.

Storm tensed. "I'm not fucking interested in her," he snarled, looking ready to rip King's head off for insinuating otherwise.

When it came to Storm and his fiancée, he was slightly insane. Just five minutes ago, he'd had his phone out, watching her at their house on one of his cameras.

"I didn't say you were," King replied with a roll of his eyes. "As psycho as you are with Briar, you don't have time for more than one pussy. I was just pointing out where your attention was. Let's get this done," he said, then slapped my back.

Not wanting to be distracted, I glanced one more time to see the blonde throw her hands in the air and squeal after she sank another ball. I really wished I had time to watch this finish. She'd lost two hundred dollars to them already, acting like she sucked. But the triple or nothing she'd suggested had her winning that back with four hundred more.

"Dancastle isn't meeting us here?" I asked, realizing what King had just said about misunderstanding why we were here.

"Nope. Stellan wanted us to handle it gently. Dancastle is a well-loved senator. If this can be done without force, it's less messy. We saw what we needed. We can go."

Storm shot him an annoyed glare and stood up. It wasn't like King to keep things from us. My dad normally outlined the details of a job, but he'd said King would fill us in. What was it we had seen?

I slapped a hundred on the bar and nodded at the bartender before Storm and I followed King to the exit. I was gonna miss the ending of the sexy little swindler's performance. Her victory cheer just before we reached the door had me grinning as we stepped outside. I wasn't as hotheaded as Storm. King might have left out shit, but he'd tell us eventually. Just wished we could have stayed in there longer. They might not appreciate the sexy-as-hell blonde, but I sure did.

My focus immediately snapped from the blonde inside to the man standing only a few feet from us.

"I told Stellan I'd have him the money next week!" Nathan Byars blurted.

He appeared frantic, and I hadn't known he owed us any money, but if he did, he needed to be more than frantic. He owned a dozen dry cleaners and also smuggled some illegal drugs. When he got tight and needed a little to get him to his next payoff, he came to us. Guessed his loan was due.

But what did this have to do with Dancastle?

King sighed heavily. "Well, you see, Nate dog, the thing is, you don't get to give us a date when you'll repay your loan. That's given to you the moment the transaction goes down, and that due date was yesterday."

The redheaded man backed up closer to his new navy-blue Ford F150. "I need some payments to go through. That's all," he stammered.

It was obvious he thought he could get into his truck before we reached him. The sound of the doors unlocking from the key fob in his hand was a careless move. If Thatcher were here, Nathan would already be on the ground bleeding out. My brother had no patience.

"Seems you had enough money for that new, shiny truck," Storm drawled before pulling out his Glock and pointing it at the idiot's head. Not that he'd kill him. At least until we had what he owed us.

He paused a moment before reaching for the door handle on his truck.

The silenced shots from Storm's gun took out his front and back left tires.

"Come on now. Did you really think you'd be able to get away that easy?" he asked.

"Might want to think real hard about where you can get that money," King suggested.

• SMOLDER •

Nathan had gone pale now that he knew he wasn't going to be able to get away on flat tires. "Listen, one of my dealers had a bad run-in. Lost some product. He's getting it back. I just need a couple more days."

King glanced at me. "Hear that, Sebastian? He just needs a couple more days. Reckon he can run and hide from your brother?"

Threatening anyone with Thatcher got the point across.

"He'd be the first," I replied. "Crazy son of a bitch. Doubt Nathan here wants to involve Thatch."

Even if Nathan hadn't looked back over my shoulder, giving himself away, I'd have known we had company. I'd heard them already. Storm didn't look at me, but there was the tiniest nod of his head that told me he also knew there was someone behind us.

Sliding my gun out of its holster as I turned to face whoever had been dumb enough to interfere, I heard the click of Storm's gun and Nathan's pained cry. He'd shot some part of Nathan's body.

The two idiots who I'd watched the blonde swindle had joined us. This was Nathan's backup? Seriously? Could he not have gotten better men?

The larger one's eyes widened as he looked at whatever Storm had just done behind me, but the other one pointed his gun in my direction. I didn't wait to see what he planned on doing since he wasn't very bright. I put a bullet in his forearm, causing his gun to fall to the ground as his knees buckled from the pain.

His friend went down almost at the same time from King shooting the man's right thigh.

"It didn't have to get messy. Look what you made us do," King drawled with a shake of his head. "Damn. Who's gonna drive the three of you? And now, there is all this blood."

• 13 •

"I'll get it!" Nathan cried out. "Tell Stellan I will have it by the end of the week. Just need a couple of days."

I smirked, glancing at the man as he leaned back on his truck, holding his wrist as blood dripped from it onto the pavement. "Thatcher will come for it next. I suggest you have it ready."

"I will," he said, wincing through the pain. "I swear."

The man that King had shot glared at all of us, then began to limp toward Nathan. I turned my attention to the other man. It wasn't my business, but I had to make sure.

"Did you pay the blonde inside what you owed her?" I asked.

He narrowed his gaze at me. "I didn't owe that little bitch shit. She was playing us. I just wanted to fuck her."

That pissed me off. Again, not my business, but she'd worked hard for that money. I'd sure been entertained.

"I'll give you about sixty seconds to go back inside and pay her the six hundred you owe her, plus an extra hundred for a game well played," I told him, aiming the gun at his thigh this time. "Or I'll give you a limp to match your buddy's."

He glared at me. "What the fuck?!"

Storm's low chuckle only seemed to make the man angrier.

"Just do it!" Nathan barked at him.

"I'd go pay the girl. Sebastian is real big on chivalry. He won't let this go," Storm said with amusement.

The guy cursed and held up his arm. "You want me to go inside, bleeding from a gunshot?"

"He's got a point," Storm said. "No need to cause us any more annoyance. Just get the money off him and deliver it yourself."

I stuck my gun back in the holster at my waist as I closed the distance between me and the bastard who was going to walk out without paying up. His eyes followed me warily as I approached him.

Bending down, I picked up his gun, then tossed it to Storm. "Now, you want to tell me which pocket, or do you want me feeling you up?"

The man clenched his teeth as he inhaled through his nose. It was a grimace that was somewhere between pain and anger. Both were battling for first place, it seemed.

"Front right."

I reached inside as he tensed up even more and pulled out his wallet. Opening it, I saw his license. Calvin Cebourn Edwards.

"Damn, your parents hated you, Calvin Cebourn," I mused, then counted out eight hundred-dollar bills instead of seven since he had a wad of cash. Might as well tip the girl proper for an excellent performance.

I dropped the wallet to the ground in front of him, right on top of a pool of his blood. "You understand if I don't stick my hand back in your jeans," I said, then headed toward the door of the pool hall.

The lit-up sign above the door read *RAILHOUSE*, but the *E* was blinking on and off. Someone needed to fix that.

Shoving the door open, I entered the building and scanned the place until I saw the blonde talking to the bartender. She laughed at something he'd said, and I wished I were close enough to hear it. I was almost to her when those unique eyes locked on me. She studied me, unsure if I was headed for her or not.

The bartender said something to her, and she blinked, then glanced at him before turning her attention back to me. The tip of her pink tongue came out to do a quick lick of her lips. I wouldn't mind tasting them myself. It was a shame I had business to handle tonight.

I laid the money down on the bar in front of her. "This is yours," I told her.

She frowned, looking at it. "What?"

I nodded my head toward the pool table she'd used earlier. "The men you so beautifully hustled—they left without paying you."

She still didn't touch the money, and her arms crossed over her chest as she stared at me, looking offended. It was cute as fuck.

"I didn't hustle anyone. And I'm not taking your money."

I wanted to laugh, but I didn't because I wanted her to like me more. "It's not my money. Like I said, it's from the dicks you played and beat."

Her gaze dropped to the money, and she took a deep breath before looking at me. "How did you get it if it's theirs? Do you know them?"

I shrugged. "Not exactly. But I swear I took the bills directly from the smaller one's wallet. I even added a tip for such an entertaining performance."

Her body tensed, as if my pointing out it was a performance insulted her. This one was feisty. She looked like a fucking angel, but she was swindling men for cash. I respected it. Hell, who wouldn't? It was hot.

"Why are you the one bringing it to me?" she asked, still not picking it up.

"Because it's yours and the other men are"—I paused—"indisposed at the moment."

Her eyes widened and cut toward the bartender, who was watching me as he poured someone a beer. She was young. Not illegal young, but possibly too young for me. Which meant she was sure as hell too young for him. He was several years older than me.

"Do I want to know what you mean by that?" she asked, uncrossing her arms and finally picking up the money.

I smirked. "Probably not."

She counted it, then lifted her eyes to mine. "That's two hundred too much." She held out two bills to me.

I shook my head. "No, Ace," I said. "That's the tip."

Then, I turned and headed for the door. I'd already been gone too long. No need to draw out something with a girl I couldn't have—at least tonight.

King's eyes were on me the moment I stepped back outside. The other men had gone, and all that was left of them was their blood on the pavement.

"Storm went to handle the security camera footage," King said, then cut his eyes back toward the bar. "You give the girl her money?" he asked.

I nodded, not sure what to make of his tense expression.

He took a deep breath. "Well, I guess that settles who is gonna be the one to get close to her."

My gut tightened. I didn't like what I'd just heard him say. "What do you mean?"

"She's why we're here. Nathan's men showing up and alerting him was just a bonus. We had been going to see him next. Saved us a trip." King patted my shoulder, then squeezed. "Sorry. I could tell you were into her, but if it makes you feel better about this, she's already taken. Dating Dancastle's son. And I doubt hustling folks at pool is all she does. She is who Stellan wants us to use to find out what Dancastle has his hands in. We already know he's using Nathan, but we need to know how big and deep it gets. The blonde is our easiest way in."

To think, I'd already decided to come back and see her when I wasn't working. Damn, I was real bad at picking out females. Not only was this one taken, but she was also in on some fucking dangerous shit.

I glanced back at the door. "You sure that's her? Hard to believe a senator's son is dating a girl who hustles men at a pool hall."

King nodded. "From what all Stellan had Wilder pull on her, she's not someone Dancastle approves of for his son. But he's going through a rebellious stage, it seems. Could be he's found a way to use her in the underground trafficking and infiltrating drugs nto the colleges around here. If it's the laced shit that was causing hallucinations and cannibalism that we shut the Miltos down for, then it's only a matter of time before the Feds step in. Keeping them in our pocket is vital. We have to stop this before it goes any further."

"Well, damn. This took a turn I hadn't seen coming," Storm drawled as he returned from clearing the footage off the security cameras.

"That's why I had to come then? Dad sent me instead of Thatcher because I'm single. You know Wells is too. Why didn't he send Wells instead of Storm?" I asked, annoyed.

They hadn't told me before I got a look at her and thought for a moment that she might be worth getting to know.

"Wells? Come on, Sebastian. You think Stellan would trust Wells with this?" King asked.

I knew this wasn't a request, and I had no option out.

"You're the best Romeo we got now that King is off the market," Storm replied with amusement.

I glared at him, then stalked past them both toward the parking lot before the jokes started up. I wasn't in the mood. If they'd told me the plan first, then I wouldn't have been attracted to her, and the disappointment that she was dirty wouldn't be an annoying sting in my chest.

THREE

I always started out having bad luck, and once they got drunk enough, my luck always turned.

ROYAL

Opening the faded burgundy canvas carrier bag that I'd bought at a consignment shop last year, I pulled out two papers on religion and its influence on Colonial America as Petra approached me. Her silky, long, dark brown hair swung back and forth from the high ponytail she had it in, and her brown eyes glinted with mischief.

I'd met Petra through her boyfriend, Spence. They were your typical Greek life students, but even if I didn't do their papers for them, I'd like them.

"God, you are a lifesaver," she said when she reached me. "I completely forgot we had this stupid essay."

I handed her both papers. "Not a problem. I already had Spence's finished when you texted. It didn't take much time to get yours done. You are focusing heavily on the family values of the religion, and Spence pushed the political side of it in his."

She groaned. "Ugh, I hate this class. Who gives a shit about Colonial America?"

I did. I found it interesting, but I decided to keep that to myself.

"Here," she said, sliding the money into my hand.

"Thanks."

She put the papers into her Louis Vuitton backpack, then glanced up at me. "Are you going to the Alpha Epsilon Tau party tomorrow night?"

Yes, but not the way she thought I was.

"Milo mentioned it," I told her.

Milo was my *in* with the Epi Taus and a couple of other fraternities on this campus and the university in town. He handled the planning of the card games, and then I showed up to play. I'd met him the summer after I graduated high school. He'd come into Railhouse, and I'd won some money off him at a game of pool. But instead of being mad about it, he was impressed.

Then, he asked me how good I was at Texas Hold'em.

When I told him I wasn't too bad, he laughed and invited me to a game. Not a friendly one or a legal one. An underground one that they had on campus, even during the summer, in the basement of the Alpha Epsilon Tau house. That night, he watched me take everyone's money.

Since then, he'd been setting up the games, in which he also played for twenty percent of my winnings. The more the rich frat boys drank, the sloppier they got, making it even easier. I always started out having bad luck, and once they got drunk enough, my luck always turned.

"Merce mentioned you last night," she said, watching me warily, as if the mention of Merce Dancastle's name was going to send me into a spiral.

"That's a shame," I replied, putting my bag strap back on my shoulder. "I'd have thought he had better things to talk about."

Petra grinned. "I want to be you when I grow up."

No, she did not. She'd never survive without her daddy's money.

"You should strive for higher goals," I replied, causing her to laugh.

"That right there—you're a complete badass who happens to be gorgeous. You don't need anyone. I think it's why he loves you," she said, then paused. "He does, you know … love you."

Merce had proven he did not love me more than once. But I again said nothing.

"I gotta get to Social Theory," I told her, glad my building was behind me and I could escape this conversation.

"See you tomorrow night then?" she asked as I started to walk away.

For a few minutes possibly, but I never actually stayed upstairs at the party. I was only ever there for the game.

"Yeah," I called out with a wave.

The one thing I dreaded about tomorrow was seeing Merce. I hadn't seen him since he'd broken it off with me two weeks ago. With the gambling ring starting back up, I'd be forced to run into him, possibly play a game or more with him.

Merce was the president of Alpha Epsilon Tau. Just like his brother and father before him.

The Dancastles were a powerful political family. His father's upcoming reelection campaign was why he'd broken up with me. I wasn't the kind of girl he needed attached to his name. His father had told him to end it with me, so he did.

During the eight months that we had dated, I'd never been to his house or met his parents. He kept me completely separate from them.

It hadn't really dawned on me that he had kept me a secret until I saw a picture of him and Opal Dalton, the governor of

South Carolina's daughter, at a benefit gala in DC this past weekend on the Campus Happenings website and socials. The speculation that the two were dating was an actual article. It wasn't as if I wanted to be photographed and have my love life shared with the world, but I realized that he had never intended for us to be more. Why he had pursued me so hard for more than a year before I gave in and went on that first date with him was beyond me.

He hadn't hurt me, not really. It stung my pride. But that was about it. I hadn't been in love with Merce. We just had fun. Then, he'd ended it. Which was for the best.

It was hard to have a relationship and survive my life. I had to stay focused.

This semester, I was taking more classes than allowed—for a student who was actually enrolled. But the more classes I attended, the more essays and papers I could write. I needed the money.

Tad, one of the football players I had met last semester in one of my classes, waved me down before I reached the door to the building. I stayed put while he jogged over to me. We had one class together this semester—History of Ideas.

"Hey, Royal," he called as he slowed to a stop. "I lost your number. Got a new phone over the summer. My old one was sacrificed in the ocean—long story, but beer was involved," he said with a grin.

"Sounds tragic," I replied.

He chuckled. "Yeah, kinda was. I've been looking for you. By the time class was over, you were gone, and I need help."

"The philosophy distribution of ideas paper," I said, already knowing that was what he was going to say.

He nodded. "Yes. I have no fucking idea what Page is talking about. She scares me, looking out of those glasses with that disapproving scrunch of her nose."

Professor Page was one of the best at the college. She had been teaching here for over thirty years. I was pretty sure she was aware I wasn't a student here, but she never said anything.

"It's gonna be two fifty. That's not an easy assignment, and it takes a good deal of research," I told him.

He nodded. "Sure, yeah, anything. If you don't do it for me, I'll fail, and I need this scholarship."

He was here because he was talented at catching a ball and running. Nothing more. I liked him and all, but I did wonder what his GPA had been in high school. There seemed to be little knowledge swirling around in that head of his.

"It's due in two weeks. I'll have it to you two days before," I assured him.

"You're the best," he said, then opened the door for me. "See you later," he added as I walked inside.

In response, I lifted a hand in a wave and hurried to get to my next class.

• FOUR •

"I just don't have time in my life for a stalker."

SEBASTIAN

The details that Wilder had pulled up on Crown "Royal" Shelton were limited. It took me a few minutes to get over the fact that she was named after a Canadian whiskey—and a fucking awful one at that—to realize how lacking her background information was. Typically, Wilder had every detail of a person's life after he did his research. He'd said that was all he could find right away, but he was still digging. She didn't even have bank accounts in her name. Her high school transcripts were impressive though, and she'd been offered several scholarships to colleges in other states, but she hadn't taken any of them.

Her home address was in the information, so that was where I started. It wasn't much to look at—that was for damn sure. The place was falling apart.

When she walked out of the front door, I was relieved. I'd wondered if Wilder had gotten it wrong.

Merce Dancastle attended many of the same functions I was forced to go to with my father. He always had some elite socialite on his arm. Most of those females had fathers in politics, like him. This girl checked none of those boxes.

She climbed on the back of a red Vespa, and momentarily, I caught myself questioning her safety, then remembered I wasn't here to protect her. I stayed far enough behind so that I wasn't noticed, although I didn't think she was paying any attention to who was following her. I did ease in, narrowing the distance, making sure other cars didn't get too close, when some fucker in a sports car almost ran her off the road. Hell, I couldn't help it. That electric scooter thing didn't look safe enough to have out on the main roads like she was doing.

Why was the Dancastle douchebag letting her drive that?

I'd question why she didn't have a car, but from the looks of her house, I assumed she couldn't afford it. Another thing Dancastle Junior could have given her easily.

When she turned onto the Howison College campus, I was surprised. There were no records about her attending any college, much less an elite private one. This was an expensive college. The Vespa was out of place with the luxury vehicles packing the parking lots.

I hadn't gone over all Merce's information like I should have. Maybe this was where he attended.

When she parked, I did the same but several rows over from her. She seemed oblivious to anything else happening around her. Someone should talk to her about paying attention to her surroundings. I began trailing her as she made her way toward a science building.

Instead of going inside, she stopped by a large oak tree and leaned back against it before digging into the worn crossbody bag she was wearing. I tried not to focus too much on the way the strap pushed her tits up, revealing a distracting cleavage. I wasn't here to lust, even if her ass looked fantastic in those jeans.

A guy slowed down close to her, and she pulled out some papers, then held them out for him. He snatched them quickly to tuck into his backpack. The grin on his face as he spoke to her was annoying. His gaze dropped to her tits as he reached out his hand toward her again. The money that he tried to slyly slide into her palm before pulling his hand away and tucking it into his front pocket made this even more interesting.

Had he just paid her for the papers she'd handed him? There wasn't any other reason for the transaction.

Puzzled, I tried to move in closer.

Two more guys stopped by after that one left, and the exact same process played out. She handed over papers, and they slipped her cash. I couldn't see what was on those papers, but we were on a college campus, which led me to believe that she was either selling them answers to tests or doing their actual assignments.

It seemed pool wasn't her only hustle. She could very easily be writing their papers or essays. I'd seen her high school GPA, which had gotten her full-ride offers to several universities.

When the last guy walked away, she started back to the sidewalk and headed down to another building. I stayed where I was until she slowed and turned. Keeping my eyes on her, I followed until I saw her go inside a history building.

What was she doing in there? She didn't go to school here. I was positive she wasn't enrolled. That wasn't something that Wilder would have missed. I assumed she was just here to hand out papers and get paid.

I waited several minutes, and she didn't emerge, so I debated on going inside to check on her. I had been planning on following her to the pool hall to "run into" her again.

Was she going into classes? Possibly sitting in on them? But why would she go sit in a class she got no credit for? Just to write papers for others? That seemed like a living hell. There were better ways to make money. From what I knew of her, it seemed more likely that she was hacking into the system and getting test answers to sell.

Before I reached the door, I decided going inside was too risky. I didn't want her to know I was stalking her. That would mess things up. Instead, I went over to find a spot to sit in the shade, keeping me partially hidden from view.

> Double-check that Royal isn't enrolled at Howison College.

I sent the text to Wilder. He'd probably be insulted that I was questioning, him but I had to know.

> She's not. But give me a minute, and I'll break into their system and check the records.

He was never wrong. And I knew that, but if she was going into college classes, then, well, it was gonna fucking change the way I was trying to look at her. I'd tried to focus on her being several things. A con artist, a liar, drug dealer, but not someone who wanted to learn even if they didn't get credit for it. That required something more, and I didn't want her to have it. Not if she was going to let me down in the end.

> She is not in their enrollment, but the boyfriend is. I've already given you that information though. If she's on campus, it's to see him. You need to stay on that. See what they are doing.

No shit. That was why I was here. But he was right, I had to go inside.

> I am.

Sticking my phone back in my pocket, I headed for the entrance to the history building. If she was in there with Merce, then it would make sense. I had been letting my hidden hopes that she wasn't what we thought she was start to take over. Maybe Dad should have sent Wells. I clearly couldn't look past her looks to keep focused on her actions.

The inside of the old building smelled like pine and lemon. I looked around, and the halls were empty, but there were several closed doors. This was just the first floor. I was going to have to check every fucking room until I found her. I should have followed her inside. Luckily, most doors had a window to see inside. I started with those.

When I reached the end of the hall, I hadn't found Royal, but I did find a lecture hall. There were hundreds of people inside, and it went up to the second floor with an entry up there as well. I stepped back and headed for the stairs I'd passed earlier. She'd been in the building for almost thirty minutes at this point, and I knew I had at least forty-five minutes left before classes started to let go. The second floor was similar to the first, but had fewer doors with viewing windows.

I slowly opened the door to the lecture hall and slipped inside, staying against the back wall to scan the place without being noticed. It didn't take me long to spot the familiar blonde head, as she sat near the back on the opposite side, writing in a notebook with a serious expression as the professor continued to speak.

Every few minutes, she'd pause and glance up, appearing to be entranced by whatever the man was saying about Colonial America before going back to her note-taking. She looked like a student. One who was diligently trying to get all the information she could. There was no sign of Merce. She wasn't sitting near any guy at all for that matter.

Taking a seat where I had a direct view of her, I decided to stay and watch.

One hour and thirty minutes later, she walked out of the door closest to her. She didn't speak to anyone, nor did she notice the heads that turned to watch her when she passed. I followed her to the mass communications building, and I let a few people go in behind her before I, too, went inside. She was entering a class when I spotted her, and I decided to stay back and wait out here this time. I paid close attention to everyone else who also went inside the room, but none of them were Merce. Once the hallway emptied out, I headed back outside and found a less obvious location so that I could watch the door.

> Dancastle has a Political Theory class in two hours.

I read the text Wilder had sent and figured that was what I would wait for. See if she went to him then.

One hour and twenty-three minutes later, she walked out, talking to a girl on her left with glasses and short brown hair. They seemed to be discussing something from class, and Royal talked with her hands animatedly. I wished like fuck I could hear what she was saying. There was no sign of Merce, and if he was on campus for his upcoming class, he hadn't come here, looking to find her.

The brunette waved and walked away as Royal started in the direction of the parking lot. Moving to her far left, I placed a row of cars between us so that I'd reach mine by the time she got to her Vespa. Her lack of awareness continued to bother me. She didn't even glance my way when I pulled out onto the street behind her. Since she was dating Merce, she needed to fucking pay attention to her surroundings. Especially if his father was messed up with what Stellan believed he was.

When she parked outside the library, I figured this was going to take some time. Once she was inside, I headed in close behind her. The smell of books hit me the moment the doors closed, and I was going to have to fight off the urge to go explore. I loved that smell almost as much as I loved a good book.

Some other time.

Scanning the area, I found her talking to a redhead, who pulled out several books from behind the counter and slid them over to her. They talked quietly, and then Royal grinned before going around the counter and following the girl to the back. That was off-limits, except for those with a pass. I knew I could get by anyway, but again, too risky.

I glanced down the row of fiction books before taking a seat to wait.

In the three hours that I sat there, four different females approached me. One was bold enough to ask me if I wanted to go to her dorm room.

Wilder sent more info he'd found on Royal. Her mother had skipped out when she was six months old.

Jill Brinkley Clifton now lived in Little Rock, Arkansas, with her husband, Eli, and ten-year-old son, Alvie. She'd had three husbands before she married Eli, it seemed, but only the two kids. They lived in a two-story brick house in a middle-class subdivision with a chocolate Lab. From the photos, it was a hell of an upgrade from the shithole Royal lived in.

I didn't get much further into the rest of her mother's life when Royal reappeared with books, which she gave back to the redhead, then tucked a stack of papers in her bag before heading for the exit. When I got up to follow, my eyes met the redhead's. She smiled nervously, then ducked her head as she blushed. At least she wasn't paying attention to the fact that I was following Royal.

Instead of heading toward her house, Royal went in the direction of the downtown area. Several cars got too close to her, and again, I felt a protective urge to run each of them off the fucking road. Definitely not where my reaction needed to be. Not with this one.

The taken females seemed to be my unlucky lot in life. Except, in the past, they had just been emotionally taken. This one wasn't just physically claimed, but she was a mark. Someone I was supposed to use for information. Liking her wasn't an option.

She pulled into a narrow space between two buildings, disappearing from my view.

I was able to park my car close by and get out to go see if she had stopped in the alley or used it as a shortcut. When I saw her red Vespa parked, I was relieved I hadn't lost her. She was standing outside a door, and I looked back at the building I was in front of and realized it was a diner—Rise and Dine. One of those buffet ones that did mostly breakfast and lunch.

I went back to watching her as the door opened, and a blonde with chin-length hair stepped out, glancing back behind her before handing a large plastic bag to Royal.

She took it, and the blonde shooed her away and then said something to make Royal smile before closing the door.

What the fuck was in the bag? It wasn't carryout.

This was the first sign all day that she was mixed up with drug trafficking. A sour burn rose in my throat.

Royal went back to the Vespa with the bag, and I started for my car in hopes that she pulled back out this way and not through some other exit. I glanced at Rise and Dine to see it'd closed almost two hours ago.

Dammit, Royal, just when I started to think you just might be innocent in all this shit.

I climbed into my Porsche as the Vespa shot out and took off in the opposite direction.

Turning around, I sped up until I could see her again. After her second turn, I knew she was headed back to her house. I had hoped she'd head to the pool hall so I could stop stalking her and have an opening to talk to her. Get this ball rolling now that I'd caught her picking up something questionable in an alleyway.

I pulled over and parked several houses away. I watched as she carried the bag inside the house. Sitting here seemed pointless, and I couldn't keep coming back to follow her around all the time until she went somewhere that I could casually approach her.

I'd just about talked myself into leaving when her door opened back up, and she came walking outside.

Here we go.

Was she going to Merce now?

She'd taken the bag inside though, and she wasn't carrying anything with her. She didn't move in the direction of her Vespa. She was walking out to the road.

No. She was headed for me.

Well, fuck.

I hadn't been expecting that, and I wasn't sure if this was an issue or not. Her hips swayed slightly as she made her way directly for my car. The jeans she'd had on were replaced for some short cutoff sweatpants that showed a whole lotta legs. Long, smooth, tanned …

I had to snap out of it. Time to lay on the charm.

I rolled down my window as she got close and waited.

She stopped and bent down, then looked me in the eye. "You," she said as recognition lit her expression.

"Me," I replied, leaning back and realizing I was enjoying this, even when I knew I shouldn't.

I'd been sloppy, it seemed. When had I ever been sloppy? I tracked people regularly and had never been caught. But this girl had noticed me. If Storm found out, he'd laugh at me for months. No, make that *years*.

"What is it? What do you want? Who are you? And why the hell are you following me?" She tilted her head to the side as the silky strands fell over her right shoulder. "Are you a cop? Is that it? Because what you saw at Railhouse was just a onetime thing. They were asking for it."

I was gonna laugh. She thought I was a cop. God, this was priceless.

"Maybe, but I'd say doing others assignments or giving answers to tests for money would be frowned upon by Howison," I drawled, unable to help myself.

I still wasn't sure how I was going to spin this to work in my favor. I figured I would throw her off first.

The flicker of panic in her eyes made me wish I hadn't said that.

"You have no proof," she said defensively. "And I have never given anyone answers to a test. I wouldn't even know where to get that."

There was no guilty quiver in her voice, only fear and determination.

"Actually, I would have proof easy enough it if I wanted it. But for your sake, probably best you handle your transactions off campus."

She blinked, and her confused look made me grin. I couldn't keep a straight face.

"I'm not a cop," I told her. "I can't believe you think I look like I could even be a cop."

Her shoulders eased, and she ran her gaze over my car. "Well, I wasn't sure. I don't think a Porsche like this one would be on a cop's salary, but then if you were undercover, it would fit in at Howison." Her eyes snapped back to me. "Then, you're just what, stalking me?"

I was in fact stalking her, but not for the reasons she believed. Letting her think I was a psycho with an attraction to her would probably work against me, but it was better than the truth.

"Not exactly," I replied. "I was curious."

She narrowed her eyes at me again. "About what?"

"You."

She took a moment to study me.

"Listen," she started. "I need to get back inside and make sure my Grams eats her dinner instead of hiding it or trying to wash her dish in the washing machine. I came out here because you have been tailing me since the library, and I wanted a reason why. So, either tell me what it is you want or leave me alone."

"The washing machine?" I asked, still working my head around that comment.

She nodded. "Food and all. Do you have any idea how hard it is to get collard greens and niblet corn out of a washing machine?"

I shook my head. Was everything that came out of her mouth supposed to be so damn fascinating?

She laughed. "Of course you don't. Do you even know how to work a washing machine? No! Never mind. I don't care. I just don't have time in my life for a stalker. Even one who looks like you and drives a car like this."

I raised my eyebrows as her high cheekbones pinkened slightly.

"Who looks like me?" I asked, entirely too pleased by that comment.

She rolled her eyes and crossed her arms over her chest. "You know what you look like."

I mean, yeah, but I wanted her to tell me what she thought I looked like. Maybe that was all I needed. I'd found females did stupid things when they were attracted to a man.

"Not necessarily," I drawled.

Her pouty lips pursed as she looked down at me. "What do you want with me?"

I wanted to fuck her. At least, that was all I'd wanted when I saw her at the pool hall. But now, shit had gone south, and that wasn't happening. Even though I still wanted to fuck her.

"Do you have plans tomorrow night?" I asked.

She opened her mouth, then closed it. Was that really that surprising to her? Guys flirted with her all fucking day. I'd watched it. Their eyes followed her when she walked by.

"Yes," she clipped.

"You gonna swindle some more men out of their money over a game of pool?" I asked.

She shook her head. "No."

She probably has plans with Merce, I thought sourly.

Although she hadn't mentioned the fact that she had a boyfriend. She was either protecting him or planning on using him to get rid of me.

"You can't change your plans?" I asked.

She bit her bottom lip like she might be considering it, then shook her head. "I can't."

Yep. She had plans with Merce. Well, I'd have to follow them and be more discreet. Not sure I actually wanted to witness them together, but it was why I was here.

"All right then," I said with a nod. "I hope you have a good night, Royal."

She frowned. "You know my name?"

I shrugged. "I did follow you all day."

Her nose scrunched up. "I thought you started at the library."

"Nope. Started right here at eight a.m."

She sucked in a breath. "How did you know where I lived?"

"Google," I lied.

"And my name?"

"Chatty waitress at the pool hall."

She sighed with an annoyed grimace. "Bet I can guess who that was."

Telling her my name would tip off Dancastle. He'd question why a Shephard was suddenly in Athens and sniffing around his girlfriend. I couldn't have that. The less she knew, the more I'd get out of her.

I held out my hand through the car window. "Amory Blaine," I told her, using a name from one of my favorite novels.

She looked down at my hand, then slowly slid her hand in mine to shake it. There was a slight crinkle between her brows as she lifted her eyes back to mine. "Amory Blaine—was it your mother or father who chose to name you after the protagonist in *This Side of Paradise*? Or was one of them just a fan of Fitzgerald?"

Damn. I wanted to smile. She was well read. She remembered what she'd read, which meant she'd enjoyed it.

"My father," I lied.

The right corner of her mouth tugged up. "Last name was Blaine, so he chose Amory to go with it. Or Amory Blaine is your first and middle and you're leaving out your surname on purpose?"

I was leaving out a lot on purpose. "Surname in Blaine. My dad wanted to name me Amory because of it."

When she dropped her hand from mine, I pointed toward her house, which was in desperate need of a good power wash, paint job, and new windows—at least three that I could see from here.

"I'll let you get back to dinner," I told her before she could ask me any more about myself.

She was smart, and I was going to have to be smarter. Starting with getting my attraction to her under control. I liked beautiful women, but I fucking loved intelligent ones who were well read. In order to keep from getting distracted by this girl, I was going to need someone else to keep me sated sexually.

She nodded, but said nothing as she watched me closely. Too perceptive. I winked as I rolled up my window.

She stepped back and then turned to walk toward her house, only glancing back once when she reached the yard. I lifted my hand in a wave, then pulled out onto the road and drove away. Leaving her behind and forcing my thoughts elsewhere.

It was time I asked out the Dolvin Cosmetics heiress my mother had kept pushing me to do. Just because Hattie Dolvin was a wealthy socialite that did some modeling didn't make her shallow. I needed to give her a chance. This seemed like the perfect time.

• FIVE •

"I mean, you said it all. I heard it. Life moved on."

ROYAL

So far, I'd been lucky. Not one sighting of Merce while I'd been upstairs, showing face at the Alpha Epsilon Tau party.

Milo had rescued me from a nosy Omega Theta—I believed her name was Becky, but I wasn't sure. She'd been panting after Merce for over a year, and the word that he had broken up with me seemed to make her giddy.

I sighed in relief as we reached the basement to the frat house. The noise from upstairs had faded, and the only thing other than the damp smell of the room was the round poker table and bar set up beside it, stocked with expensive bourbon, gin, and cognac.

Cody, Witt, and Julian were already down here with their drinks sitting at the table. Cody had his signature cigar in his mouth, but he'd yet to light it. He always waited until the first hand was played. Some superstition of his. I didn't always win these games. If I did, then they'd figure out the hustle. The nights I let them win, Milo covered the loss for me by giving me the money to play.

Tonight was not one of those nights.

I was here to take them all to the cleaners.

"Might as well start out the new school year with a bang," Milo had told me.

Witt raised his eyebrows when he saw me. "Royal, didn't expect to see you here tonight. Seeing as how things went down with you and Merce," he said.

Cody shoved him. "Fuck, man," he scowled. "That's harsh."

Witt shrugged. "What? We were all thinking it."

"I wasn't," Julian said, then winked at me. "I was hoping our little card shark would still come around. Makes game night a hell of a lot more fun."

Cody snorted. "You say that now, but when she's walking out with your five grand, you're gonna be cursing her and every relative she's ever had."

Julian glared at him. "Shut up and light the damn cigar. You look like a moron with it hanging out of your mouth like that."

This was typical. All of it.

"I missed y'all too," I chirped with a bright grin.

Two hands landed on my shoulders and squeezed. "You came. That's my girl,"

I recognized the voice. It was Landon McGill. His father was a big-time CEO of a large appliance company.

"Heard you were free of Merce," he said, entirely too close to my ear. "I'm claiming my turn now. Before you take my money."

Milo grabbed my arm. "All right, Landon, take your overused, diseased penis over there. She's not here to mess around with another one of you fuckers. She's here to play."

I moved closer to Milo as Landon walked down the last stair and gave me a smirk. Landon was beautiful in a pirate sort of way. There was a Jack Sparrow look about him. But Milo was right; Landon was also popular with the ladies and had been known to sleep with several a night—often at the same time. When you played cards with the guys, you learned all about their sex lives.

"She's out of your league, Baset," Landon told Milo as he walked toward the bar.

"She's out of all your leagues." Merce's voice caused me to tense.

Taking a quick glance at the stairs, I found Merce standing there, his eyes locked on me. There was a pleading in them that seemed ridiculous, considering the situation. It wasn't as if I'd broken up with him. He was the one who had ended things. I gave him a tight smile, then turned my attention back to the table of very nosy males.

"Who else are we waiting on?" I asked.

Witt's eyes shifted from Merce to me. "Just Topher. The others have pussy lined up."

"I brought that bubbly lemonade you like," Milo told me. "Want a bottle?"

I nodded. I'd never had carbonated lemonade until I started coming here to parties. The first time I tried it, I fell in love. The girls used it for a mixer, apparently, for their vodka. It'd become my go-to drink on game nights since I wasn't drinking alcohol. My dad had made the idea of drinking unpleasant for me. I rarely touched it, and I'd never been tipsy.

"Thanks," I told him when he handed me the cold bottle from the mini fridge at the bar.

"Royal."

Merce's voice made me tense again.

Why was he down here? He sucked at cards.

If I ignored him, it would seem as if I cared. That he'd hurt me. I didn't want him or any of the others thinking that was the case. Turning, I looked at him, but said nothing. If he wanted to clear the air or whatever, fine. Get it over with.

"Can we talk?" he asked.

His green eyes that I'd once been affected by no longer held any power over me.

"Not really any time for that, Merce," I replied.

His eyes cut to the table, then back to me. "I just want to talk," he said. "It won't take long."

Why? We had talked. It was done. Nothing more to say.

"Eh, I can't think of anything we need to say. I mean, you said it all. I heard it. Life moved on." I glanced over at the others, who were watching us like a live-action movie. "Don't y'all agree?"

Landon was grinning with an amused twinkle in his eyes as he leaned back in his chair. He held up his glass of bourbon. "Cheers to that, mate," he said.

"Gotta say, I agree with her, man," Julian added with a knowing look in my direction.

Cody held up his hands. "Not touching this one. His bedroom is across from mine. I have to see him more than the rest of you fuckers."

"What did I miss?" Topher asked, and all eyes swung to him as he descended the stairs into the basement.

His dark red hair and Scottish accent made him popular around campus. He just needed a kilt.

"Just agreeing that it's time to play," I told him, walking past Merce to go take a seat at the table.

"Like hell you were," he replied. "I missed the drama, didn't I? Dammit."

"No drama," Milo told him.

"Royal, please," Merce said behind me as if we were the only ones in the room.

"See!" Topher exclaimed. "I knew it! I missed it!"

"Shut up," Cody drawled.

I turned back around to see Merce still standing where I'd left him, his eyes on me. If I had loved him, this would be hard. I'd feel something. But there wasn't anything stirring in my chest.

"Like I said, it's all been said," I told him, then gave a nod to Milo to let him know I was ready to get this thing started.

• SIX •

Come on, Ace. You know you want to.

SEBASTIAN

Hattie Dolvin was currently in Paris on a photo shoot for her father's cosmetic line. She was returning next week and had invited me to a new release party for one of her father's products. The same one she was modeling for now. It had been entirely too easy. We'd flirted some at different events we both attended, but never anything more. It seemed one call from me was all she'd been waiting on.

I finished the drink in front of me and set it down just as the bartender returned. Royal hadn't lied to me about having plans tonight. She wasn't at the pool hall. Hattie had taken a hell of a lot less work to hook than Royal. I wasn't going to be able to tail her again. She'd be looking next time. I needed a plan, and right now, I hadn't come up with shit.

"Another one?" the bartender asked.

He was the one who had been talking to Royal last weekend. I could tell he remembered me.

"The blonde last weekend, the one hustling the guys at pool," I began.

His expression tightened, and he said nothing as he continued to pour my whiskey.

"She come here often?"

He set my drink down in front of me. "Lots of blondes come through here. I talk to them all."

I smirked. "You know who I'm talking about. The pool hustler."

He glanced around, and then his eyes came back to mine. "No hustling happens here."

Liar. He knew goddamn well that she had hustled those men. He was protecting her. That damn face and body made men do stupid things.

"I'm not here to cause trouble. I'm just curious. That's all."

He placed both his hands on the bar, and his jaw stood out as if he was clenching his teeth. I was pissing him off.

"I'm Rodney McVeagh. I own the place. Like I said, lots of blondes come through here. Whoever that girl was last week—"

"Royal." I supplied her name, and he appeared pained that I knew it.

Not a very good bullshitter, Rodney.

"You know her name," he said, then inhaled deeply and released it. "Look, Royal is a good girl. She's got a lot on her, and she handles it better than most men I know. She don't need, uh, someone, uh, like you coming around her."

Ouch. What the fuck had I done to Rodney?

"Someone like me being what exactly, Rodney?" I asked, then took a drink from my glass, curious as to what had made the man dislike me.

His eyes darted around again. He was uneasy. "You know …" he said.

It didn't really matter what Rodney thought about me. Not really. I just wanted him to give me some idea of when

Royal might be walking back in those doors. I figured I could convince him I was safe.

"I come from a family that breeds and races thoroughbred horses. On Sunday, we eat brunch at my grandmother's house with the rest of the family. It's a big, tight-knit Southern bunch. I was raised to work in the family business. I love horses and racing.

"I'm just curious about Royal. She intrigues me. I'd like to get to know her."

I'd laid it on thick. Taken the truth and made it sound pretty.

His brows drew together. "That might be the case, but Royal, she's worth protecting. She's already messed around with one like you. Wealthy, elitist, someone who has no idea what she's been through or the life she's been forced to live. My fiancée would slit my throat if I didn't try and keep Royal safe from any more pain. Her little sister is Royal's best friend. They grew up together. She's watched Royal struggle her entire life. Your kind will never understand or respect her the way she deserves."

His fierce expression as he spoke about her made me want to believe him. But the darkness of the world was often wrapped up in a pretty package to deceive. Being blinded by beauty was a mistake I couldn't afford.

"Okay," I said. "I can respect that. But you still don't know me."

He shifted his feet, and his Adam's apple bobbed as he swallowed. "No, I don't. Just like I don't know where the bloodstains in my parking lot came from. And I should, but my security cameras seemed to have missed that."

I frowned. "Security cameras?"

Storm had missed something. That wasn't like him. What had this man seen? Fuck, I hated to take him out, but if he was an eyewitness or had any footage, I'd have to make sure he never talked. We were too close to Dancastle's trail for that.

He nodded. "Yeah. The security cameras I have outside. They should have shown me where that blood came from that night. The night you and your friends were here. They don't though. One second, the pavement is normal, and the next, there are small pools of blood in several places. Weird, huh?"

Smarter than he looked. That was Storm's mistake. He'd underestimated the man.

I shrugged. "You can't tell me you've not had blood in your parking lot before."

He shifted again. "Yeah, but the other times, I had footage of who had caused it." Rodney sighed and gave me a wary look. "I don't want no trouble here. And if it were anyone other than Royal, I might answer your questions just to make sure you don't cause an issue. But she ain't got no one looking out for her. That sorry-ass father of hers …" He paused and clenched his teeth. "She's …" He paused again, then muttered a curse as his eyes locked on something behind me.

I glanced back to see who it was that had him so tensed up, and relief came the moment I laid eyes on her. Royal was walking in this direction—until her gaze met mine. She stopped, and her shoulders rose and fell as she looked at me.

Come on, Ace. You know you want to. It's right there in those pretty eyes.

When she started walking again, I could feel it. I was gonna get an in tonight. She didn't like to show weakness, although according to Rodney, she'd had a rough life. That would toughen someone up. I was going to find out exactly what she'd been through or if she was full of shit and Rodney just believed her stories. The man clearly didn't know about her current boyfriend being a senator's son. Seemed she only told him what she wanted him to know.

"Didn't expect to see you here," she said, placing a hand on her hip and giving me a pointed look.

I turned completely around and faced her. "I didn't expect to see you here either. Thought you had plans that didn't involve hustling men at pool."

The corner of her mouth twitched. "I did. I had plans hustling a bunch of frat boys at Texas Hold'em. Unfortunately for them, they drank too much, so it was over much faster than anticipated."

I let out a surprised laugh. "You're serious."

She nodded. "Very," she replied, then walked over and pulled out the stool beside me. "Now, tell me, Amory Blaine, why are you here?"

Rodney cleared his throat, and she swung her gaze toward him.

A soft smile touched her face. "It's fine. Down, boy. I can handle myself. You know that."

"I just thought you might want to, uh, play some pool. Those two are passing through. Heard 'em talking. They are stopping here to see a friend at the University, then headed further north."

She leaned over to see around me toward the pool tables. "The younger ones, dressed like they walked out of a Ralph Lauren store?"

"That'd be them," Rodney said.

She straightened back up and looked at me. "I googled you. Nothing. No social media. Not one small thing. That's odd," she said, narrowing her eyes. "What do you want with me?"

Straightforward. Damn, that was sexy. Hell, she'd be sexy, even without all the other shit. But that sassy mouth and no-nonsense approach were refreshing. I'd never experienced it before. At least not with a smoking-hot female. I wasn't going to let that affect me though. Hattie was also gorgeous, and she wasn't hiding shit.

This one was dangerous in ways that Merce couldn't be. He knew it, and she was his weapon. That had to be it.

"I didn't plan on it," I replied. "Typically, when a woman tells me no, I don't come back." Which was the truth, but with her, I had no choice.

She laughed then. "You got a lot of experience with women telling you no? I'm calling bullshit on that. I would even wager I'm the first one. Which is probably why you're here. I'm an anomaly. Or is it the chase? You never had one you had to chase, and it's exciting."

Dammit, she'd be fun. Why did she have to be an illusion?

"I can't say I like the idea of a chase. But you have my attention, and I find myself unable to stop thinking about you. If you did something to turn me off, then perhaps I'd go away. Instead, you're just making it worse."

Thankfully, new customers came up to the bar, and Rodney had to leave us to go get their drinks. I wanted to talk to her without his presence hovering. I had to get her interested in me, but as of right now, she seemed to be the only one who was charming anyone.

"If you knew me, you'd realize you're wasting your time. My kinda different isn't something a guy like you would want in his life. Trust me. I've dated the rich guy with a powerful family, and he dropped me the moment his dad told him to." She reached over and picked up my glass, then took a drink.

"You saw my house. I'm not one of you. My dad is a drunk, who I have to pick up from Miller's Bar almost every night and get him home. I don't know my mother, and my Grams, who was my only real parent, is slowly going batshit. Still interested?" she asked with sarcastic smile.

I took my glass from her hand and took a drink from the exact spot where her mouth had been, then licked the taste of her berry-flavored gloss that had transferred to my lips. Her gaze dropped to my mouth, and for a moment, she didn't breathe.

She was lying to me, and I was still getting hard. Damn her.

"How old was he?" I asked her.

How far was she going to play this game?

She blinked, and her eyes shot back up to meet mine. "Who?" The one word came out breathy.

Finally, she was distracted. I'd gotten to her, if only a little. Or perhaps that was part of her act.

"The pansy-ass whose daddy told him what to do."

She let out a deep breath, and her shoulders slumped. "Twenty-one."

I smirked. "That's the problem. You were dating a boy. I'm a man."

She let out a nervous laugh. "I can see that."

I reached out and brushed the pad of my thumb over her cheek. "How old are you?" I asked even though I already fucking knew not only her age, but also that her birthday was in four weeks and she'd be turning twenty-one.

"Twenty-one—well, I will be in a few weeks," she replied.

She was honest about some things. Good to know. I wasn't dealing with a habitual liar. Just one who covered up what she had to.

"What about you, old man?" she quipped. "How old are you?"

"Twenty-nine," I replied dropping my hand back to the bar.

"Damn, ready for a walker soon." Her eyes twinkled as she said it.

Keep that up, Ace, and I might fuck you to get you out of my system.

She glanced over my shoulder and then back at me. "I didn't come here to drink and flirt with old men," she told me. "Might as well go see if those two want to play a round."

I hadn't been able to watch her finish the last game, but then I'd not known what and who she was. I did now. Studying her and learning her tells would be good leverage.

"By all means. I'll enjoy the entertainment."

She rolled her eyes with a curl of her lips as she stood up.

I had her interest. Next step was to gain her trust. I didn't see why fucking her couldn't play a part in that. Might as well enjoy something about all this.

SEVEN

"Working as in hustling frat boys at cards?"

ROYAL

> Is Royal a nickname?

I was smiling at the stupid phone in my hand. I shouldn't have agreed to exchange numbers with Amory Blaine. Sure, he was older than Merce, but he drove a Porsche and wore designer jeans. I wouldn't ever fit into his life. This was a game to him. I just couldn't figure out why he was playing it.

> Nope. It's my name.

As if anyone would nickname me that. Nothing in my life was royal.

The clanging of pots in the kitchen had me jumping up from the sofa, where I had been reading a book for one of my classes.

"What are you doing in there, Grams?" I called as I headed to the kitchen.

"Oh, just making a chicken potpie. You know how much my Vinson loves that. Thought he might want something nice and warm when he gets home from work."

I opened my mouth to tell her that my father hadn't worked in years, but I stopped myself. She was living in the past again, and maybe that was just easier for her.

The text that lit up my screen asked:

> First name or middle?

I had long since stopped getting embarrassed by the name my mother had given me. It was part of my story.

I looked back at Grams as she pulled out the Crock-Pot that had been behind the pots.

"We don't have the ingredients for chicken potpie right now. Why don't I go run and get us something to eat?" I told her, walking over to take her arm and help her straighten back up before she fell.

"I was sure I'd gone grocery shopping just yesterday," she replied with a frown.

Grams hadn't been grocery shopping since my senior year of high school. I did the shopping and tried not to spend money on meals for dinner. That was an expense I couldn't add to the others weighing on me. Having connections at a few places where I could get their leftover food at closing time helped keep hot meals on the table. Otherwise, we'd be eating grilled cheese and canned tomato soup every night.

"You were planning on it, but never made it," I lied, leading her back to the living room. "*Wheel of Fortune* is about to come on, and you can't miss that," I reminded her.

Her eyes lit up. "Oh, I almost forgot!"

She hurried up her shuffling until we reached her green chair. I covered up her legs with the afghan she had once made, then turned on the television.

"Who is that man? Where is Pat?" she asked, looking almost frantic.

I had explained this to her almost every night since Ryan Seacrest had taken over Pat Sajak's place on the show, but rarely did she remember.

Amory's text read:

> It can't be that bad.

I smirked. He had no idea.

I glanced back up at Grams. "Pat retired, Grams. That is Ryan Seacrest. He's the new host."

She scowled. "Well, that's a shame. Pat was still young. Why would he do that?"

I knew better than to get into this with her. She refused to believe the man was almost eighty now because she didn't realize she was eighty-two.

> Crown Royal. I was conceived after my father and the woman who gave birth to me got drunk at a bar. She was drinking Crown Royal that night and said that was the only reason she was careless enough to have sex without protection. So, when I was born, she decided that it should be my name. Think it can't be that bad now?

I hit Send, then glanced back up to see Grams still scowling at the television.

> You're serious.

I stifled a laugh.
Why would I make something like that up? Admitting it is bad enough.

> It's unique, but then so are you. What are you doing tonight?

I looked over at my book that I had to read in order to finish two papers for students.

> Working.

He immediately began to type his response, and the fact that it made me giddy was a red flag.

> Working as in hustling frat boys at cards? Or is it the pool table you're working tonight?

Smart-ass.

> Neither. Reading a book for one of my classes so I can do two papers on it for a frat guy and a football player.

There was a pause, and I wondered if that was it, if he was going to stop texting, but then the dots showed up again.

> What book?

"WINDOW!" my Grams shouted at the television. "It's a candle in the window, you idiots!"

How she could figure out the phrases on that show, but couldn't remember how to brush her own teeth, I didn't know.

Glancing at the clock on the wall, I knew it was almost time for Bruce to start shutting down the food counter at Zoom Way—the service station about a mile from our house. Rise and Dine had been closed for hours, and I knew they were all long gone. I couldn't text my friend who worked there for the leftovers off the buffet. But Bruce, the manager at Zoom Way, would always give me the pizza, hot wings, potato salad, corn dogs, and fries they had left over at the end of the day.

I sent Bruce a text, then replied to Amory's.

> A boring one.

I closed the book and placed it on the side table before going to put on my shoes. While Grams was interested in the television, it was a good time for me to get dinner.

> Okay, then for which class?

Grinning, I typed as I walked to the door.

> Social Theory.

"Be right back with dinner, Grams!" I called before heading out to the car.

I wanted to wait and see what Amory sent me next, but Bruce had responded, telling me he would package it all up for me now. I needed to hurry. *Wheel of Fortune* only had about twenty minutes left.

• EIGHT •

"I wasn't going to let her make me look like a fool."

SEBASTIAN

King walked into my father's office, holding up a stack of papers. "Wilder just sent these," he announced and glanced at me. "Seems you're off the hook."

Frowning, I waited for an explanation. *What did he mean, I'm off the hook?*

"Perfect timing," he added. "Since you got a date with the makeup princess coming up."

I should have never said a word about Hattie. They were all going to stay in my fucking business about it now. Mom was bad enough. I didn't need them doing it too.

My father took the papers, then sat behind his desk, going over them.

King went over to pour himself a glass of whiskey, then glanced over at me. "Want one?"

I shook my head. "What am I off the hook for?" I asked him.

"Canadian whiskey," he replied, then took a seat in one of the high-back leather chairs across from me.

That got Wells's attention, and he looked up from his phone. "Are we good then? Meeting over?"

King's gaze swung to him, making it clear he'd said the wrong thing.

"What?" Wells asked, then shifted his eyes to my father, who was looking in his direction with disdain.

Wells never did know when to shut the fuck up and wait.

"Am I taking up too much of your time?" Dad's voice was so cold that it could have cracked steel.

Wells shook his head. "No ... sir," he replied.

"Merce Dancastle ended things with the girl a few weeks ago and has been seen with Governor Dalton's daughter several times. However, this photo shows him within several feet of Royal two days ago, and his complete attention is on her. Then, this one from yesterday, the same thing. And these, he is following her out of a frat house, clearly trying to get her attention as she's walking away." He dropped the pictures onto his desk. "He might be dating Dalton's daughter like he was told to do, but he's not done with the Crown girl. She's our in. This isn't over."

When my father's eyes met mine, I realized what King had been saying.

Merce had broken up with her? Was he the one whose father had told him to? That would make sense and prove she hadn't lied to me about it.

"She told me a guy had broken up with her because his father had told him to," I informed my father. "She didn't tell me who, and I hadn't realized she and Merce were no longer an item."

"How did you leave things with the girl?" he asked me.

I shrugged. "Good. I mean, we had just started to talk. She's guarded as fuck and sharp. Doesn't let much get by her."

My father leaned back in his chair. "Meaning what exactly?"

It felt wrong, telling him—any of them—the things I'd learned about her. Like I was sharing her private life. Yet that was normal for us. We invaded the privacy of everyone around us. She wasn't who I was protecting. I had to keep that straight in my head.

"She's a hustler, which you knew already. She not only hustles men at pool, but she is also involved in some underground poker ring at the college. She goes to classes there, even though she isn't enrolled, and does assignments for others for money.

"And"—I really fucking hated to admit this, but it was important that he realized she was savvy as well as smart—"the day I followed her, she noticed me. Walked right up to my car down her street and confronted me about it."

King covered up a laugh, and I ignored him. I'd known that was going to amuse them. The guys, not my dad. He was not amused. To him, I had fucked up.

Dad took a deep breath. "Well, that can only mean if Merce knows anything about what his father is doing, then she does too. Especially since Wilder also found this," he said, picking up a piece of the paper and shoving it in my direction.

I reached over and picked it up. There was an older man, balding, looked like he needed a shower, a shave, and to lay off the beer. He was with Merce, standing outside Royal's house.

Dad then tossed another picture on top of it. In that one, another man was putting a box into the Volkswagen Beetle that was sitting out front in Royal's driveway while Merce had a hand on the balding man's shoulder, talking.

"Who's the man he's with?" I asked, looking up from the photo to my father.

"Vinson Shelton," he replied, then cocked an eyebrow.

I'd seen that name on Royal's background check. It was Royal's father. Fucking hell.

"The plot just got real damn thick," King muttered.

She was too smart for this to have been going on under her nose. She had to know about it. There was always the chance that box was something like dime bags, but there was only one way to find out. I was going to get deep into her life. Yes, I wanted to fuck her, and that would be a part of it, but I was going to have to get her trust. Doing so meant I'd be around her a lot.

"I have a few favors to call in. Go back to Athens in the morning and be outside her Modern Literature class at eleven fifteen. The class will end, and the students will begin to leave, but the professor will hold her inside the room to speak to her. He's going to call her out on not being a student and mention the papers she has written for other students. You go inside, introduce yourself as George Blaine's son, and save her ass. That's step one. You will have almost made it to her next class when she gets a call from her father. He will have been picked up for driving with a revoked license. Her grandmother will also be home alone, and the red scooter she drives will have two flat tires."

He was making her need me.

"Talk about a shitty day," Wells mumbled.

"She will be desperate, and you will be there," my father replied, then turned to King. "Where is Thatcher? I have something the two of you need to handle in Atlanta."

That was it. In twenty-four hours' time, he was going to make Royal think I was her hero.

Keeping my head on straight was a priority. I'd watched her work a room. She was good at it. That was what I had to remember. She was a job for me, and I wasn't going to let her make me look like a fool. I had no doubt she could one-up me if I didn't stay focused.

• NINE •

"I take it, you won't believe that I came to charm you?"

ROYAL

It was slightly hard to breathe. I was sweating. As in my hands were so damp that it was hard to make notes. Every time I looked up and found Professor Brereton's gaze pause on me, my heart rate sped up. He'd never paid much attention to anyone in this class. I always sat in the back, never asked questions, blended into the crowd. Today, he saw me and only me, it seemed.

By the time he dismissed the class, I felt slightly ill. I gathered my things, trying not to look in his direction, but I could feel his eyes boring into me.

He had been tipped off. Had I made someone mad? What was so different about today that he was suddenly very aware of me?

His monotone voice and apparent boredom with everyone had been working so well for me.

"Excuse me, Miss Shelton, is it?" he asked.

I felt the blood drain from my face. He knew my name. Which meant he knew I wasn't on his class roll.

Oh crap, oh crap, oh crap. I needed to think fast. I had to come up with something.

He could find out about all the classes I attended. I needed the money I got for the papers, but this was also my way of getting educated, even without the degree to go with it. This was something I enjoyed. It helped with accepting that I couldn't take the scholarships I'd been offered because the schools were too far away for me to live at home. Grams needed me. Leaving hadn't been an option.

Straightening my shoulders and taking a deep, calming breath, I tried to regain my composure as I held my books to my chest and turned to look at Professor Brereton. He was in his late fifties, I'd guess, with silver hair that he kept neatly trimmed. He wasn't unattractive, but he wasn't necessarily attractive either. He just was.

"Yes, sir," I replied, smiling as if I had no reason to be concerned. Possibly arrested. Could I be arrested for this? Was it illegal to do what I'd been doing? Sure, the papers for other students were bad, but not jail-time bad. I didn't think. Why hadn't I checked into that?

He crossed his arms over his chest. "It strikes me as odd that you are always here, in the back of the class, yet it's been brought to my attention that you aren't actually registered for this class. In fact, after some digging, I found you're not even enrolled at Howison. Would you like to explain?"

I was going to vomit. Right here, on the floor at his feet. Then possibly faint while he called security to escort me off campus. Remaining calm was something I was typically good at. I had an excellent poker face, which was one of the reasons I was so good at it. But right now, that technique had left the building. I was in full panic mode. I opened my mouth, but no words came out. I couldn't get one single sound through the panic clenching my throat.

"Nothing to say?" he asked.

He raised both gray eyebrows at me. He had a mole over his left one. I wondered if he'd gotten that checked. It didn't look good.

Why was I thinking about his mole?

I needed to say something. Get myself out of this mess. I had four hundred dollars' worth of papers in my satchel that I had spent hours on. That was money I'd planned on using for the electric bill and part of the phone bill.

"I, uh …" The words came out in a stammer.

"Yes, I'd love to hear what you have to say about this and the fact that you are doing essays for students at a price. That makes this even worse. Don't you think?"

Oh God. Oh God. How did he find out?

I needed a good lie—no, an exceptional one—but nothing was coming to me.

I heard the door to the room open, and I wasn't sure if I should look. What if it was campus security—or worse the police?

I sucked in a breath, on the verge of tears.

"Professor, sorry to interrupt," the deep, familiar drawl startled me.

I spun around to see Amory walking toward us.

What was he doing here? Was it him who had told on me? No, surely not. I mean, unless he'd been working undercover for the college. Did they have those here? Why would they? Why had I trusted this man?

His smile shifted to me. I held my breath, afraid of what was coming next. I'd trusted the wrong person. He knew too much. Was it because I had turned him down for a date? This was a little drastic of a response, if so. We'd been texting some. It had been friendly. What else had I told him?

"I'm handling a situation, Mr. ..." Professor Brereton replied sharply.

He didn't know Amory, but that didn't mean he wasn't the one who had ratted me out.

"Yes, I can see that. The problem, however, is, you're holding up my friend who I've come to visit, and she has another class soon."

Then, it wasn't Amory who had told on me? Or was it?

I watched in confusion as he turned his attention back to the professor.

"Your friend, it seems, is in some trouble," the professor began.

Amory shook his head. "No, I don't think she is," he replied.

"I'm sorry, but who are you, and why do you think you have the authority to waltz into my classroom and tell me what is or is not going on?" the professor snapped at him.

Although deodorant wasn't my biggest issue right now, I hoped mine was equipped for this kind of sweating. If I didn't have a full-blown panic attack in the next five seconds, it would be a miracle.

"Forgive me," Amory replied. "I should have introduced myself. I'm Amory Blaine. I believe you've heard of my father, George."

There was a polite arrogance in the gleam in his eyes as he stared down Professor Brereton. One that briefly distracted me from my building anxiety.

"I see," the professor replied, sounding impressed.

I swung my gaze back to the professor, who now appeared to be nervous.

What was going on? How was the mention of Amory's father causing Brereton to change so rapidly?

The professor cleared his throat. "I was unaware that Miss Shelton was a friend of your family."

"Indeed, she is, and if you would be so kind as to"—he glanced at me with a smirk, then back at the professor—"forgive and forget whatever it is that has her so worked up, my family would appreciate it. I hate to see her upset like this, especially with another class to attend."

If I had been speechless before, then I was full-on mute now. All I could do was stand there and watch in shock—or horror.

"Yes, of course," Professor Brereton replied, taking a step back. "She is free to go."

Wait. What?

I stared at him, waiting for him to say he was joking or pick up a phone to call security.

He glanced at me. "Excellent job on your paper," he told me, although I hadn't turned in a paper.

Two other students had turned in papers that I'd written for them, but my name wasn't one either of them.

"Excellent," Amory replied, and I looked back at him.

He held out his arm to me. "Ready?"

No. I was not ready. Professor Brereton knew what I had been doing. Walking out that door would not get me out of trouble. No, out there, I'd have to face it and deal with it.

Why he was letting me go with Amory, I didn't understand, but I also knew Amory wouldn't be here for the next class.

"I—he was—I mean, Professor Brereton was—" I was bumbling up my words, not sure what to say exactly, but knowing I had to say something.

"He was accusing you of not being enrolled here and doing other students' papers for them," Amory said as he held my gaze.

There was a twinkle of mischief in his eye, and once again, I wondered if he'd done this. Told on me. But why would he do that, then show up here, using his father's name like a weapon? I didn't understand.

"Yes." My voice was just above a whisper.

Amory shifted his gaze back to the professor. "I'm sure Professor Brereton has forgotten all about that. Haven't you?"

I watched as the professor nodded his head jerkily, his expression somewhat grim.

"Really?" I asked, not trusting that this was actually going to be dropped.

"Yes," Professor Brereton replied. "You're an excellent student, and your work is exceptional."

"That sounds about right," Amory replied. "If you want to get a milkshake—aka what you call a coffee—from the cart, we need to hurry up. Can't be late for your next class."

Perhaps it was shock or just sheer bewilderment, but I nodded my head. Amory waved a hand for me to walk in front of him, and my legs began moving, thankfully, as we headed for the door. I kept going, not stopping until we exited the building completely and were several feet from it.

Turning back around, I gawked at him. He just stood there, all relaxed, in his snug-fitting blue shirt that matched his eyes a little too well, faded jeans, brown leather belt, and boots.

"What was that?" I asked under my breath, not wanting anyone to hear us.

He leaned slightly closer to me. "It's called saving your ass. At least, that is what most would consider it to be."

I shook my head, and a short, unamused laugh fell from my lips. "That—how—I was—where did you come from? Were you the one who told? Why were you here?" My head was filled with a surge of questions and emotions. I didn't know what to think or feel.

His dark brows drew together. "Me? You think I told someone? Why the fuck would I do that?"

I shrugged. "I don't know. But you were right there. Barging in and scaring the man with the mention of your dad's name—which, by the way, I'd also like an explanation for. None of what just happened makes sense."

Amory reached for my books. "Here, let me carry these," he replied, taking them from my arms. "Let's walk so you can get your caffeine, and I'll answer your accusatory questions—even though they sting."

I pointed to the building behind him. "You were in there. What would you have me think? That you swooped in like Superman and saved me? Sorry, I'm not that naive."

He chuckled. "No, you're definitely not that. I take it, you won't believe that I came to charm you? Waiting outside your class when you exited. Take you to get a coffee as I walked you to your next class."

I shook my head. "Too much of a coincidence."

He nodded toward the path. "I'll talk as we head in the direction you need to be going. You'll have to stop me when we reach your building though. I don't know which one it is."

He started to walk, and I fell into step behind him because he had my books. He was right; I didn't need to be late. After what had just happened, walking into a class last would make me stand out. Although I wasn't sure my heart could take another class today. I might need some time to accept that I wasn't headed for jail after all.

"Truth is, I did come to charm you. You were on my mind all weekend, and I wasn't ready to give up on getting you to agree to a date with me. I had it all planned out. Show up, perhaps make you laugh. Spend some time with you between classes. It was a well-laid-out attempt.

"But when you didn't come out of the building when the class mass exited, I decided to see if you were inside. I thought perhaps I'd gotten your class wrong today. I parked a few cars over from your Vespa, so I knew you were here. When I reached the door, I looked in and saw the professor scowling at you with disapproval, and you were pale. I also knew the professor speaking to you when you weren't a student enrolled in this college was bad." He sighed, then paused to look down at me.

"My father is not only a Howison College alum, but it was also his endowment that built the football stadium. He golfs regularly with the president of the college. I'll need to make a call to my father as soon as I get you to class and let him know what just happened so that he can help out and do some damage control, but his name was enough to shut down the professor from whatever he was about to do. Momentarily. He'll hit a wall when he goes higher up with this, and that will be the end of it."

It all sounded too easy. I didn't trust easy.

"How can you be so sure? You think you can just call your dad and he'll help me out? A girl who is sitting in classes here that she doesn't pay for and doing assignments for other students at a price?" Saying it aloud made it sound even more unlikely. I was screwed.

"Technically, what you are doing is a self-audit. Many colleges even allow it. You might be sitting in them for free, but you aren't getting a degree or credit for the courses. As for the work you are doing at a price, I'd call that using your skills, working with your strengths; it's enterprising. My father respects an entrepreneur."

I let out another laugh and shook my head. He was dead serious. There was no teasing laughter in his expression. He believed what he was saying. I, on the other hand, didn't have as much faith in his father. That, and my heart rate still hadn't returned to normal. I needed to go home and regroup. Decide how to proceed.

"If you are full of shit, then you are really good at the delivery," I told him.

The corner of his mouth lifted into a crooked grin. "Thanks. I think. But I'm not full of shit. Just so we are clear."

Whatever. My head was starting to hurt. I had to accept he'd been there at the right time and gotten me out of a bad situation even if it was temporarily.

"I'm not going to go to the next class. My head is pounding, my heart is still racing, and I need to think. Thanks for coming and for what you did back there. I can't imagine I am worth the effort you are putting into trying to get me to go out with you. I must warn you that I'll probably be a disappointment. Whatever you think about me is a lot less interesting than the reality. But you did save me, and I owe you one. So, text me later—tomorrow, whenever—and I'll give you that date so you can see that chasing me isn't worth your time."

His smile deepened, and it was hard not to simply gaze at the man. He was gorgeous. Over six feet tall, muscular, broad shoulders, a square jawline that made his aristocratic features seem more masculine. Otherwise, he'd be entirely too pretty.

"Deal. I'll walk with you to your Vespa," he replied.

Since he was parked near me, there was no reason to argue with him about it. We were going in the same direction.

"Sure you don't want that coffee milkshake thing you like to drink?"

I glanced up at him. "How do you know about that?"

He winked. "Stalker, remember?"

A laugh bubbled out of me, and the tension slowly eased. Maybe this wasn't the end of my college career. He sure seemed to believe his dad would help me out with this. I was struggling with it, but then, with a father like the one I had, I didn't have much faith in parental figures.

My phone vibrated in my pocket, and I stopped walking to pull it out. I'd put it on silent for class, but I had to keep it on me in case something happened with Grams. A number I didn't recognize lit up the screen. That was never good.

"Hello?" I said into the phone, trying not to jump to the worst-case scenario.

Dad was home with Grams until I got back today. *It was fine. She was okay.*

"Is the Royal Shelton?" a man asked.

I tensed up, gripping the phone tightly. My eyes lifted to meet Amory's.

"Yes," I replied.

"This is Sergeant Phillips, down at the police station. One of my officers brought in your father, Vinson Shelton, about twenty minutes ago for driving with a suspended license. He asked that we call you. Your grandmother is home alone, and he is saying she has dementia. He is being, uh, rather difficult, or he'd have called you himself. There is a fine for him to be released if you want to come here and pay that."

I was already walking toward the parking lot again, almost at a run. *How long had Grams been home alone? When had he left her? Why had he been driving? I should have taken the car, not my Vespa. This was what I got for saving money on gas. Damn him.*

"How much is it?" I asked, realizing I hadn't said anything.

"It's one thousand for this offense. The next time, it will be higher with jail time included."

Shit! We didn't have that kind of money to blow on this right now. Bills were coming due. I had enough to cover them all, but not that much left over.

"Okay, he'll have to stay there for the time being. I need to get to my Grams. I'll figure something out," I told him as my Vespa came into view.

"Yes, ma'am," the officer replied.

I ended the call, shoving my phone into my pocket, then glanced over to see Amory was beside me. He still had my books.

"I have to go. I need those," I told him, reaching for them.

"What's wrong?" he asked, concern etching his face.

I might as well tell him. He was the one coming here, doing all he could to get me to go on a date. If he saw what a shit show my life was, he should back down quick enough.

He didn't hand me my books.

"My dad has a suspended license and was pulled over, then arrested. He was supposed to be with my Grams, who is home alone and has been alone for God knows how long. I need to get to her, then figure out how I'm going to come up with a grand to get him out, although I'd like to just leave him in there. I would if it wasn't because Grams needs someone with her when I'm not home." I reached out for my books. "Please, I need to go. I have to hurry."

He held out my books and opened my satchel to shove them inside, then turned to my Vespa.

"I can give you a ride. It'll be faster. Not sure it's safe to drive when you're worked up like this. Especially that thing."

Nope. I'd told him the truth, but he wasn't about to witness it firsthand.

I shook my head and turned to my Vespa. "Thanks, but I'm fine." Which wasn't the truth. This day was just getting worse.

"Uh, no, you're not. Looks like you've got a flat front tire," he told me, and my stomach instantly sank as my eyes dropped to the tire.

"Are you kidding me?" I asked.

"Back looks low too. You must have run over something on the way here this morning. Come on. My car is right over here."

Fantastic. I had no option. Amory Blaine was stepping in to fix all my problems. Well, some of them at least.

I nodded, no longer able to argue. I had to get to Grams.

"Thanks," I said as he led me over to his shiny silver Porsche.

I heard the doors unlock as we reached it, and then he opened the passenger side for me.

"Just glad I'm here," he said.

Sometimes, I was sure fate hated me. Today, it seemed to have some pity on me and toss me a sexy, wealthy, tall man to make some of the shit that was being thrown at me less difficult. I'd thank it for the mini break, but since I still had to deal with my dad in jail and the possibility that Grams had burned the house down, I wasn't going to be that generous yet.

I buckled my seat belt as Amory walked around to get inside the driver's seat. My hands were balled into fists on my thighs as he started the car up and backed out of the parking spot. I would have to come back here and deal with the tires at some point today. Leaving it here would cause attention I didn't need. Which meant spending more money that I didn't need to spend.

"Can you call the house? Check on your Grams?" he asked me as he headed toward the main road.

I shook my head. "No house phone. We had one a couple of years back because she refused to use cell phones, but when she got worse, the sound of it ringing confused her and caused her to get upset."

He glanced over at my seat belt. "You buckled up tight?" he asked.

I nodded, unsure why he was asking until the car shot off, causing me to be pressed against the smooth leather. My eyes closed when he swerved around a car going slower—at the speed he was going, every car was going slower.

"If we end up in jail for speeding, it's not gonna help Grams," I said.

A deep chuckle had me opening my eyes to look at him. He seemed amused, as if he was above the law.

"We won't. Trust me."

Oddly enough, I found that I was starting to—trust him, that was. I wasn't one to trust, but Amory was making it easy to give in and believe him. He'd done nothing but be there for me today when things could have been much worse. Perhaps he was above the law. He seemed to make others bend to his wishes. Even me.

"That seems to be the mantra of the day," I replied.

He cut his eyes at me. "What?"

I pointed at the road. "Please, if you're going to drive like you stole this car, then keep your eyes straight ahead. We might not go to jail, but death is a possibility."

He grinned, but he was looking where he needed to be now.

"Trusting you," I told him. "The mantra. I don't have any other choice but to trust you."

He started to jet around another car, and I held my breath until we were safely in front of them.

"Don't make me regret it," I added.

Because I had trusted before, and I'd been burned. Too many times. I had trusted friends, who let me down; my father, who had taught me at a young age not to trust him with anything; and then I'd trusted Merce.

My thoughts went to Merce. Could it have been him who told on me? Would he do that? I hadn't broken up with him.

He was the one who ended it. But I had refused to talk to him in front of the other guys in his fraternity on Friday night. He stayed the entire game, then followed me out, pleading with me to let him explain. There was nothing left to explain. It was over. What had he expected me to do? I was moving on with my life. He'd told me to, and I was.

He had an ego the size of Mount Rushmore. Would my not speaking to him have caused him to retaliate like this? I didn't want to think he would blatantly hurt me this bad, but then I'd learned he couldn't be trusted, hadn't I?

"Whatever you're thinking, I hope I'm not in it," Amory said.

I swung my gaze to him. "Why?"

"The scowl on your face is fierce."

I took a deep breath and tried to relaxed my clenched fists. "I told you to keep your eyes on the road."

"It was barely a glance," he said defensively.

We were almost there. My heart sped up some more. What if Grams was hurt? She could have tried to cook something and burned herself. She could have fallen. She could have broken glass and cut her hand and be bleeding to death.

"Easy. Less than a minute. Don't go having a panic attack on me. Let's get you inside and make sure all is okay first." Amory's voice eased me some, but not enough.

He slowed the car as we neared the house, and it was a straight-up miracle we hadn't been pulled over. Amory had to be the luckiest person I had ever met. Things seemed to always go his way. *Must be nice.*

As soon as the car came to a stop, I unbuckled, shot out of the car, then sprinted for the front door, digging out my keys from my bag as I ran. I heard Amory getting out behind me, but I didn't have time to stop him. If he was coming in, then so be it. I might need help in here anyway. I had no clue what I'd find inside.

Shoving open the door, I left the keys hanging from the lock and rushed inside. "GRAMS!" I called out, running past the empty living room, where I heard her favorite soap opera playing on the television.

I was in the kitchen when I heard the shuffle of her feet. I swung my gaze to the small hallway to see her coming toward me, and I almost fell to my knees and wept in relief. No blood. Nothing was cooking. She appeared to be fine.

"Grams!" I said, going to her. "You're okay?" I scanned her body for any signs of a problem.

"Course I'm okay," she chided. "Just got the beds made up and was gonna start on the apple pie that Vin loves so much. Thought he might want a slice when he gets back from work. Why don't you go wash your hands? I'll let you peel the apples while I work on the crust." She patted my arm, smiling, lost in the past as she walked on by me. "Scrub them up good now. Ain't no telling what all you touched at school."

I leaned against the wall and took a deep breath, then let it out. It was okay. She was okay. All that could have gone wrong hadn't. I rested my head against the wood paneling and took a moment before going after her to stop whatever mess she was about to make. We didn't even have apples, much less the stuff she needed to make a pie. If we did, I might just help her make one. Not that Dad would be eating it. As it was, I had no extra money for ingredients. I needed to make a grand if he was going to come home anytime soon.

Turning my head toward the kitchen, I saw Amory standing there, watching me. I'd forgotten he had followed me inside. Straightening, I forced the embarrassment of our home from my thoughts. I would not go there. Not again. I'd been so ashamed of it when Merce came here the first time.

But this was a home that my grandfather had bought. He'd taken care of it with Grams. She'd loved this place when I was a kid. She had been proud of what she had. My being embarrassed by it was insulting to them both.

"Seems all is well," I told him. "Except I need to make sure she doesn't burn anything down, trying to make a pie."

His lips quirked, but he didn't smile. He seemed to be thinking or perhaps trying not to make any expression to give away how he felt about the place where I lived. I was sure he lived in some mansion to go with his fancy car.

Walking back into the kitchen, I found Grams standing in front of the refrigerator, staring at it like she was lost. This was common.

I put my arm around her shoulders and closed the door. "Hey, Grams, your story is on," I told her. "I can hear it playing in the living room, and you don't want to miss it. Someone could always return from the dead. And who knows what Victor is up to today?"

She nodded. "Oh, yes. I need to watch it, don't I?"

"You sure do. Let's go get you seated in your chair, and I'll heat you up a slice of pizza."

She scrunched her nose. "Not the pizza. Do we have any pork chops?"

Gran couldn't eat pork chops with her dentures, but by the time I had her meal fixed, she'd have forgotten about the pork chops.

"Sure," I agreed and walked past Amory, who was standing silently.

Grams, however, stopped and turned back around to look at him. "Aren't you a handsome young man?" she said, her eyes widening. "Isn't he handsome, Royal?"

I glanced up at him, and he was giving her one of his female-slaying smiles. He closed the space between us and took her hand, then pressed a kiss on the top of it. "Amory Blaine, ma'am. It's nice to meet you. I can see where your granddaughter gets her beauty from."

Grams giggled. She actually giggled. I rolled my eyes, but I couldn't keep from grinning at him. Merce had never spoken to her. He'd only come inside once. Amory had said he'd come today to charm me, and I had to admit, he was successfully doing so.

"Well, isn't that sweet?" she said, smiling at me with a pleased look on her wrinkled face. "I like this one. He's a sharp boy. Just like your father."

I grimaced and patted her shoulder. "Let's hope not," I muttered under my breath and turned her back around toward the living room. "I believe I hear Victor now," I told her.

"You do? That scoundrel. There is no telling what he's doing."

She hurried over to her chair and sat down, her eyes now glued to the television.

I left her there and looked back at Amory. "Thanks for that. She won't remember you tomorrow—or in ten minutes probably—but thanks."

His gaze went from her to me. "I was just being honest. You can tell a beauty, no matter what the age. I'm sure she had the men falling at her feet back in her day."

I headed back to the kitchen. "Oh, she did. Back when she could tell me the stories. My grandfather was four years older than her and would come to her high school and buy her lunches. He worked at the coal mines, and she was from a poor family, much like his. He knew she didn't have much in the lunch she brought from home. Normally, a cold biscuit from breakfast or an apple, if she was lucky. So, he wooed her with hot lunches from the cafeteria."

I'd heard that story so many times that I knew every detail by heart.

"If only a hot lunch was all it took these days," Amory replied teasingly.

I opened up the refrigerator to get the last piece of pizza out to heat up. I needed to go get some more food tonight. I hadn't been by Rise and Dine in a week. Anya could probably hook me up with the leftovers this afternoon.

"It was more than the food, I assure you. Grams loved him so much that even though he died before she even turned sixty, she's never looked at another man. We once had a neighbor, Mr. Burnswell. He had a thing for Grams. Brought flowers and chocolates over. When he had a good watermelon crop, he would bring us fresh ones all summer long. But not once did she give him more than a *thank you*. Poor guy finally gave up."

I placed the piece of pizza in the microwave and prayed it worked today. It had been struggling lately. Sometimes, it was fine, and other times, it wouldn't stay on for longer than five seconds before cutting off. Due to it being difficult, I'd been using the oven for almost everything. It continued to cook, so it seemed that Amory's luck was rubbing off.

"I thought she wanted pork chops," he said.

I cut my eyes over to him. "We don't have pork chops, and even if we did, she can't chew them with her dentures."

He raised his eyebrows slightly. "But she will forget she asked for one," he guessed.

I nodded. "Yep."

· TEN ·

"I tried dating out of my league, and it didn't end well."

SEBASTIAN

My phone rang, and I already knew who it was. I leaned up against the front of my car and answered it.

"Already miss me?" I asked.

"I didn't say I needed groceries," Royal snapped on the other end of the line.

I smiled. I wished like fuck I hadn't reacted to her, but after today and all I'd witnessed, I knew there was a part of me that liked her. Even if she was a con artist.

"You didn't have to. I saw the contents of your fridge."

A deep sigh on the other end. "Amory, I'm not a charity case. I can buy food. I was going to get us dinner tonight."

"With what? Your Vespa?" I asked, reminding her that we'd left it at school with two flat tires. It had new ones now and was currently being delivered to her house, but she didn't know that yet.

"I would have figured it out," she replied. "This is entirely too much food. There are twelve full bags. Twelve. I don't know if we have room for all this. And the delivery guy said he couldn't take it back."

I glanced over at the door to the police station. "Guess you'll have to find room for it then."

She let out a frustrated growl.

"Come on now," I replied. "It's not so bad. There's even an apple pie from the bakery in there. I figured you could tell your Grams she made it."

A short laugh came through. "One afternoon with her, and you know all my secrets to handling her."

She was pretty damn great with her grandmother. I'd not wanted to be impressed, but I had been. If she was involved in this shit, I didn't think I could let her go down with them. That old lady needed her. Now, as for the son of a bitch I was about to get out of jail? They both could do without him. But unfortunately, we needed him free to fuck up so we could see who was behind the laced drugs.

"I'm a quick learner," I told her.

"Someone else is at the door," she said, sounding slightly miffed.

I heard her open it, and then a man spoke—the same one I'd talked to, who had changed her tires, then put it on his trailer to bring to her. She asked him who he was, and I wanted to laugh. He ignored the question and left her the keys, then told her to have a good day.

With the click of her door, I waited for her to say something first.

"My Vespa arrived. It miraculously has new tires and was dropped off, all free of charge. How odd," she drawled.

"Seems you've got luck on your side today," I told her. Although I felt a little guilty since we had been behind everything that had gone wrong today.

"Thank you," she said, sounding almost pained.

I chuckled. "You're welcome."

"Whenever you want that date, just let me know."

Even if this was a job, my ego was feeling slightly bruised. She hadn't been this accommodating before I righted all her wrongs today.

"I didn't do all this for a date. Sure, I'd come to see you, hoping to charm you, but as for all the other things, I wanted to help. I like you, Royal, but my pride is still intact. If you are agreeing to this because you feel like you owe me, then don't. Just accept it as help from a friend."

My dad would probably slam me against the wall while holding me by my throat if he heard me right now. But he wasn't here, and I had to make sure she was going to go out with me because some part of her wanted to. Even if in the end, it didn't matter one fuck what she felt or wanted.

"My not wanting to go out with you wasn't about you. Look at yourself. I told you, I tried dating out of my league, and it didn't end well."

The sincerity in her tone made my chest tighten. She was probably full of bullshit right now. The woman had a mirror. She could see herself. She had to know guys drooled all over her. But that speech was pretty damn convincing.

"Like I said, he was a boy. I'm a man. I want to get to know you. Spend time with you. As for leagues, no one is out of yours. Wealth doesn't measure a person's self-worth."

A small, breathy sigh came over the line. "Okay. Yeah. I'd like that too. Although I can't believe that you'd still feel like this after what you witnessed today."

It's a game, Sebastian. Play it. Don't get hustled by the hustler.
"I'll pick you up tomorrow night at seven. Is that okay?"

"Oh, uh, my dad. He's not here, and I can't leave Grams."

He'd be there. But I wasn't trusting that bastard with her Grams either. If there was anyone I did feel protective over in that house, it was the grandmother.

"Let me handle that. Just be ready at seven."

"What do you mean, you'll handle it?"

"Do you trust me?" That was a bit of a gamble. My dad's plan today had set this in motion—the winning her over—but I wasn't sure it was enough.

"Yeah, I guess I do."

Grinning, I stood back up and headed for the door of the police station. "Tomorrow night at seven. Wear something short."

She laughed. "Okay."

"Bye, Ace," I said.

"Bye."

Ending the call, I opened the door to the station and walked inside.

The officer up front recognized me and motioned for me to come around the desk. "You sure you want this ornery bastard?" he asked.

I hadn't made the call; my father had. I'd been too busy getting everything else handled for Royal.

"Unfortunately," I told him. "It's for his daughter."

He smirked. "Ah, yeah. I've seen her. She's been in here to get him before. Knockout and hard to forget."

"Yeah," I agreed.

"Makes more sense now."

I bet it did. I was sure he'd hit on her when she was in here before. She got fucking hit on all the time. The bullshit about being out of her league was something she used to make a man think she didn't know she was beautiful. Well, I wasn't the dumbass who had written that song. A gorgeous woman knew she was gorgeous, and she knew the power that came with it.

"Someone's here to get you out, Vin," the cop said as he unlocked the cell.

I watched as the asshole looked at me.

"About time," he said, standing up. "Who are you?"

"A friend of your daughter's."

His gaze narrowed. "Where is she at? Sending some man to come get me. Mean little fucker, that one."

Okay, so Royal might be a lot of things that were questionable, but this was her father. He felt it was okay to call his daughter a fucker. I tensed, ready to knock him back down with my fist.

"You can't be talking about Royal. Maybe I got the wrong guy. Because the woman I am referring to is at home, taking care of your mother."

His eyes widened slightly as I took a step toward him, not trying to hide the disgust or anger in my tone or expression.

"You got the right guy. I didn't mean nothing by it. Just joking a bit. Course she's taking care of her Grams. She's a good girl." Unlike his daughter, he was a terrible fucking liar.

"Come on, before I change my mind," I told him, then turned to stalk back out the way I had entered.

"Who are you?" he asked. "Did you pay for this? 'Cause we ain't got the money to pay you back. She didn't promise you we would, did she?"

I hadn't paid shit. He was here because of a call my father had made.

"Why don't you shut up, Vin, before you are back in there and I have to listen to you bitch all night?" the cop snarled at him.

I didn't look at him until we reached the exit, and then I shoved open the door and turned to him.

"No one owes me anything," I told him.

He nodded and studied me before walking out past me out the door. "You a friend of Merce then?"

I shook my head. "I'm a friend of Royal's."

The truck pulled up, and I walked over and jerked the door open.

"Get inside," I told him.

"Who is that?" he asked, his eyes shifting from Wells to me.

"A friend. He's taking you home. Now, get in the goddamn truck," I ordered.

He climbed inside. "Ain't no need to be rude. I can walk back, you know."

But he wasn't walking. He was getting inside.

I slammed the door, then headed for my car. Tomorrow night's date had to be planned, and it needed to be one she couldn't stop thinking about. I had an idea, but I should run it by a woman. Pulling my phone out of my pocket, I dialed Storm's number.

"Yeah?" he barked into the phone.

"I need Briar's help."

"With what?" The possessive tone was amusing.

"Planning my date."

"With the Shelton girl?"

"Yep."

He groaned. "Fine. Come to the house."

"On my way," I replied, then hung up.

I'd probably just interrupted some kinky-sex shit they were doing, but he had about thirty minutes before I got there. They could wrap it up.

• ELEVEN •

He was going to see soon enough that I was a hassle.

ROYAL

Dad's barreling into the house last night had surprised me only for a moment. Honestly, I should have expected it. Amory was the one to fix everything else yesterday. He had been thorough.

Grams had been in bed already, so she'd missed his cussing and accusing me of spreading my legs like a whore to get him out of jail. I took it, knowing he'd calm down soon and go to bed. When he stopped with the threatening to kick me out—because we both knew that he'd never do that, that he needed me here—I was free to go back to the bedroom I shared with Grams and send Amory a text, promising I'd pay him back as soon as I could.

He said that if I tried, he'd use the money to have groceries delivered weekly until it was gone. I wanted to argue, but I was too tired, and for once, I could close my eyes without worrying about the bar calling me to get Dad or how we were going to afford groceries after I paid the bills and got Grams's medication.

Merce had claimed to love me, but not once had he done anything close to even one of the things Amory had done for me yesterday. It was as if someone had dropped a fairy godmother on me, but they'd made it a hot, sexy male.

I had taken the time to go to campus today to deliver the papers I had, but I wasn't ready to face a class just yet. I was still waiting to see if Amory had really stopped Professor Brereton from turning me in.

My Vespa was running smoother than ever, even when I'd bought it. The slight pull to the right in the steering was gone, the jerk when I sped up after stopping was no longer there, and the wheels made the road smoother. What all he had done to it, I didn't know, but it wasn't just new tires.

Amory was going to be picking me up in an hour, and Dad had already left with a friend to go to Miller's. When I had asked if he'd stay home tonight, he had yelled at me about going out to spread my legs and that he wasn't helping me do that. If Amory had planned for my dad to stay with Grams, then this date wasn't going to happen.

I took the slice of pie I hadn't heated up in the oven out, then placed it in a bowl before adding a scoop of vanilla ice cream. Grams was in the living room, watching *Wheel of Fortune* and complaining about Ryan Seacrest again. She'd called out answers twice, then asked me where Pat had gone and if he was on vacation.

Just when I reached the living room, the doorbell rang, and I paused to glance at it, then went on in to give Grams her pie.

"Here, Grams," I told her.

"What's this?"

"The apple pie we made together, remember?" I replied, heading for the door.

"Oh, yes. Well, it sure smells good."

I checked out the window to see an older lady outside. That was odd. I unlocked the door and opened it up. The lady was petite with a white bob and kind eyes. I hoped she wasn't here to sell me something or tell me about the Lord. I didn't want to be rude to her, but those folks were often hard to get to leave.

"Can I help you?" I asked.

"If you're Royal Shelton, you can," she replied.

I nodded. "That's me."

"Wonderful. I'm at the right place," she told me, then held out her hand. "My name is Maeme. Amory is one of my many grandsons."

Oh. OH! Why was his grandmother here?

I shook her hand, waiting for her to explain why she was at my house. My head was spinning with reasons and the fact that I might have to let her come inside. I'd not straightened up yet today. And she was probably as rich as Amory.

She looked around me. "He says you need a little help tonight," she began as she shifted her eyes back to me. "I'm here to meet your Grams and stay with her while the two of you have a night out."

He'd sent his grandmother to sit with mine. I didn't know if I wanted to hit him or hug him. It was incredibly sweet, but he'd seen this house. What was she going to think? She'd tell his parents, and that would be the end of that. Just like Merce's parents didn't approve of me. I didn't care if Amory was a grown man; he wouldn't want to date someone his family disapproved of. But then wasn't I, just yesterday, trying to get out of going on a date with him? Perhaps this was for the best. End it before I got attached or started feeling things for him.

I stepped back and motioned for her to come inside. "That's very kind of you," I said.

She came inside and smiled brightly as her gaze drifted over the place.

"My boys know I'd do anything for them, but from what he tells me, your Grams is a real treat," she replied.

I guessed that was her way of saying she was aware Grams had dementia.

"You could say that," I replied.

"Is that Rosie? Tell her to come have some of the pie we made," Grams called out.

I licked my lips before explaining, "Rosie is her sister, who died when I was three. Grams often lives in the past."

Maeme's eyes softened. "I imagine it is easier there anyway. With happy memories."

Yes, for my Grams, it definitely was.

"Come this way," I told her and walked into the first room on the right.

"Grams, we have company. Her name is Maeme. Do you remember the attractive man who came to see us yesterday?" I doubted she did, but she nodded, her eyes wide with curiosity. "Well, this is his grandmother, and he told her all about you. She wanted to come for a visit."

Maeme clasped her hands together with a big smile. "Your home is just lovely. Did you make that afghan yourself? The colors are brilliant."

Grams's eyes lit up as Maeme complemented her home and blanket. "Well, yes, I did. I make them for the children's group home auction every year, don't I, Royal? They bring them a real nice price too."

Grams was sitting up straighter with pride sparkling in her eyes. "Royal, dear, go get, uh …" She paused, forgetting her name.

"Maeme," I offered, and she nodded with a soft laugh.

"Yes, my memory isn't what it used to be these days," she explained, having no idea how sadly accurate she was. "Anyway, go fetch her a slice of our pie. We made a delicious one, and you must have some of it."

Maeme walked over to the sofa across from Grams. "I'd love some," she said. "Now, tell me about that afghan. I'd love to hear about it. I used to do needlework years ago, but knitting and crocheting I never could get right. Certainly not like that. You've got a talent."

Grams looked so giddy with the praise; her smile was the biggest I'd seen it in years. Maeme glanced at me and winked, then made a movement with her hand slightly to tell me to go on.

"Once you get the hang of it," Grams began as I left the room quietly.

I stood just inside the kitchen, listening to Grams go on about the yarn quality and color choices before making my way back to the bedroom. Leaving Grams with someone other than my dad and me had never been an option. But it appeared Amory's grandmother knew exactly how to handle her.

I felt a warmth in my chest, and a smile played across my lips as I stared at myself in the mirror. This guy really liked me. It was intimidating to think about. He was going to see soon enough that I was a hassle. Had he not gotten enough of that yesterday? It had been a day full of hassles.

Reaching up, I took a strand of my hair and wrapped it around my finger. I had good hair. Grams had always loved my hair when I was little. Letting the strand fall, I touched my lips, then my cheeks, and studied my nose. I saw the flaws, but I also knew that no one else looked as closely as I did. I wondered if my mom looked like me at this age. The photo I had, she was older than me now, but there were resemblances.

No, I wasn't going to think about her. She wasn't my mom or even my mother. Grams was.

Dropping my hand back to my side, I turned around to find something to wear. It seemed this date was happening, and I wanted to at least look nice. He'd put a lot of effort into it getting his grandmother over here to sit with Grams. I was gonna wear something short. Not too short though. I didn't want his grandmother thinking I was a hussy.

My phone dinged.

> How did I do?

That was all Amory texted me.
Biting my lip, I smiled.

> The sundress is short, and the heels are high.

I hit Send and waited as the dots appeared.

> God, I love Maeme.

A laugh bubbled out of me as I held the phone for a moment more before putting it down and going to do all I could to make that man's heart flutter.

TWELVE

"That would be lame. I was gonna get you a car. Preferences?"

SEBASTIAN

Holy hell.

I'd not been prepared for this.

Jesus, was she even wearing a bra?

I reminded myself that my grandmother was in that house and I couldn't walk inside with a boner. But fuuuck. Her legs looked endless, and those tits … Goddamn.

"Wow," I said after eye-fucking her in silence for a touch too long. "You're gorgeous."

A slight blush touched her cheeks, and I bit the inside of my jaw hard enough to snap me out of it. That wasn't a real blush. This wasn't a real date. And this female was not what she appeared to be.

The black-and-silver dress clung to her tits and small waist, then flared, hitting just a couple of inches past her ass. The heels were enough to make a man sweat when paired with those legs.

Snap out of it! I was looking again.

"Thanks," she said. "You're rather jaw-dropping yourself." Then, she glanced back. "Do you want to go and say goodbye?

Your Maeme has my Grams's full attention right now. I'm not sure we should interrupt."

I held out my hand. "Then, we won't," I said.

She slipped her palm over mine, then stepped out onto the crumbling porch. I didn't want her breaking either leg in those heels, so I held on to her until we were safely on the cracked sidewalk.

"I can't believe you sent your Maeme to come stay with Grams."

I glanced at her and smirked. "She was happy to. I told you I'd handle it."

A soft laugh fell from her shiny pink lips. "Well, I guess I hadn't expected that. I figured you meant Dad when you said you'd handle it. And he's already gone to Miller's."

I wouldn't trust her father to stay with her Grams for five minutes.

I shook my head. "No. I met him last night," I replied.

She dropped her gaze to the grass. "Yeah," was her response.

I took her elbow to steady her as she stepped over the broken concrete that was sticking up just before we reached the driveway. She gave me a small smile, but the shyness in her expression confused me. Was that part of the act?

When we reached the passenger side, I opened the door for her. The short dress rode up her thighs even further, and my eyes locked on the exposed golden skin longer than necessary. Closing the door, I mentally scolded myself as I went to get in the driver's side. Briar had helped me with my idea, and it was a pretty damn good one. This date was going to win her over, and I'd be locked into her life. Trusted with secrets. Hopefully.

"How hungry are you?" I asked once I was inside.

"Um, not terribly. I mean, I could eat now if that's your plan, but if not, I can wait."

I chuckled. "Let me try again. When was the last time you ate?"

The corner of her lips curled up. "I had some pie an hour ago."

Perfect.

"All right then. Eat later."

"Where are we going?" she asked.

I backed out of her driveway. "Best I show you."

"Why? Is explaining it difficult?" The hesitant sound of her voice was amusing.

I cut my eyes at her. "I thought we covered the *you can trust me* thing."

She lifted a bare shoulder. "It's a work in progress."

Not what I'd wanted to hear. "Seriously? After yesterday, you are still unsure about me?"

She leaned back on the seat, relaxing, and I knew I'd see her bare thighs if I just looked down at her lap, but I refused to do it.

"You were quite the white night," she replied. "Almost too good to be true. So, you see why I'm not ready to toss all my good sense into the Amory Blaine pot."

I laughed. I couldn't help it. She was funny. She was sexy, smart, challenging, interesting, and not to be trusted. I'd experienced some unfair shit in life, but this might take the cake. Even when I'd been in love with Oakley and she'd loved Wilder. This beat that. First, I had been young, and looking back, I didn't think that had been love. It was lust, respect, and I'd taken her virginity, so I'd felt somewhat possessive over that. But marriage would have been a mistake.

This girl was all the things Oakley had been and more. She was savvy, not in love with another man, and a complete smart-ass.

"Did Grams like the apple pie?" I asked, changing the subject.

She nodded. "Oh, yes. She was bragging to your Maeme about how good it turned out."

She thought that Maeme was the name we called her because she was a grandmother. Most people did. But her name was actually Maeme, and she was not my grandmother. She was King's. But she was the oldest in the family, and no one stood against her. Not even my dad.

I didn't correct her.

"Good," I replied.

"We are leaving town?" she asked me when she saw me turn north.

"Not far," I assured her.

"This is a test of trust, isn't it? You're gonna take me out into the woods and see if I freak out."

I grinned. "No, but that does sound entertaining."

She rolled her eyes and shifted in her seat. My eyes dropped to her lap of their own will, and I bit the inside of my cheek again, tearing my gaze off those fucking pretty thighs.

"When's your birthday?" I blurted out. "You said you were turning twenty-one soon." I knew this answer, but I needed to be distracted.

"October 28. Why? You're not gonna have a cake delivered to my house or anything, are you?"

I shook my head. "No. That would be lame. I was gonna get you a car. Preferences?"

"That had better be a joke," she warned, sounding truly pissed.

I glanced at her. "Why? What would you do? Run me over with it?"

"Maybe! Don't tempt me."

"Easy, Ace. I'm not buying you a car. But if you want a cake, I can make a call."

She let out a sigh of relief. "I just don't know what to believe with you after yesterday."

Yeah, well, unless my father decided I needed to buy her a car, I wouldn't be doing that. Actually, he'd be the one doing it if that happened.

Her phone dinged, and she snatched it out of her purse quickly. I tried not to watch her, and I knew I'd see what the text said soon enough. All texts and calls she received were now sent to my phone. Wilder had sent me the info on how to program the spy software into her phone, and I'd done it yesterday when she was dealing with her Grams in the bathroom.

A frown drew her brows together.

"Everything okay?" I asked.

She nodded but quickly turned the screen off and stuck the phone back in her purse. All right, that was odd and possibly a lead. It was definitely a reminder that she wasn't a real date and this night wasn't real romance.

The apple orchard was up ahead, and I could check my phone once we got there. See if it was anything I needed to forward to my father. I realized I was gripping the wheel too tightly and made myself relax.

"Are we"—her eyes stared out the window as I slowed the car to turn into the deserted parking lot—"going to an apple orchard?"

"Yep. Nighttime picking. They are closed on weekdays, but they made an exception for us," I explained.

"You can pick apples at night?" she asked. Her smile made her eyes twinkle in the moonlight.

"Look out there. See the lights? Each row is lit up, and"—I reached behind her and took out a flashlight to hand to her—"I brought this in case you wanted extra lighting."

She took it from me, then reached for her door handle.

"Wait, you might want to change into these too," I added, getting the pair of rain boots I'd borrowed from Briar. "I think they'll fit. I guessed your size." Her feet were small, like Briar's, so I figured this would work. If not, I had two sizes up that I'd gotten from Maeme.

She looked at them, then at me. "You thought of everything," she replied, then bent over to slip off her heels.

I almost asked her to hand those to me so she could put them back on when we got to the dinner portion of the evening, but the way they made me forget what I was doing, it was probably best they didn't come with us.

"Perfect fit," she said, then turned to climb out of the car.

A flash of shiny silver panties—barely covering a smooth, round butt cheek—had me mentally cursing as I turned to get out too. I didn't need to know what her ass looked like. From that small glimpse, it was world-class.

The click of her flashlight reminded me that I hadn't gotten out to check the damn text. I'd been too busy looking at her legs and ass. Shit.

THIRTEEN

"Then, you've been dating the wrong men."

ROYAL

This was like walking into a fairy tale. The lighting along the ground lit up the trees, which were heavy with red apples, with a warm glow. Nothing too bright, but just enough to see what we were picking. I had never been apple picking before. I'd heard friends talk about it in the fall, but it wasn't something I'd ever done. Trying not to act giddy about it was difficult.

Standing on my tiptoes, I reached for a shiny one to take from the branch and almost fell forward, losing my balance. Amory came up so close behind me that I could feel the warmth from his much larger body, and it caused me to shiver.

"Like this," he said as his hand took the apple, then twisted it before easily plucking it free. "Twist and pull." His breath was hot on my ear as he leaned over me to drop the apple in the white paper bag I was holding by the sturdy handles.

I didn't trust my voice just yet since his being in my personal space was causing my heart to flutter in my chest. I nodded my head instead. When he moved away, I wanted to spin around and tug him back to me. I wouldn't do that, of course, but the scene playing out in my imagination was having a fine time with the idea.

"Just up ahead is our stop. Do you have enough, or do you want to fill another bag?" he asked me.

I stared down the row of trees to see the end was more lit than where we were now. What was up there that was going to be a stop for us?

Curious, I held up the bag. "These are great."

His hand touched my lower back, and I bit my bottom lip, holding in the sound that was about to slip out if he kept this up.

"What is up there?" I asked him, hoping I didn't sound as affected as I was.

"Dinner," he replied.

I turned my head and looked up at him. "Dinner? How? We are in the middle of an apple orchard."

The corner of his mouth inched up slowly. "I have my ways."

This wasn't my first date by far. I'd been on many dates since Grams allowed me to start dating at seventeen. However, this was the most unique, romantic, and well-planned thing any guy had ever done for me. Granted, there might be a blanket with a bag of fast food up ahead, cold from him having left it here hours ago, but somehow, I doubted it. Amory was thorough with everything he did. Including his pursuit of me. I was starting to question why I'd fought against it so hard.

I liked him, and the more I was around him, the more that like was turning into affection. Maybe it was closer to lustful emotions because the man was all the things. Whatever it was, I didn't see a reason to keep pushing him away. He hadn't run off once he got a look into my home life. He'd even bailed my dad out of jail.

"What are you thinking? You've gone quiet." His voice was slightly husky.

"That if charm were an Olympic sport, you'd get the gold."

His deep, smooth laugh gave me chill bumps. Oh, yes, he was getting to me. There was no way out of this now. I wanted to be here. I wanted him. I'd never wanted Merce like this. Thinking of him put a slight damper on my mood. He'd texted me in the car, saying he missed me and wanted to see me. I still wasn't convinced he wasn't the one who had told Professor Brereton about me.

We stepped into the clearing. I stopped, taking it all in, and a gasp escaped me. It wasn't a blanket on the ground, nor was there a bag of food. Instead, there was a small table with two chairs, a lit candle, and two silver domes covering what I assumed were our meals on each side. The trees surrounding it were filled with twinkling lights, giving the entire setup a magical ambiance.

"Wow," I whispered.

"I hope you like Italian. I felt like it was the safest bet."

I nodded. I liked whatever he wanted me to eat. This was … this was incredible.

"How …" I paused, shaking my head in amazement. "How did you do all this?"

"Made a few calls," he replied simply, as if this had been easy to pull off.

"You made a few calls?" I asked, smiling at how ridiculous that sounded.

He'd done more than make a few calls. He had spent a lot of time and money on this.

"I've worked up an appetite," he said, leading me toward the chair to my left.

I watched as he pulled it out, then nodded at me to take a seat. I didn't move, but just stood there, soaking it in. Him in. This entire moment in.

He frowned. "What's wrong?"

I licked my lips, then laughed. "Nothing. I'm just … this is all …" Pausing, I tried to think of the right way to say this. "No one has ever done anything like this for me before."

He flashed me a cocky grin. "Then, you've been dating the wrong men."

"Boys," I supplied, walking over and taking a seat. "I've been dating boys."

He pushed my chair in, then leaned down close to my ear. "Let's change that."

I sucked in a breath and inhaled his clean scent. Mint and spice. Whatever it was, I wished I could bury my head in his chest and stay there.

Amory lifted the dome in front of me to reveal a pasta dish—I didn't know the name of it, but it was creamy-looking and smelled divine.

"Spaghetti alla carbonara," he told me. "It's one of my favorites."

He set the dome down on the grass beside us, then walked around to sit in the chair across from me. The small candle between us was in a crystal holder that kept it safe from the evening breeze. He'd had to have help. It hadn't been lit very long, and the silver bucket—filled with ice and a bottle of wine—was clearly chilled, but the ice wasn't melted. I looked around us for any way someone could have gotten here without me seeing or hearing them pass by. The only option I could tell was that they had come from the other side of the property. It was dark, so I couldn't see, but I assumed there was a road or building out that way.

He reached over to pick up a long, narrow dish that had a linen napkin over it, and he removed the cloth to reveal bread, along with an oil, then placed it between us.

"I'm not a wine drinker," he told me. "But Minna informed me that white wine would be the best choice." He pulled it from the bucket and looked at it. "Frascati. I'm sure it's good. She's excellent at pairing the best wines with foods."

I had no clue what that was, but it was white wine and probably cost a fortune.

"Who is Minna?" I asked, trying not to sound like a jealous female.

He took the wineglass in front of me and began to fill it. "Minna is our cook. She's been with my family a very long time. To be honest, Mexican is her specialty, but she agreed with me that Italian was a better option for tonight."

He had a cook. Of course he did. His father had built the college football stadium. They probably had an entire staff at his house.

"It smells amazing," I told him as he handed me my glass.

"She's the best," he replied, then poured his wine.

I lifted the glass to my lips and tasted it. Oh, yes, this was expensive. No wine I had ever tasted went down so smoothly.

"Good?" he asked.

I giggled and nodded my head, setting the glass down. "Not the right word. I could drink the entire bottle." Not that I would. One glass was going to be my limit.

He grinned and reached for the bread, tearing off a piece and then dipping it into the seasoned oil before holding it out to me. "She makes this from scratch. Both the bread and the oil."

I needed a Minna in my life. I took it from him. "If you watch me eat this, I won't be able to enjoy it properly."

He tore off another piece, then soaked it in the dip before putting it into his mouth and taking a bite. I watched his jaw as he chewed and the way his muscle flexed in his neck. God, that was nice to look at.

Realizing I was gawking at him, I quickly looked down at my plate and took a bite of my bread, feeling my face grow warm. I was out of my depth with this man. He was much too worldly, sexy, and sophisticated for me to handle. I was going to mess it up. He would never be able to take me out in public.

"Relax, Royal. It's just me and you. Whatever has you all tense, stop thinking about it. Enjoy the meal," he told me.

I looked up at him. "Sorry. I'll try."

He picked up his fork and twirled the noodles with it. "What's your favorite type of music?" he asked.

I pressed my lips together and shook my head.

"What?" A curious gleam sparked in his eyes.

"Fine. But you're gonna laugh."

"Never."

I stared at him for a moment. "Classic country," I admitted.

"What's wrong with that? George Strait is a king."

I shook my head. "No. *Classic* country. As in George Jones, Waylon Jennings, Johnny Cash, Loretta Lynn, Willie Nelson, Hank Williams Senior, not Junior."

His eyes widened. "So, *classic*, classic," he said. "And you're almost twenty-one. I wasn't expecting that."

"Grams loves them all. She has at least a hundred albums. I grew up listening to them. I didn't hear other music until I was older. Whenever I hear 'You Ain't Woman Enough,' I can still see Grams holding her wooden spoon in the kitchen, singing it like she wrote it."

Feeling a real smile stretch across my face, I realized my shoulders weren't tense anymore, and I wasn't battling with my lack of self-confidence. Amory was giving me an odd look. As if he didn't recognize me or was confused. That made me laugh.

"What?" I asked, amused.

His gaze softened. "Nothing. I just like listening to you talk. Hearing about your life."

This man was going to ruin me for all the others.

FOURTEEN

"Life isn't a fairy tale, Royal."

SEBASTIAN

This was not what my father had been thinking when he set his plan in motion. He'd taken over and used me like a damn puppet on a string. It had worked. The way Royal was looking at me right now, she was feeling something. And I fucking liked it. I wanted it. But knowing it had all been manipulated meant this wasn't real. Whatever it was she thought she felt for me was because my father had spoon-fed it to her.

Dinner had been fun. I found myself enjoying her laugh, feeling warm shit in my chest when she smiled at me. I wasn't so sure the family was right about her. There were facts, and then there was speculation. What we thought fit. But they didn't know her. They hadn't sat and listened to her talk about her Grams or tell stories of her childhood. She was a hustler, swindler, whatever you wanted to label it, but it was how she survived. I could respect that. Hell, I'd done much worse.

She let out a squeal and jumped when a rabbit crossed in front of our path. I pulled her against my side with my arm over her shoulders.

"Easy, Ace. It's just a bunny. Last time I checked, those aren't killer around these parts," I teased.

"You never know."

A phone started ringing, and I knew it wasn't mine. I'd never read her last text message, and until this moment, I'd forgotten all about it. She had that effect on me. It had become just us. No ulterior motives.

Stopping, she reached into her purse and pulled out the phone. The screen said *Miller's*. It was the bar her father went to often.

"Hello?" she said.

She began walking quickly back toward the car, as if to get space between us, not realizing my stride was much longer than hers.

"Already? Jesus, Glenn, how much has he had?" she asked, sounding frustrated.

It was just after ten, and she was getting the *come get your drunk father* call. I didn't like that fucker, but hearing what she dealt with on a regular basis had pushed me to the verge of hating him. She was on a first-name basis with the bartender, it seemed.

"I'm out. I'll need to go home and get my car first." She paused. "Please don't call the cops, Glenn. I can't handle that again."

After letting out a sigh, she thanked him and ended the call.

"I'm sorry," she began when she turned back to look at me.

The pained expression on her previously happy face pissed me off.

Damn that asshole.

"No need to apologize," I told her.

She chewed on her bottom lip and nodded, continuing to walk at her fast pace. As much as I wanted her tucked against me with my arm around her, this was probably saving my ass from doing something stupid. Like pressing her against the side of my car and jerking up that short dress until I could get my fingers inside her panties.

Nope. Don't think about it.

We were at the car in minutes, and I did my damnedest to watch the road as I started driving back to her house while she took off the rain boots and began putting her heels back on. All that skin I didn't get to touch. Teasing me with it. Yeah, I didn't care if this was for the best. I hated that motherfucker for ending the night before I wanted to.

She was silent most of the way back, and by the way she held her body, I could tell she was tense. Unable to resist any longer, I reached over and took one of her fisted hands, then flipped it over. With the pad of my thumb, I caressed her fingers, and she relaxed them, slowly opening until she wasn't pressing her nails into her palm anymore.

I glanced at her, and she was watching me rub her hand. I ran my fingers from the tops of hers, all the way down to the base of her palm, then back up, continuing the pattern. The sound of her breath hitching made my cock start to stiffen again. I bet she sounded fucking amazing when she got off.

"Better?" I asked her.

She nodded. "Yes," was her whispered response.

"I'll go with you to get him," I said.

Her head snapped up, and she looked at me, wide-eyed. "No. No, you don't have to do that. It's fine, really."

I'd go straight there, but he wasn't fitting in the back of this car. She could argue with me all she wanted, but I was going to Miller's with her. Mostly because I hated thinking of her dealing with him on her own, but there was also the thought of her walking into that bar, dressed like she was, that wasn't helping my mood.

"I want to," I told her.

"I don't want you to."

I cut my eyes at her. "Ready to get rid of me so soon?"

A sad smile touched her lips. "No, it's not that. I wish …" She sighed. "I was enjoying the evening. I don't want it to end with you seeing my drunk father, acting like a jerk at the bar."

I laced my fingers through hers and held her hand. "Life isn't a fairy tale, Royal. We all deal with real shit. I'm not going to go running when I see what yours looks like."

She laid her head back against the seat as her fingers curled around my hand as if she needed me. That one little move triggered an odd reaction deep inside me. I didn't recognize it, and I wasn't sure this was a good thing. The closest description I could think of to label it was *pleasure*, but that wasn't strong enough. There was a dangerous edge to it. Almost as if a predator had been lying dormant in my soul and it had just been woken up for the first time, currently sated.

But what would happen when it wasn't?

FIFTEEN

"He can't breathe!"

ROYAL

Not only was he determined to go with me, but he was also driving the Bug. If I wasn't so stressed about him seeing my dad like this, I would laugh at the picture he made. His tall body and broad shoulders sitting behind the wheel of my Grams's Volkswagen Bug.

Before we had left in this car to head to the bar, Amory had convinced Maeme to go on home since Grams had taken her meds and was asleep. I hated having to rush off instead of thanking her properly and asking her about the evening. She had been so kind to come stay with Grams. I needed to get her address so I could send her a thank-you card.

"This place?" Amory asked as he slowed in front of Miller's Bar.

"Yeah," I told him. "Pull around to the back door. They normally have him back there so it's easier for me to get to him."

Amory nodded, but his jaw was clenched tightly. Not only did it stand out more, but the veins in his neck were also prominent I wanted to make that look go away, but I knew there was nothing I could do. He disapproved of my dad doing this. So did I, but this was life. It wasn't like I could stop him.

The moment he stopped the car, I was already unbuckled. I opened the door to bolt out and get to the bar first. I wasn't sure if he'd stay in the car or not. Hopefully, he would. My dad wasn't a nice drunk. If he decided to go on one of his rants about me, then I didn't want Amory to hear him. It was bad enough that the bartenders at Miller's had more than once.

The door swung open, and Glenn, one of the younger bartenders, came out, holding my dad's arm in a firm grip as he stumbled and cursed.

"Don' wan' no help from you!" he shouted.

Glenn ignored him, looking past me to the car and Amory, who I'd heard just get out of it. I hadn't turned back and asked him to wait inside because it wouldn't have done any good. The longer I stood out here, the more my dad would have a chance to do or say something.

"Let's go home, Dad," I told him, reaching to take his other arm and relieve Glenn.

"He got here earlier than normal," Glenn said. "I tried to keep a watch on him, but he's not easy."

It wasn't Glenn's fault. He had a bar full of people to serve and wasn't my dad's keeper.

"It's fine," I assured him.

Glenn didn't look so sure.

"Stop talkin' 'bout me like I ain't here!" Dad snarled at me. "Jus' get in the damn car and take me home, you good-for-nothing slut. Look at ya, dressed like a whore. Look just like your momma did when I met her, and she's a whore too."

I felt Amory behind me and took a deep breath before pulling my father's arm so he would start moving toward the car.

"Heard it all before, Dad. Let's go," I replied calmly.

The shame of hearing his hateful words was hard with Amory standing there, listening. I'd thought I was immune to it, but the sick knot in my stomach that came this time told me I wasn't.

Dad pushed me, and I stumbled because of the heels I was still wearing. Normally, I handled his aggressiveness without issue, but I wasn't dressed for it tonight.

"Whoa," Amory said, grabbing my waist to steady me as he glared at my father.

"I'm fine," I told him. "It's fine."

Amory didn't even glance at me when he released me, then grabbed my father's other arm and jerked him hard enough that he was the one falling forward this time. His arm was snatched from my hold as Amory basically carried him by his arm to the car.

My father began cursing and crying out in pain. I glanced at Glenn, who stood there, watching. He raised his eyebrows at me, then nodded his head before turning to go back inside.

Hurrying over to the car, I got the door and opened it to put him in the passenger seat.

"Lean the seat forward," Amory ordered. "He's going in the back."

"Don' sit in the back in my own fucking car!" Dad told him.

"You do tonight," Amory replied, then forcefully shoved him into the car, where he fell onto the seat face-first.

He didn't wait for my dad to get straightened out before moving my seat back and squishing him into the small area. The things my drunken father was gonna say on the ride home were going to be bad. Especially now that he'd been handled this way by someone I'd brought with me.

"Get in," Amory said to me in a gentler tone.

I lifted my eyes to meet his and expected to see pity or disgust. Instead, I felt a chill run down my spine from the enraged gleam in his brown eyes.

I didn't try to soothe him, but then I had no idea what to do or say. I sat down, and he waited until I adjusted my dress before closing the door.

"You think I don't know you're spreading your legs for that man? Only reason he's here, ain't it? Your Grams would be ashamed of you if she knew." The slurred speech was low and held the disgust that it always did.

When he was drunk, he made no attempt to hide how he felt about me. All my mother's transgressions were blamed on me.

I said nothing, but kept my focus straight ahead at the poorly lit parking lot. Amory climbed back into the car, and I remained tense, waiting for my father to start in on me or possibly him next.

Amory fixed the rearview mirror until it was aimed at the back seat. "Say one more motherfucking word to her or about her, and I'll pull this car over, jerk you out of it, and beat your sorry-ass face in."

I sucked in a breath, staring at him. Surely, he was joking.

No words came from my dad. He grunted in response. If I was lucky, he'd pass out before we got home.

Amory started the vehicle and shifted it into drive before he reached over and once again coaxed my fist open with the soft brush of his fingers. My stomach went from the tight knot it was in to once again fluttering wildly from being touched like this. Simple, kind, and reassuring, all at once.

I opened my fingers, and his hand slid over mine. Then, he threaded our fingers together before firmly closing his large hand over mine with a sturdy grip. Just like before, my body began to relax. It didn't feel lonely when his hand held mine. The desperation evaporated, and the world seemed less fraught with obstacles ready to leap out at me. I knew that wasn't the case. I would wake up tomorrow with all the same troubles from today and more, but in this moment, I didn't fear them because we had this connection.

The drive back home was quiet. I waited to hear my father's snore, but it never came. It wasn't until we pulled into the driveway and Amory's hand left mine that the heaviness reappeared. Dad was still awake, and Amory would be leaving. My father was going to make me pay for this.

It wasn't anything I hadn't dealt with before, but I normally tried to avoid setting him off. Too late for that. Amory had done enough that he'd be ready to unload the moment the Porsche pulled out of the driveway.

We opened our doors at the same time. I climbed out, then turned to move my seat forward and get Dad, but Amory had already done so on his side and was roughly snatching my father out. I winced as my dad groaned, staggering onto the broken pavement.

I hurried the best I could in the heels, not wanting to trip over any of the cracks, but needing to get to the two of them before it got worse.

"Thanks for your help," I told Amory. "I've got it from here."

The moment my father's palm connected with my face in a loud smack and I felt the familiar sting from his slap, I realized my mistake. It was one of those things that I should have been prepared for, but since the routine was different, I was off my game.

"Stupid bi—" my father started, glaring at me, but he was slammed back against the car hard with Amory's hand gripping his throat so tight that his face was instantly red.

"AMORY!" I cried out as he lifted my dad off the ground like he weighed nothing.

He couldn't breathe. My dad's eyes bugged out, and my heart was slamming against my chest so hard that I thought it might crack it open.

"STOP!" I begged, grabbing his arm and pulling it, trying to free his hold on my dad.

He wasn't letting him go. *Oh God.*

"AMORY!" I shouted again. "LET HIM GO!"

Amory looked down at me, and that terrifying darkness I'd seen in his eyes before, in the parking lot at the bar, was back.

Tears stung my eyes, and I pleaded with him to let my father down. "He can't breathe!"

There was a small flicker there that I hoped meant he was going to listen to me. When my dad was lowered back to his feet, I heard him gasp for air, although Amory hadn't released him yet; he'd eased his grip enough so my dad could get oxygen.

He swung his eyes back to my dad. "When I let you go, you'll get your sorry ass in that house and go to bed. Don't touch her. Don't speak to her. Don't look in her goddamn direction. If you do, I'll find out. And the next time, I won't stop."

I crossed my arms over my chest even though there was no real chill in the air. The sinister sound in his voice had caused a disquiet to settle over me. The shadows that lurked in his eyes now were eerie.

His hand fell away, and my dad started to turn to look at me when Amory grabbed his face and snatched it back to focus on him instead.

"Don't look," he reminded him.

I shivered.

While holding on to his face, Amory pulled him forward, then shoved him toward the house. Dad managed not to fall, although it was several steps before he righted himself.

I'd brought this here. Amory was my fault. If I'd known he was like this or that he even had this kind of behavior behind that charming smile, I wouldn't have gone anywhere with him. I couldn't date a man who was going to end up killing my father. Because it didn't matter what Amory said to him. When he wasn't here, I'd be slapped or tossed around some. My dad never truly hurt me when he was drunk. Just some bruises here or there, but he didn't deserve to be choked to death.

Amory's gaze finally shifted to me when my dad reached the front door. I licked my lips and straightened my shoulders. A tear rolled down my face, and I wiped it away. Guilt, disappointment, and anger all warred inside my chest.

"Please leave," I told him.

His gaze softened, but I'd already seen enough. This wasn't something I had room for in my life. I needed support and understanding, not brutality.

"Royal," he began, but I shook my head.

"NO! You need to leave. Now," I shouted, pointing at his car.

Another tear rolled down my face, and I hated that I couldn't stop them. For a moment, I'd thought I'd found something good in my life. That perhaps I was going to be happy. Not alone. I should have known not to be fooled. All I ever seemed to get was the ugly of the world.

He took a step toward me, and I backed up.

"Amory," I warned. "I need you to get in your car and drive away."

Not wanting to stand out here any longer while all the things I'd been wishing for had gone up in a blaze, leaving nothing but ashes behind, I walked toward the house. His footsteps didn't follow me, and I was relieved, although every move I made farther away, the layers of disillusionment thickened, making the magical time I'd had with him earlier a painful regret.

• SIXTEEN •

"We fuck the hot pussy. We don't love it. How many times do I need to remind you?"

SEBASTIAN

I poured my third full glass of whiskey. I hadn't gone up to the house, but stopped at the stables instead. Other than the horses, the buildings were empty. While I lifted it to my lips to drink it down in one long gulp, hoping to numb the shit roaring inside me, the door opened, and I cut my eyes in that direction to see King walk inside, followed by my brother. I finished the drink and leaned against the bar.

"What's got you drinking Jack like it's water?" Thatcher asked.

"I'm gonna toss out a guess here and say she's about five-seven, blonde, and excellent at pool," King replied with a smirk as he walked behind the bar.

"The girl you're supposed to use to infiltrate the Dancastles?"

I didn't like the way he'd said it or how he'd said it. Grabbing the bottle, I poured more whiskey into my now-empty glass.

"Fuck, if you're gonna drink it like that, at least drink something better than Jack," King said to me, sliding the bottle he'd just poured from in my direction.

I glanced down at the five-hundred-dollar bottle of scotch. "Why waste it?" I replied. "It's not like I'm drinking for enjoyment."

"He has a point," Thatcher agreed. "Don't give him that. But pour me a glass."

The door opened again, and Wells came walking inside with Teller, his younger brother. He'd just turned twenty this summer, but unlike the rest of us, he hadn't been pushed into the family workings just yet.

"What the fuck is Teller doing here?" I asked.

"Stellan and Roland were informed that it was time Teller made a decision. He's a part of this, or he isn't," Thatcher replied.

I didn't have to ask who had informed them. It would have come from the top. Blaise Hughes would have made the call, taking Roland's decision to let his youngest son finish college like a normal student out of his hands.

Wells slapped his brother on the back. "It's about time Momma's best boy got his hands dirty," he said with a mocking grin.

Teller had always been their mother's favorite, and it chafed the hell out of Wells. His narcissistic personality didn't handle it well. Unlike Thatcher, who gave not one fuck about the fact that I was our mother's favorite.

"Easy, brother. Your envy is showing," Teller replied with a cocky grin, then walked over toward me—or rather the bar.

I liked Teller. He'd been annoying as fuck when he was a kid, always getting into our shit, but he hadn't seemed to inherit all the bad traits that made Wells hard to like.

"Fuck off," Wells shot back at him. "At least I wasn't raised to be a pussy."

"Could you not come in here with that shit? Keep your family drama at home," King told them both. The irritation was clear in his voice.

"Sorry," Teller replied. "Can I have some of that?"

King moved the scotch over to him. "Drink up, little Jones."

Thatcher nodded his head toward Teller while looking at me. "You know, he could take your current job if you want out of it."

I stared back at my brother, trying to gauge what he was attempting to do here. I'd come to get drunk so I wouldn't have to deal with tonight. Not because I wanted to be rid of Royal.

"Are you trying to start shit with me?" I asked him.

"Fuck," King muttered behind me.

Thatcher cocked an eyebrow. "You tell me."

"What's the job?" Teller asked, but I didn't look at him.

"One you won't be taking," I said through clenched teeth.

Thatcher cut his eyes to Teller. "He's closer to her age. It would make more sense."

I slammed my glass down on the bar. Thatcher's lips twitched like he might smile.

Fucking asshole.

"He's not going near her," I told him.

Thatcher chuckled that deep, sadistic sound that was rarely heard. "All right then. I was just trying to be helpful."

"Bullshit! You are never helpful," I snapped.

"Sebastian, please don't tell me you went and fell in love again," Wells said with a roll of his eyes. "Jesus, dude, what is your deal? We fuck the hot pussy. We don't love it. How many times do I need to remind you?"

I narrowed my eyes as I glared at his smug face. Like he knew shit about anything. "I'm not in love. I've never been in love. But Royal is complicated, and I'm not sure …" I paused because I wasn't saying she was innocent yet. I had to do some more investigating before I announced her innocence in all this. "She's different."

Wells laughed. "You weren't in love with Oakley when you asked her to marry you?" he accused.

I wasn't the one who had taken his first love from him; that was his cousin, Wilder. I had dated her years after Wilder and proposed. But I now knew it wasn't love.

"No, I was young and felt possessive of her." I left out why. I didn't need to rub that in his face even if it had been another lifetime ago when he was the one in love with her.

"Because you had her cunt first. Popped that cherry," Thatcher said as he grinned wickedly over the rim of his glass.

"Where is Capri?" I asked him. "Don't you need to be standing guard over her like the psychopath you are?"

King snorted behind me.

"You took her virginity?" Wells asked me, sounding surprised.

Was he really asking me this? Who the fuck cared?

I took another drink.

"You want to get under Wilder's skin? Bring that shit up. He'll get that feral, enraged look in his eyes, and then he'll probably go and fuck the hell out of his woman, reminding her who's fucking it now," King said with a chuckle.

Wells shook his head. "Damn, I thought for sure she'd lost it before you. God knows I tried like hell to get in it. Probably wouldn't have cheated on her if she'd just given my horny teenage ass some. Hell, we might be married with kids by now."

Teller barked out a laugh. "She would have never married you! I was a little boy, and even I could see her panting after Wilder."

Thatcher walked over and set his empty glass down beside me. He looked from King to me. "You're right. Need to get back to Capri."

Our little jockey had him so wound up that he was almost a different man. Almost.

Last week, he'd taken off one of our stable hand's fingers for touching Capri's arm on fucking accident. Thankfully, King had walked in on it and convinced Thatcher that Capri would be very upset if he kept it up. Or else he probably would have taken the guy's whole hand or killed him, slowly slicing the man to pieces. She still had no idea it'd happened.

"Where are the girls you said we'd get tonight?" Teller asked, looking at Wells.

Wells pointed toward King. "Not while he's here. The ones who have shackled themselves don't want the bitches around anymore."

I picked up the bottle of Jack. I could use the distraction myself. "You staying here long, King?" I asked, hearing a slight slur in my voice.

"Nope. I'm leaving," he replied, then finished his scotch. When he was done, he set it beside Thatcher's glass. "Enjoy your night, boys."

I watched him stroll out the door.

Wells looked at me. "You want Fall?" he asked me.

I thought about it for a minute. The stripper was always willing to please me. She had the wrong color hair now though. All the things she could do to me weren't appealing. I wanted to fuck, but it just wasn't her face I was thinking about.

"No," I finally replied. "Not up for it tonight. But Teller would enjoy her."

Wells sighed. "Don't do this to me too."

"Do what?" I asked him, already starting toward the door.

"Get your head up some chick's ass."

"Just tired tonight," I replied.

"Bullshit!" he called out as I left the room.

Taking my phone from my pocket, I pulled up my texts, then remembered I'd never checked Royal's text from earlier tonight. Seeing her as a job was becoming harder, and my brain wasn't working that way anymore where she was concerned.

I opened the app that sent me all her texts and calls.

> Merce: Please stop ignoring me. I miss you. I fucked up. You know I love you, Royal. Talk to me, baby.

My hand tightened on the phone, and I stopped walking.

I scrolled to the next text; it was him again, only thirty minutes ago. He'd called her, but she hadn't answered as well.

> Merce: If you will talk to me, we can fix this. Us. I've had time to think, and I can't live without you.

Royal hadn't texted back.

I went back to my texts and found the last one she'd sent me. I almost smiled—until I remembered how our night had ended. I'd wanted to watch the life drain from that motherfucker's face. He'd called her names, taken the glow from her cheeks. The sadness in her eyes did me in. The driving force to mutilate the man who had caused it was alarming, even to me. I'd never reacted that way before.

> I stepped out of bounds tonight. I'm sorry. The things he said to you were cruel, and I was already on edge. Seeing him hit you caused me

> to snap. I shouldn't have. I handled it poorly. Please forgive me.

I read over the text one more time before hitting Send. It was a lie. I should have done more than I had, just not in front of her. That was the real reason I was apologizing. He deserved much worse, but she didn't deserve to see it.

I didn't expect her to text me back. Tomorrow, I was going back to Athens, but not to see her or talk to her. I was going to follow her. Properly this time. In another vehicle she wouldn't notice or suspect. There were some things I needed answers to. I wanted her name cleared from any involvement with the drug distribution. Then, I'd find out if Merce and her father were involved. But I wasn't going to use her to do it. I had another plan.

The thought of using Royal made me physically ill. She'd been used enough by the man who should have been protecting her. But she didn't need him anymore. She had me. Even if she didn't want me at the moment.

There was no response from her that night, and it took all my willpower not to send another text. Beg if I needed to. However, the next morning, just as I was arriving in Athens city limits, I got an alert that she'd sent a text, and it wasn't to me.

Pulling over, I picked up my phone and read it. She had texted someone named Anya.

> Are you working today? If so, would you mind bagging me up all the leftovers?

I read that twice, confused. *What leftovers?*
A response came through.

> Not today! I'm sorry. Dareen is

> working, and she wouldn't mind doing it if it wasn't for Alice being on shift. She's terrified of the old hag.

I wasn't getting something here. Was she talking about food? Getting leftovers from a restaurant?

She sent another text.

> That's okay. Thanks anyway! I understand. Grams was wanting the Rise and Dine cheese grits. LOL.

The bag from the back door of the diner. She was getting their leftovers for food. Fucking hell. I should have been relieved that it hadn't been the laced drugs, but my chest felt so damn tight that I couldn't take a deep breath.

> Does she not like the ones at the cafeteria? You know Ethel loves you there and will bag you up whatever you ask for.

So, she wasn't just getting food from Rise and Dine. The little charmer didn't just use her skills to keep her family's bills paid, but she also had places that would give her the food that they'd otherwise toss out.

> I'm heading to classes today. I'll stop and see her. Thanks! Enjoy your day off!

Was Ethel at the Howison cafeteria? Not that it mattered. Grams was getting her cheese grits from the diner. I'd make sure they got a delivery of everything on the buffet.

SEVENTEEN

Amory Blaine in a cowboy hat was porn-worthy.

ROYAL

Grams was beaming at the food on her plate.

"You say we have strawberry cheesecake and pecan pie too?" she asked me, her eyes lit with the excitement of a child.

I nodded. "Yep."

I hadn't even known the Rise and Dine had strawberry shortcake and pecan pie. The only desserts we'd ever gotten there were stale cookies and soupy lemon meringue that had sat out too long.

The fried fish was also something we'd never gotten before, as well as the soft, flaky butter rolls with honey or the twice-baked potatoes. Those all had to be items that were eaten up by customers.

I looked back at the four large bags sitting on our kitchen counter. It had been delivered an hour ago. Not only was it warm and fresh, but the delivery boy had said that it was everything they had on the menu today, just like requested.

I had been so flabbergasted by it all that I stood there, speechless, then remembered he needed a tip. When he said he had already been tipped two hundred dollars, I knew exactly who had sent this. I hadn't thought it could be him because how would he know about the Rise and Dine?

Once I closed the door and had a moment to think, I realized he'd seen me go get the leftovers that day he followed me. Anger, frustration, and embarrassment hit me all at once. That was, until Grams saw all the food from the bags. There had to be at least two pounds of the cheese grits. She had giggled like a little girl, holding the container tight to her chest.

Score one for Amory.

Between this and the text he'd sent last night, which I had read more times than I could count today, the resolve to stay away from him was slipping. In the light of day, it looked a bit different in my head. I had been tired and upset last night, then made it a much bigger deal. My dad wasn't in bed when I walked into the house. He had been waiting on me.

I touched the long sleeves I'd worn today to cover the handprint bruises on my arms.

After he'd finished his tossing me around and cursing me, I'd sat on the floor of the living room, where he'd had thrown me. All the anger from outside had started to fade away even then.

Amory had been defending me. Something my father had never done.

Grams shoveled another forkful of cheese grits into her mouth.

"Easy. It's not going anywhere. Don't choke," I warned her.

Another knock on the door, and then the bell rang.

"Better get that. It might be more food," she said, smiling.

We were going to be eating what we had now for a week at least. I walked over to it and opened it up to see Amory standing there. His dark hair, with the slight curl to it, was tucked behind his ears, and his brown eyes were lined by thick lashes. His almost-too-perfect high cheekbones, nose, and mouth were turned masculine by his jawline.

"Can we talk?" he asked.

I stepped out, closing the door behind me.

"Thanks for the food," I told him. "Grams is inside, eating it now."

His brows drew together. "How did you know it was from me?"

I let out a small laugh. "Because it's a ridiculous amount of food and you tipped the delivery boy two hundred dollars. I don't know anyone else who would do that."

The corner of his mouth lifted slightly. "You dated guys like me before. I'd think you were used to a man spending money on you."

I really wanted to laugh at that. "Uh, no. Merce did not send my family any food. Ever." I hadn't meant to say his name, but I didn't think it mattered. He wouldn't know who Merce was.

"The food seems to have softened you up some," he said as he studied me closely.

I licked my lips and nodded. "Yeah. I won't lie; seeing Grams that excited did help, but so did your text and sleep. I saw it a little differently this morning."

He didn't try to mask the relief in his eyes. "I am sorry," he said as his hand cupped the side of my face. "I shouldn't have reacted like I did."

I nodded. "I know."

He leaned his head slightly closer. His eyes locked on mine. "So, I'm forgiven?"

"Yes."

Amory took another step toward me, and I sucked in a breath as his eyes darkened. He bent down, taking my face with both his hands, and pressed his lips to mine.

To say the world felt like it had fallen from beneath me was an understatement. His tongue licked where I had just done so myself, and I opened my mouth to his obvious request.

The taste of mint had never been so good, but then I'd never had it via Amory Blaine's tongue. I wrapped my hands around his arms, feeling slightly off-balance as he pressed closer to me. His spicy scent and larger body seemed to consume me, and I went willingly.

"You taste even sweeter than I imagined," his deep, raspy voice said before he sucked gently on my bottom lip.

I heard the sound of a small moan, and I thought it must have come from me, but I wasn't sure of much right now. Just that I wanted closer. I wanted more of this.

Amory dropped his hands to my waist and tugged me up against his hard body with a groan that sent a tingle straight to the area between my legs.

His mouth left mine, and he began kissing a trail along my cheek over to my ear.

"What time does your Grams go to bed?" His husky voice in my ear made me tremble.

"Eight," I breathed, arching my neck for him to do more of that.

"Can I come see you then?"

I nodded. Yes. Definitely, he could do that. If I wasn't afraid my dad would come home, I'd pull him inside right now and convince Grams she needed a nap.

He let out a long, ragged breath as he slowly straightened up, and his hands eased their tight grip on me.

My chest was rising and falling so fast, and I knew he could tell, but there was no way I could control it. His eyes seemed to soak me in like I was his last meal as they drifted over my chest and down my body.

He took a step back, then another. "I'll be back tonight. If I stay here much longer, I'm not sure I can keep from shoving you against that door and giving the neighbors a show."

I let out a strangled laugh, then coughed, covering my mouth as I stared up at him.

His eyes twinkled with amusement. "You'd better go inside," he told me.

I didn't want to. I wanted to stay here with him. But Grams was alone inside, and I needed to be sure she wasn't eating too much. She'd get sick, and then the night really would be ruined.

"Okay," I replied, touching the knob behind me with my back still against it.

Reluctantly, I tore my eyes off Amory to turn around.

His hand closed around my arm, grabbing me, and I let out a cry and winced. Shit. Instantly, he let go of me. I was trying to think of what to say to him as I looked back at him, but he was already shoving my sleeve up.

I attempted to stop him and tug it down, but it was no use. He pulled it up until the handprint bruise was visible.

"Your father?" he asked, not taking his eyes off it.

"Don't," I replied as I finally got my shirt free of him and tugged it down so he'd stop looking at it.

His shoulders rose and fell. The veins in his neck stood out, and he took several deep breaths before he lifted his eyes to mine.

"Last night." It wasn't a question. He was stating what he already knew.

"He was drunk and angry," I told him. "Please don't do anything. Don't ruin what happened. The kiss."

He shook his head, and his shoulders relaxed. "I won't. I'm sorry if I was the cause of that. I messed up last night, and you paid for it."

"No!" I said fiercely, placing a hand on his chest. "This isn't your fault. Just forget it, okay? I bruise easily. It didn't even hurt."

Amory nodded. "Okay." Then, he reached out and ran his knuckles down my cheek. "I'll be here at eight."

That hadn't been bad. I wanted to throw my arms around him and thank him for not making a big deal out of this. He winked at me with a small smile, then turned to walk back to his car, which I realized wasn't the Porsche.

How many vehicles did he have?

I'd never pictured him in a truck, even an expensive-looking one. He opened the door, then picked something up. I watched as he placed a black cowboy hat on his head and then glanced back at me.

Amory Blaine in a cowboy hat was porn-worthy.

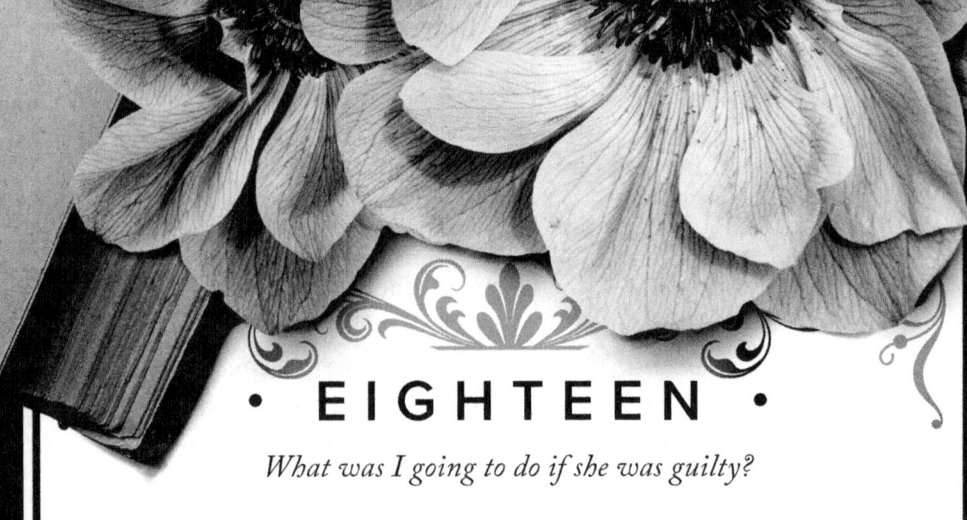

• EIGHTEEN •

What was I going to do if she was guilty?

SEBASTIAN

The only thing keeping me from taking that bastard out myself was knowing Royal was waiting on me.

"You look like you're considering burning the place down," Storm said beside me.

I tore my eyes off Miller's Bar and looked at him then at Thatcher, who was leaning against the driver's door of the Escalade with his arms crossed and a cigarette in his mouth. I'd asked him specifically to do this. If I couldn't be here to do it, then I wanted him. Not because he was my brother, but because he'd not restrain himself. He'd make it hurt. He'd enjoy it. Until I could get there.

"I gotta go," I told him.

Thatcher nodded his head once, then clenched the cigarette between his teeth. "Go on then. We got this."

I took one last glance at the bar, then headed for my truck. It was ten until eight, and I didn't want to be late. Thinking about how fucking incredible Royal had felt in my arms today and the sweetest-tasting mouth I'd ever had was what kept me from ripping things off the walls after I saw the bruise on her arm.

My plan had been approved by my dad. He liked it and agreed it would speed things along. He just wanted to be sure I could handle Royal. I'd assured him I had the situation with her under control. Which I did. I just didn't know what tomorrow would bring and if I was ready for it. Whatever she did or said though, I was going to make sure she stayed clueless and safe.

Forcing thoughts about everything except her out of my head, I did my best to relax. She'd notice if I was tense. My being distracted, however, wasn't going to be an issue. The moment I saw her, I'd forget this shit, or at least it would be moved aside. She always managed to claim my complete attention.

Pulling into the driveway, I smiled as the front porch light came on. I wasn't even out of my truck yet when she opened the door. I almost swallowed my damn tongue when I got a look at what she was wearing.

Please let there be nothing on under that oversize, long-sleeved shirt.

I wouldn't think about why she had on sleeves. I knew she didn't want to remind me about her bruise. It was probably best I couldn't see it.

I made long, swift strides up the beaten, weathered sidewalk until I reached the porch. I skipped two steps and was in front of her in moments.

She smiled shyly up at me. The places I wanted to see those pretty lips. Starting with them wrapped around my cock.

"Just a shirt?" I asked hopefully.

She blushed, then tugged it up. "Shorts on too."

Dammit. We'd have to fix that.

I nodded my head at the door. "Grams asleep?"

"Yes," she said, then turned to go back in the door.

I followed so close behind her that our bodies brushed.

I shut the door and locked it before reaching for her waist. She spun around and laughed.

"Shorts off," I told her as I reached under the shirt and took the offending item, then pulled it down her legs.

She lifted her feet one at a time without argument. This obedient side of her had me thinking I should have taken the panties off too.

Standing back up, I pressed a kiss to her lips. "Much better."

She let out a breathy laugh.

"We'd better get in the living room," I told her. "All I've thought about since I left is how sweet that mouth is, and if I start kissing you right here, we won't ever make it in there."

Her eyes widened slightly, and the excitement in them only made my hardening cock stiffen even more.

"I don't think I'm ready to have sex with you," she blurted out, as if she had been struggling to say it. "I mean, I want to. It's just … well, I don't move that fast. I'm not a virgin or anything but sex creates an attachment and feelings that I don't think I'm mentally prepared to have with you."

That was not what I'd wanted to hear. I disagreed. I'd fucked many women, and only once had I had any attachment to one. Maybe it was her age. I had to remember how young she was.

I ran the pad of my thumb over her bottom lip. "Whatever you want, Ace."

She let out a relieved sigh. "Thank you."

Don't thank me yet.

I hadn't agreed to play fair. She'd need to ask me to fuck her, and I was positive I could make that happen.

I took her hand and walked her into the living room. Sitting down on the sofa, I pulled her onto my lap. "Since I got my first look at those legs, I've wanted them straddling my lap," I told her as I guided her legs on either side of me.

Her breath hitched, and I watched her face as she lowered herself. When my erection was pressed against her cunt, she gasped slightly. I brushed her hair out of her face.

"You make me hard. I can't control that," I told her before bringing her head closer until I had those lips on mine again.

She opened immediately, and I savored her with slow flicks of my tongue. Keeping my hips from lifting and pressing against her harder was difficult as she returned my kiss hungrily. Moving my hands down her shoulders and then her arms, I continued until I found the hem of the shirt.

She stiffened as my hands slid underneath, and I pressed one flat against her stomach.

"You said no sex," I reminded her with my mouth still on hers. "And you're not wearing a bra, which means you want me to play with these titties."

A sexy little moan came from her, and my dick twitched in my jeans. I nibbled on her plump bottom lip before thrusting my tongue back into her mouth just as I filled my hands with her heavy tits. Hard nipples poked my hands, and I squeezed.

"I wanna see," I urged, rolling each hard nub between two fingers. "What color are they?"

Her hips rocked then, and she let out another sexy sound. My rigid dick was rubbing her clit. I'd known exactly how to sit her on me for it to work to my advantage.

I started lifting her shirt up, and she didn't try to stop me, only wiggled more on my lap, panting. If she wanted to dry-hump me, I'd gladly let her, but hopefully, she'd at least let me get my jeans off to do it.

When I dropped her shirt to the floor, I tried not to look at her arm, but my eyes went there anyway. She was too lost in her building orgasm to realize she'd given me a view of her arm. My gaze swung to her other arm, and I tensed as my blood roared in my ears. That arm was worse. She'd not told me he'd hurt both her arms.

What had he done? Grabbed her and shaken her? Thrown her down? I was going to kill him.

"Amory." She said the name I'd given her as she touched my face with her hand, turning my attention from her arm to look up at her. "Don't," she begged.

I wasn't going to let that bastard ruin this, but he would pay for it.

I swallowed hard and nodded, then focused on the two perfect, bouncy breasts with hard pink nipples in front of me.

"Look, how pretty," I praised, taking them both, then pulling one nipple into my mouth and sucking on it.

Her mouth was slightly open when I looked up at her. The wiggling had turned to hard rocking as her eyes took on that glazed gleam of pleasure. She was gonna orgasm like this, and I wanted to feel it. Shoving my hand down the front of her tiny pink panties, I slid my fingers into the hot, wet warmth.

"Oh God!" she cried out the moment my middle finger made contact with her hard, swollen clit.

"That's what you needed," I said, licking at the pulse in her neck before moving back to her tits. "Your pussy is dripping. It wanted some attention."

"Amory," she moaned.

Hearing another name on her lips like this was not good for my sanity. Even if the name she was saying was who she thought I was.

I moved my hand further down until two of my fingers pushed inside her tight cunt.

"AH!" Her head fell back as she began to fuck my fingers. "Yes, yes," she panted.

"That's it, baby. Come all over my fingers. Give me a taste."

She looked at me, and then her mouth opened, and her body jerked as she pulsed around my fingers, coating my hand with her release. I wasn't sure I'd ever simply watched a woman get off. I was normally too busy getting my own nut to pay attention. But, damn, that was beautiful. Her face was flushed, lips swollen, and her lashes fluttered as she closed her eyes.

I eased my hand out, careful to keep her juices on my fingers. She stared at me, looking stunningly sated. I ran my tongue up one finger, then sucked it into my mouth. Her taste reminded me of melted sugar, drizzled over a ripe peach. I wanted that covering my face.

The flare in her eyes made me want to smile. She liked seeing me do this. I made sure to clean the other finger just as thoroughly. She watched with fascination.

"I'll spread your legs and get you off with my mouth next," I said when I finished.

She blinked then, as if broken from a trance, and then a smile played at the corners of her lips. "I can't believe I did that."

"What?" I asked, confused.

She ducked her head. "Had an orgasm like that."

I put a finger under her chin and lifted her eyes back up to me. "Why wouldn't you?"

She pulled her bottom lip between her teeth for a minute, then scrunched her nose. "I normally have to do that."

I still wasn't following her.

"I don't understand what you're telling me."

Her shoulders rose and fell with a heavy sigh.

"Orgasms aren't easy for me. I have them, but I have to be the one that does it."

"You've not gotten off during sex then?"

How the hell had a man not gotten her off while fucking her?

"No, I have. I just do it. You know, I rub my clit to do it," she explained, then pressed her lips together, looking embarrassed she'd said that.

Oh, hell no. I played with one of her nipples while holding her gaze. "You won't touch yourself when I'm inside you, and you'll orgasm more than once."

A small laugh left her lips. "I would tell you not to be disappointed if I don't, but I think I believe you."

"You spread those legs for me right now, and I'll show you," I told her.

She was considering it. I could see it in her expressive eyes.

"As tempting as that might be, I still don't think I'm ready," she said, sounding as if the decision pained her as much as it did my throbbing cock.

She started to get up, and I grabbed her waist.

"That doesn't mean you have to get off me."

Her eyes dropped to my lap, then slowly made their way back up to me. "You gave me an amazing orgasm. I was just going to return the favor."

I was going to break through the zipper on these jeans.

"No favor to return," I told her, although I wanted her hands or mouth on my cock more than I wanted to breathe. "The taste of your pussy was all I needed."

She blushed some more and started to get off me again. I let her this time. When she was standing up, she moved between my legs, and I widened them, watching. This was her show now, and I'd take whatever she was willing to give me.

When she bent down to unsnap and unzip my jeans, I held my breath. The sight of her slender fingers working to get me out of my pants was one of those things I would burn into my brain to jack off to over and over again. I lifted my hips for her, and she tugged down the jeans, along with my boxer briefs, until they were on the floor, pooled around my boots.

Her eyes, as she took in my hard length, made the predator that had suddenly taken up residence in my body snap to attention.

She ran a fingertip down the side of it. "That's, uh … wow. Um, I didn't realize sizes differed so much."

I chuckled. "What do you mean?"

Her eyes lifted to mine. "This is the biggest one I've seen. It's much bigger."

"Not a good time to mention the other dicks you've seen, baby," I warned her. The thing pacing inside me, pressing too close to the border, didn't like thinking about it any more than I did.

"Sorry," she whispered.

I said nothing because she wrapped her fingers around me and began to pump slowly. Words were gone. I was solely focused on watching her pretty hand on my dick.

She eased down to her knees in front of me, and I wasn't sure if I was gonna weep at the sight or make an idol in her honor to fucking worship.

Nothing had ever looked so damn good as Royal's mouth taking my cock, her lips slowly moving down it. She had only half of my dick in when it hit the back of her throat, and she gagged.

"Fuuuck," I groaned, grabbing a handful of her hair and pulling her head back slightly. I wanted to slam her face back down on it, but I'd be damned if I hurt her.

Her lips tightened around me, and she went down further, making me lightheaded; it felt so good.

"Look at me," I told her.

She lifted her eyes back up to meet mine, and I cupped the side of her face.

"This angel face, stuffed with my cock, is the prettiest damn thing I've ever seen."

A smile tugged at her lips as she continued to work her mouth over my throbbing dick. I brushed her hair out of her face, not wanting to miss a moment of how she looked while sucking me off.

"That's it," I groaned. "Fucking amazing."

I was already close. Having her ride my dick had brought me to the edge, and this was about to finish me off.

"I'm gonna come, baby," I warned her.

I expected her to move back and use her hand, but she sucked harder. Her gagging as the head of my cock slid down her throat was it. My hand fisted in her hair, and I thrust my hips, shoving it even further, no longer in control of my body.

"FUCK! FUCK!" I shouted as my body shook.

My eyes stayed glued to her as she swallowed it all. Every jet that shot out of me. Her fingernails bit into my thighs. Another shudder ran over me, and I wasn't sure I could feel my legs.

I was still gasping when she lifted her head, letting me pop free of her mouth. Blue eyes stared up at me with a twinkle of satisfaction in them. If I could breathe, I'd laugh at her smug expression. She had every right to be. She'd just given me the world's best blow job.

Her pink tongue darted out to lick her lips for anything it might have missed. The simple action had me transfixed.

"Come here." My voice had a thick, husky timbre to it.

She stood up, and I slowly took in the view of her gorgeous body in nothing but panties. I wanted to grab her and haul her to my room. Put her in my bed and keep her there. With me. Forget this other shit.

Reaching for her hips, I pulled her to me and placed her in my lap, then buried my face in the curve of her neck and shoulder.

"Goddamn," I muttered against her silky skin.

A small laugh bubbled out of her, and I tightened my arms around her. Fucking her wasn't going to get her out of my system. It would just make this—or rather, me—worse. My soul felt as if it had started pacing impatiently. A deep rumble vibrated in my head. Warning me that I'd better protect, claim, own.

But how was I supposed to do that when, right at this moment, her father was being taken underground to be beaten and tortured for information? What if my desire for her was so damn strong that I had missed the truth? What was I going to do if she was guilty?

Her fingers sank into my hair, and she ran them through the thick curls. I closed my eyes as she soothed whatever disturbance was unraveling just beneath the surface of my sanity. I turned my head just enough so that I could see her arm. The dark purple-and-blue handprint that circled her soft skin seemed to speak for itself.

Royal needed me. She trusted me. As if reading my mind, she curled her body in closer to mine, and the side of her plump tit pressed against my chest.

I was going to have to make a choice. Unlike any I'd ever made before. One that I'd been raised to never consider. Because the family always came first.

A soft purr came from her as I ran my hand down her back. The scent of vanilla and honey was all I could smell.

She turned and slipped her arms around my neck, then laid her head on my shoulder.

"I could go to sleep like this," she whispered.

I continued to caress her back.

I'd feared this from the beginning. No, that wasn't right. I'd feared being attracted to her and getting distracted.

This I hadn't been prepared for.

"Go to sleep," I told her, then kissed the side of her head. "I'll make sure you are tucked in bed before I leave."

Her warm breath tickled my skin as she laughed softly. "I'm not very good company. I don't know why I'm so sleepy all of a sudden. But you—" She yawned, wiggling against me. "You feel safe and warm."

It took every ounce of my willpower to keep from standing up and leaving this house with her locked in my arms. I couldn't do that. But I wanted to. I wanted to take her and run. Run until no one could find us. Run until all the truths didn't matter. Until it was just us.

"I won't let anyone or anything hurt you," I told her, knowing she had no idea the lengths I would go to in order to make sure she was safe. Even if it was from her own crimes.

No one was going to hurt her again. Not even my family.

• NINETEEN •

"My little brother has had his switch flipped."

SEBASTIAN

The cry of pain that met my ears did nothing to appease the increasing darkness spreading through me. It was as if I no longer recognized myself. That the man I knew was standing back and watching the transition take place and doing nothing to stop it.

I stalked through the underground tunnel toward the sound. The smell of Thatcher's cigarette smoke met my nose before I reached the door leading into the room where they had Vinson Shelton strapped up. His wrists were tied together and pulled up tight from the chain that hung from the ceiling. There was some blood on his face, but not much. Yet.

His eyes swung to me as I walked all the way into the room, and I saw the anger flash in them at the realization that I was behind this. I was glad those eyes looked nothing like his daughter's.

"Is this about Royal?" he spit. "What did that little slut do?"

I didn't stop walking until my fist slammed into his nose, causing it to spray blood as he let out a pained howl.

Thatcher chuckled behind me, but I didn't turn to look at any of them.

"Call her one more name, and I will slice off your goddamn dick and shove it in your mouth until you choke on it," I warned him.

"Shit," King muttered behind me.

"Oh fuck," Wells drawled. "I told you not to—"

I turned around and headed toward him. He stopped whatever he was about to say when he looked at me.

A hand wrapped around my arm, and I jerked it back, ready to slam whoever had just touched me into a wall.

Storm's eyes met mine.

"Deep breath," he said. "Take a deep fucking breath." He glanced back at Wells. "You either shut the fuck up or leave."

"What is wrong with him?" Wells asked.

A deep cackle came from across the room. "My little brother has had his switch flipped."

I swung my glare to Thatcher.

He took the cigarette from his mouth and held it out to me. "Go ahead. Burn him. Enjoy it. You know you want to cause him pain."

"Broke my nose," Vinson said in a garbled voice behind me.

"Oh, he's gonna do more than that. I can see the manic gleam in his eyes. You can start talking, or he can unleash all the crazed shit building inside him on you. Either way, I'm entertained," Thatcher told him.

My gaze narrowed when I saw Teller standing in the corner, wide-eyed as he watched me. Turning back around, I studied the man in front of me. Blood clots covered his mouth and down his neck. His eyes were starting to swell. Neither made me feel peace or even a shred of satisfaction. The creature controlling me wanted anguish, torture, agony.

"You bruised her. Left your handprints on her skin." I seethed, moving back to him. Rage rolled off me as my breathing got heavier.

"She was in my face! She bruises easy! Whatever she said, it was a lie!"

A loud, animalistic sound filled the room, and I faintly recognized it as my own voice as I grabbed his arm and twisted it unnaturally until the crack of his bones met the wail that tore from his chest.

"He's gonna kill him," Storm warned.

"It'll take more than that to kill him." Thatcher's voice sounded amused.

I ignored them as I grabbed his other arm and did the same with it. Except this time, Vinson's head fell forward, and there was no sound but the breaking of his bones.

"Is he dead?" Teller asked.

"No, dumbass. He blacked out from the pain," Wells replied.

"You done? Because we need to get answers from the motherfucker before you kill him," Storm told me.

My chest rose and fell fast as I walked over to the other side of the room and placed my palms against the wall, trying to calm the violent craving taking over me.

They were right. We needed answers.

Then, I could kill him.

If she ever found out, she would hate me. He was a bastard, but she loved him. He didn't deserve it. Not her love. I wanted him out of her life. I wanted to protect her from him. But at what cost was I willing to do that?

If she hated me, I wasn't sure that I could survive it. What I'd felt earlier with her in my arms, clinging to me, had fed some fucking beast inside me that I didn't think I had control over. This thing … it needed her. It needed what she'd given me.

"What has he said so far?" I ground out through my clenched teeth.

"Not much," Thatcher replied just as the flick of his lighter went off.

"We need him conscious to talk," Storm said, pointing out the obvious.

"That's easy enough," Thatcher said.

I heard him walking, his boots heavy on the concrete floor.

A cry came from Vinson, and I dropped my hands and turned around to look at him. Thatcher was holding his lighter in his hand, grinning like a psycho. He liked to burn those we tortured when they went unconscious.

"Ah, he's awake. Now, talk, before I let my brother break all the bones in your body since that seems to be his thing as of late."

Vinson's eyes were almost closed from the swelling, but he managed to glare through the slits. "What is it you want to know?" he asked, struggling to breathe.

"I thought you said it was the grandmother losing her memory?" Thatcher said as he looked over at me. "Seems he's going too."

"Tell us all you know about the Dancastles and their dealings with drugs. Are they moving the laced crack that is causing all the hallucinations and cannibalism?" Storm asked him.

"Don't know nothing 'bout hallucinating and cannibalism," he grunted.

"What do you know? And keep in mind, if you lie, you won't walk out of here alive," Storm told him.

I was holding my breath. Not for the fucker's sake, but for Royal's.

"His son, Merce—he moves cocaine and ecstasy through the club scene. He has people working for him. He supplies it, and they get it out there. That's all I know."

"And how do you know that?" Storm urged.

"Because he dated my daughter," he spit. "He wanted me to start selling it in the bar. I didn't want to do that, so he had me make some drop-off runs for him. That was all I did. He paid me a nice chunk for it too."

Thatcher cut his eyes at me, and without him saying a word, I knew what he was about to ask. My hands fisted at my sides, and I braced myself. It had to be done, although I refused to believe a word he said.

"And what about Royal?" he began. "Was she involved? Does she know anything?"

Vinson slowly turned his head to look at me. His broken arms hung at odd angles at his sides. The blood was still trickling from his nose. He would tell her I had done this to him. She'd hate me for it. I couldn't have that. The only way to silence him was to kill him.

"They were fucking. What do you think? Of course she knew."

Blind fury exploded inside me as I shot across the space between us. My hands wrapped around his neck, and I squeezed, wanting to shut up his lies. End whatever shit he was going to accuse her of. Make him go limp and lifeless. Hanging here, no longer a threat to Royal.

I heard voices in the distance and felt hands grabbing me. Pulling me. It all seemed far away. I was detached from it. Nothing mattered but the man in front of me as his face turned a bright red and then blue.

Suddenly, I was jerked back hard, and my hands were ripped from Vinson Shelton's throat. I fought against the hold on me, but I couldn't get free.

"FUCKING LIAR!" I roared.

"Is he dead?" I heard King's voice behind me and realized he was one of the ones holding me.

Thatcher stepped forward and stuck his cigarette between his teeth, then grabbed the little hair on top of his head, lifting it to place a finger on his neck, in search of a pulse.

"It's weak, but it's there," he replied, letting the head flop forward again, then glancing back at me. "You almost got him."

"I left you down here to oversee things," King told him.

Thatcher shrugged. "Probably shouldn't have."

"If we let you go, are you going to stay back? We aren't done with him," King said to me.

I wanted him dead.

"She had nothing to do with it," I snarled.

"We can't trust him, but he can give us the information we need to find out the truth. But he has to be alive to talk. The more he talks, the more we can weed out the truth." King told me what I'd already known, but I didn't give a fuck.

"If she helped with the sale of drugs, she didn't know about the laced crack. She'd never be okay with that," I said, although I wasn't positive, I wanted to believe she was everything she appeared to be. The girl I'd spent time with was real. But I hadn't known her long enough to be one hundred percent sure.

"Let the fucker live, and we can use him. This was your idea—to take her father and bring him here and keep him until we get all we need out of him. It'll help lead us to the proof we need on Dancastle," King reminded me.

I wanted Royal free of all this. I didn't want to lie to her. It was eating me alive inside that she didn't even know my name.

I wanted to tell her the truth. I wanted her to know me. Not some made-up version of me. I wanted to pursue her, not use her. To do that, I had to find another way. Vinson was the other way.

"I can't be here when he talks," I said, knowing I'd kill him next time.

"No shit," Storm replied.

"Sebastian."

King's tone made me tense. I didn't like it. There was a warning edge to it.

"It might be best if you step back. Keep your distance from Royal Shelton. This has gotten personal for you, and that's an issue."

I stared at him. The urge to shut him up didn't overtake me. Although the tightening of Storm's hand on my arm meant the others weren't so sure I wasn't about to snap again.

King had sounded like my father. Something he would say to me. Something I was going to be told once he got word of this. He would keep me from her.

But hadn't I already known that was going to happen?

I nodded and pulled my arm free of Storm's hold, then left the room without looking back.

"Let him go and cool off," my brother told them.

Yeah, let me just go do that.

• TWENTY •

"I'd be able to stay away longer if you weren't so damn addictive."

ROYAL

I chewed on my thumbnail as I stared at my father's empty bed. He wasn't on the sofa in the living room, the car wasn't here, no one was answering at the bar, and the police station had said they didn't have him.

So, where was he?

I had woken up, tucked in my bed, just like Amory had promised. My thoughts had instantly gone to last night, and I lay there, smiling, thinking about all we'd done. How he'd made me feel. Then, I realized no one had called me from Miller's last night. I had expected them to. It had been a while since I'd slept all night without interruption.

This wasn't like Dad. Sure, he'd not come home before, but that was because he had been behind bars. Otherwise, he was here. He knew he had to stay at the house with Grams today.

Maybe he'd gone home with a woman, or he was asleep in his car at the bar. I needed to go look for him, but I didn't want to leave Grams here alone. Putting her on the back of my Vespa wasn't an option.

The sound of a glass shattering came from the kitchen, and I left my dad's doorway at a run before Grams cut herself. She was standing in the middle of the room with wide eyes and pieces of broken glass scattered in front of her. I'd moved all breakable items to the cabinets under the counter and hidden them behind the pots and pans.

"Don't move, Grams," I warned her as I went to get the broom and dustpan.

"I found my good dishes and the drinking glasses I had misplaced," she told me. "Silly me had stuck them in the cabinets. Don't know what I was thinking."

The cabinets were open, and all of the cookware was pulled out onto the floor. Why had she been digging around in there?

"Why don't you go on back to the living room and watch the morning news?" I suggested. "I will get this cleaned up and move all those things back where they belong." Which was a lie.

I'd move them to a better hiding place. She would forget about this one, but clearly, this spot wasn't good enough. I had to put them higher, somewhere she'd be less likely to go snooping.

"I was gonna make a pot of gumbo," she told me. "Just like Granny used to make. You know her people were from Louisiana. It's why she cooked so good. Yum, the stuff she could whip up. And I can make that gumbo. You will love it."

I nodded, agreeing with her. I'd had her gumbo before, and she was right. She'd made some of the best I'd ever tasted. But even if we had the ingredients she needed, which we did not, she wouldn't be able to make it. She'd forget what she was doing before she got it all set out on the counter.

"You can make that later," I told her. "I'll need to go get the bouillon paste and shrimp from the grocery first."

She frowned. "You don't get the shrimp from the grocery. Lord's sakes alive, that would be frozen, and you can't use frozen shrimp. Granny would roll right over in her grave, she would." Grams shook her head as if I had lost my mind.

We lived a good four and a half hours from the Atlantic Ocean. There was no fresh shrimp here.

"You're right. I'll go get some fresh shrimp," I assured her.

She nodded and turned to shuffle toward the living room. I let out a sigh of relief that she was safely away from the broken glass and finished getting it cleaned up. I quickly disposed of it, then tied up the garbage bag to take it outside. I didn't trust her not to go digging in the trash and end up slicing a finger.

I passed the living room on my way to the door and glanced in to see she was sitting in her chair, watching the television with a cup in her hands. I had yet to make coffee, and I wasn't sure what she had poured in that. I needed to check as soon as I got the trash outside.

Closing the door firmly behind me so Grams didn't try to follow me, I stepped around the rotten places on the wood until I made it safely off the porch. This was getting worse, and we should probably just take it all down. Get some bricks to use as steps and not have a front porch anymore. We? We who? That should be me. Dad wasn't going to do anything that required actual work.

I was almost to the trash can beside the road when an expensive matte-black SUV slowed down, then turned into our driveway. There were only two people who knew where I lived and had money to drive something like that. The Mercedes symbol on the back meant this was one of those G-Wagons that cost more than two of my houses.

Opening the lid, I dropped the trash bag inside, then closed it while keeping my eyes on the driver's door. I did not want that to be Merce, but I'd seen Amory in two different cars now. What were the chances he had three vehicles?

The familiar boot that emerged had me relieved and also caused my stomach to flutter. When Amory stepped out, his eyes were locked on me, and the sight of him seemed to make all my other problems fade away. He was already back. I hoped that meant I wasn't the only one who was feeling things.

I tucked the hair blowing in my face behind my ear as I made my way in his direction. I had no idea why he was here so early, but I didn't care. I was just glad he was.

"Good morning," I said, smiling up at him as he started toward me.

"It is now," he drawled as a crooked grin curled the corner of his lips.

I licked mine, thinking about how his had felt. Then, I remembered I hadn't brushed my teeth yet, and I stopped walking. I did not want him smelling my morning breath.

His eyes slightly narrowed as he studied me, but he closed the space between us. "You were heading toward me, all smiles and bright eyes, and then you stopped."

I put my hand in front of my mouth as I looked up at him. "I haven't had my coffee yet, which means I haven't brushed my teeth," I admitted.

A low, deep chuckle, which made me feel warm all over, came from his chest. "Morning breath won't scare me off."

Eh. Well, we weren't going to test that.

"I wasn't expecting you," I told him. "I mean, I'm glad you're here, but I just didn't think I'd see you again so soon."

He took my hand and pulled it away from my face. "Stop shielding your mouth," he told me with a gentle yet slightly demanding tone. "I want to see it."

From now on until the end of eternity, I would brush my teeth the moment I woke up. Just in case.

"It looks the same as yesterday," I quipped.

His eyes heated as he stared at it, and he made a pleased-sounding hum before lifting his gaze to meet mine. It wasn't cold out, but I shivered anyway. The dark gleam in his eyes felt ... possessive maybe, or was that just appreciative lust that I was reading too much into?

Things with him were moving fast. Faster than I'd ever allowed them to with a guy. But unlike the ones before him, I wanted to grab him and hold on.

My heart had never been broken, but I feared this might just be the man who would end up wielding the power to do it. I was helpless to stop it. There was no control over this thing that was happening to me.

"What are your plans today?" he asked me as he ran the back of his fingers down my arm.

I wished I didn't have to wear sleeves to cover up my bruises. I wanted to feel his touch on my skin directly. He stopped as he reached the tender area, and his eyes dropped to look at it, as if the shirt wasn't covering it up and he could see through the fabric. A pained expression flashed across his face, and he tenderly brushed his thumb over my bruised arm.

He had asked a question. What was it? He'd flustered me. I tried to remember what I was supposed to be saying.

When his gaze returned to my face, his dark, straight brows drew together into a scowl, and his chiseled jaw stood out more than usual. His expression caused a mixture of uneasiness and fascination to settle over me. I wasn't scared of him, yet there was often something in his eyes that seemed to warn me of things I didn't know. I should probably be put off by that, but it did the opposite. I found myself wanting to get closer to him instead.

"Your plans?" he asked, snapping me out of my wandering thoughts.

Right. He'd asked about my plans today. My problems came crashing back to the forefront of my mind, and I let out a weary sigh. I couldn't spend time with him, if that was what he was asking. I had a missing father and Grams to take care of.

"Dad didn't come home last night, and I didn't get a call from Miller's. I can only assume he went home with someone. Until he gets here, I can't leave Grams, and I was supposed to go to the library and use the computer there in the back to write two essays and print them. My friend Coral is working today, and she always lets me use the computer and printer there." I left off the *for free* part. No need to remind him how I had to live my life.

"I have somewhere I'd like to show you and your Grams," he told me.

"Me and Grams?" I asked, not sure I was understanding him correctly.

"Yes," he replied, his expression softening.

"Why?"

He slid a finger under my chin and ran his thumb over my lips. "Because I think it will benefit you both."

I had questions—so many questions—but I nodded. "Okay. Um, I'll need to change and get Grams dressed to go out. She doesn't go anywhere unless it's to a doctor's appointment, so an outing would be good for her."

He smiled. "Indeed. Which has to do with what I want to show you."

I let out a small laugh at his smug expression, then turned to walk toward the house when he reached out and grabbed my waist, pulling me back against his chest. His warm breath smelled of mint as he lowered his head until his lips brushed my ear. He inhaled deeply and let out a satisfied-sounding groan.

"I needed that," he whispered. "I missed feeling you pressed against me."

I bit my bottom lip as I sank into him more. "It's not even been twelve hours since you left," I pointed out.

"Mmm," he replied, pressing a kiss to my neck. "You shouldn't feel so good. I'd be able to stay away longer if you weren't so damn addictive."

His hand slid under my shirt slowly, and I held my breath as my eyes fluttered closed. The warmth of his large palm covered my left breast, and I felt my knees go weak.

"Amory," I gasped as the tingle began between my legs.

His hand stilled, and his body tensed, but only for a moment.

Then, he slid his hand from my shirt. "Sorry. I got carried away. Let's go inside," he said before squeezing my hips and nudging me to move forward.

It was a good thing he'd stopped us because I hadn't thought once about the neighbors or who could be watching. This man was making me do things I'd never done before. Perhaps I should be worried about the pull he had on me, but right now, all I wanted was to keep him close. Enjoy the way he made me feel. Safe, wanted, protected, desired … no longer alone.

• TWENTY-ONE •

"I've liked you since I sat in that bar and watched you play an Oscar-worthy game of pool."

ROYAL

"What is this place?" I asked, stepping out of the SUV and staring at the massive antebellum-style home in front of us.

"Haven House," he replied.

I'd read the sign at the tall gates we'd driven through after the security man opened them for Amory. But that didn't tell me what Haven House was.

Amory began helping Grams out of the vehicle. She'd been so excited about going somewhere in his fancy car earlier, but now, she clutched her favorite red leather purse to her chest as she stepped out, looking unsure.

"Is this your house?" she asked him with a touch of awe in her voice.

"No, ma'am, it isn't," he told her.

"Well, it's just glorious. Right out of a movie," she said, standing there, taking it all in. "Do we know who lives here?" she asked, then frowned at Amory. "Who are you?"

I walked over to her before she panicked. "Grams, it's Amory Blaine, remember? He brought us here. To …" I paused, having no clue why we were here or what this place was.

"It's a place with activities that you can participate in," he told her. "Art classes, board games, crafting, and even story time. There are others here about your age, and they come to socialize as well as learn new things."

My gaze swung back to the house. As nice as that all sounded, there was a price tag on that, and I knew Grams's Medicaid would not cover it. What was Amory doing? I'd just met him, and, yes, I liked him more than I had ever liked any other man, but he was stepping too far.

"I don't think showing us things like this is wise," I told him, smiling so as not to alarm Grams.

"I know the owner, and I've set up something that is free for your Grams to attend. She can come during the day while you are working and going to school," he replied.

That sounded too good to be true. I didn't trust things like that. I knew better.

"Nothing in life is free," I argued. "Everything comes with a price. This is a beautiful place, and I am sure it is just as charming inside. But I think we need to leave."

"You don't trust me," he said with a quirk of his eyebrow.

I wanted to trust him. There were things I did trust when it came to him, but this wasn't about my body. It wasn't about me at all. It was about my Grams, and I couldn't trust him with her.

"I like to paint. Can I paint in there?" she asked as she began walking toward the house.

Crap!

I hurried to catch up with her. "Grams, why don't we get back in the fancy car."

She shook her head and continued on. "I like to socialize. I'm rather good with conversation."

Once she was, yes, but now, she remembered nothing long enough to have a conversation.

"This is a place that exclusively caters to those like your Grams. It's a memory care facility. Just go inside and see what they offer," he urged. "Don't you want your Grams to have activities she enjoys and others her age around for her to visit with?"

Guilt at not being able to give her that kind of life hit me. I did the best I could for her, and, no, our life wasn't perfect or even comfortable at times, but she didn't go without. I didn't visit with her like I should, but I was always busy working or taking care of things in the house. I never had time to sit and just talk to her. I just assumed since she wouldn't remember it anyway, there was no point.

Was I wrong? Had I been neglecting her?

I stared up at the house as we reached the stairs leading up to the tall double doors.

"Isn't this home just beautiful?" Grams said as I took her arm to help her with the first step.

"Yes, Grams, it is," I agreed.

"Do you think someone famous lives here?" she asked, her eyes widening. "Land sakes, do they know we've come to visit? I should have brought a Bundt cake. My lemon one with the drizzly you love so much."

I started to tell her she didn't need to worry about that when the door opened, and a woman appeared. She looked to be in her mid-forties with short brown hair and bright blue-rimmed glasses, dressed in a matching blue shirt with fluffy sleeves and a pair of cream linen pants. She smiled at Grams, then shifted her gaze to Amory and finally me.

"You must be Mrs. Maude Shelton," the lady said, looking at Grams.

How did she know Grams's name? If Amory had told her, how had he known Grams's name? I'd never told him her name.

I swung my gaze to him, and he winked at me.

What the hell was that? Don't wink at me. Explain yourself.

"I am indeed," she replied, holding her shoulders back the best she could.

"We have been looking forward to your arrival," she said, walking out to greet us. "There is a special story time today. We have an author visiting, and she's reading her book in the silver room instead of the library. The silver room has much more comfortable seating, and there is a spot saved just for you on the coveted teal sofa."

Grams looked at me. "They have an author here," she whispered loudly. "I told you someone famous lived here."

I forced a smile and nodded. "I heard that. Do you want to go listen to her read?"

Grams turned back to the lady. "Of course I do. They have me a special seat."

"Wonderful," the woman replied, then waved her hand for us to enter as she stepped back.

Another lady met us as we walked into the foyer. She was younger with thick auburn hair, pulled up in a loose bun on her head. Her eyes went to Amory immediately, and she blushed slightly, looking pleased to see him, as if this wasn't the first time.

"Tully, if you can escort Mrs. Shelton to the silver room, please," the woman told the redhead.

She tore her eyes off Amory rather reluctantly, then smiled at Grams. "Of course," she agreed.

I wanted to reach out and hold on to Grams, but she didn't even give me a backward glance as she willingly went with Tully, the redhead who had a thing for Amory.

I watched them as they walked slowly to the left of the wide staircase.

"I'm Shari Darlington," the other woman said, and I turned to look back at her. "I'm the house manager of Haven House. I oversee everything that happens here and make sure that our residents and day guests are well taken care of."

I cleared my throat. "It's nice to meet you, Ms. Darlington."

"Just Shari, please. Now, it's Royal, is it?" she asked.

I nodded.

"I would love to have the opportunity to show you what it is we do here." She said it as if I were about to bolt and go grab my Grams.

I had to admit that Grams was safer here than at home with my dad. It wouldn't hurt to let her go listen to the author read her book. I nodded again, but I didn't look at Amory. I wasn't sure how I felt where he was concerned right now. He'd blindsided me with this, and I didn't appreciate it. Even if he had been trying to do something nice for Grams and help me. He should have asked me first. We weren't his charity case, and I didn't want to feel like one. Not to anyone, but especially not to him.

Dad was probably home by now, and I hadn't left him a letter to tell him we'd gone out. Not that he deserved one since he'd stayed gone all night and not called or texted. Served him right if he worried. Although I highly doubted he'd worry.

"We adapt an ability-centered enrichment approach for each resident and day guest. We believe in a whole-brain-fitness lifestyle, where they not only exercise their body and brain, but they also participate in social activities. If someone suffering from dementia is left without that, their mind goes faster. They lose themselves at a rapid pace. We give their golden years more time, along with a richer experience. A reason to hold on to things and enjoy their moments."

I listened as she spoke, and the ache in my chest grew with each word. Grams didn't have reasons to hold on. When her memory was clear, she was often sad. I couldn't blame her for allowing her mind to go. Especially when the home she'd lived in with my grandfather was falling apart and her son did nothing to help out.

"We have chef-prepared dining with delicious courses that meet all their dietary needs. The things they need to strengthen their bodies and even their minds. There are seven licensed skilled nurses on-site with twenty-four-hour supervision. Daily wellness checks and medication management. We have an on-site fitness center with physical therapists," she continued.

I stiffened as Amory's palm touched my lower back, but I didn't look at him. I didn't want to look at anyone really. Hearing Shari talk, I felt my heart sink more and more. All the things that my Grams needed, and I'd never even thought about it. Even if I had considered it, I'd never been able to supply it for her.

"We have several brain-fitness programs with a highly trained and dedicated staff. We do small group exercises seven days a week. There is a bird-watching group that goes out every morning after breakfast to the lawn where the bird feeders are located. It's a favorite activity around here."

Grams would love that. She loved to look out our back window and watch the birds that came to the bird feeder I'd made for her one year at a vacation Bible school she'd sent me to at her church.

"Would you like to see the activity rooms?" she asked.

"Yes," I replied, although I was sure this was only going to make it even harder on me. Seeing all that Grams could have. What she could experience instead of being left in front of the television often with no one to talk to.

"I need a moment with Royal," Amory said.

Shari smiled. "Of course. I'll be waiting just down there, in the first room on your right. No rush at all."

"Thank you," he replied, but I could feel his eyes on me.

I waited until Shari was out of sight before finally looking up at him. I wanted to slap him for this. Showing me all that was available and unaffordable. Dangling this in front of my face, knowing I'd want it, but hating the idea of being charity.

"Stop grinding your pretty teeth," he scolded me. "I didn't bring you here to upset you or anger you. I had the resources available, and I wanted to share that with you and your Grams."

I sucked in a deep breath through my nose. "This can't be free. And I will not take a handout from you."

His brows drew together. "This isn't a handout."

"Okay, fine. Charity then. It's … it's embarrassing enough. My house. My life. Compared to yours." I felt my eyes sting, and it angered me more. I would not cry. "We've been on one date. And you feel so sorry for my pathetic life that you're pulling strings to get my Grams into some elite … home. Or whatever this is. I just …" I pressed my fingers to my temples and closed my eyes. "I want this for her. And I hate that she has to live the way she does. But at what cost do I get it?"

I dropped my hands and looked back up at him. "I like you, Amory. I do. A lot, okay? But this is new, and we are just getting to know each other. I don't want you to see me as … some problem or weight on your shoulders. My life isn't yours to fix. I just want to get to spend time with you."

He cupped my face and took a step closer to me. "You like me a lot."

"Is that seriously all you got out of what I just said?"

The corner of his mouth lifted slightly. "No. I just wanted to clarify."

I let out a sad laugh. Wishing that, for one day in my life, I could be happy. The entire day. Not have something remind me of the shitty hand I'd been dealt.

"It just so happens that I like you a lot too, Ace. I've liked you since I sat in that bar and watched you play an Oscar-worthy game of pool. The more I get to know you, the more I'm around you, the more I fucking like you. Not once"—he stopped and leaned down closer to me, his eyes darkening—"not one time, have I ever considered you a charity case or a problem. I've been impressed by how fucking clever and ingenious you are. How you have taken your strengths and found a way to make money with them. You juggle more roles than anyone I know, and you do it like a badass. I don't see you and think needy or weak. I just have the ability to help you. Help your Grams. I can do that, and I want to. Let me. Please, Royal. Please. Let me do this."

I sniffled, and he wiped a lone tear that had escaped with the back of his finger. He was very good with words. In just a few sentences, he'd made me feel strong and impressive rather than needy and pathetic.

"Do you promise me this will cost you nothing?" I asked him, still struggling with that. This couldn't just be free.

"This house—not Haven House and what it does, but the house it is in and the property it sits on," he said, "my family owns it. Haven House leases it from us."

I blinked, letting that process.

They owned this house? Why wouldn't they live in it? What in the world could their house look like if they owned one this incredible that they just leased out?

Again, I was in over my head. This man was a kind of wealthy that had to surpass even Merce's family.

"You own this house," I repeated.

He nodded. "Yes. It's been in our family for over a hundred years."

So, they weren't just rich, but they were old-money rich. Well, I was old-money poor, and this was a lot to take in.

"Trust me, Royal." His tone sounded pleading.

Trust him? I didn't trust people. I knew better than to do that. Yet I had done nothing but trust this man from almost day one. Okay, week one. Not day one. But still, that was a big deal.

Finally, I nodded.

I wasn't sure I'd ever really had a choice. He was claiming me at a rapid pace with every action, touch, and word that came out of his mouth.

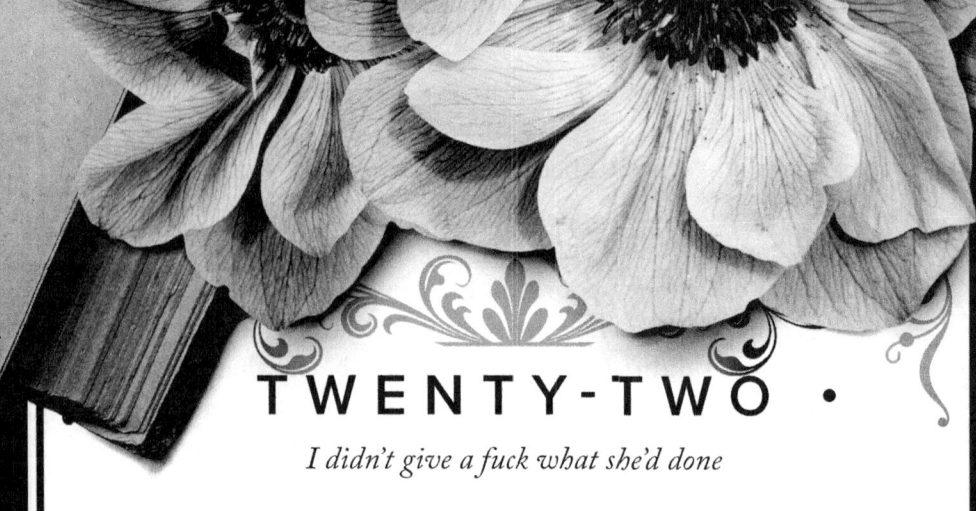

TWENTY-TWO

I didn't give a fuck what she'd done

SEBASTIAN

Standing by while Royal frantically searched for her father was hard. I hated seeing her worried. Why she was so damn concerned about the piece of shit, I didn't know. He sure as fuck had no concern for her.

His car was missing. That was the first thing she'd discovered.

When she had gone to talk to her Grams about leaving her there to visit and her Grams smiled, then waved her off so she could go back to the easel she had been painting on, Royal's expression immediately appeared lighter. As if a weight had been lifted—and it had. One she'd been carrying by herself for too long.

She had then asked me to go to Miller's to see if her dad was there or if they knew who he'd left with. He wasn't there, he wasn't at home, and he'd walked out last night, alone. All things I had known already. But she had to find this out on her own.

"Where would he have gone?" she asked, standing in the parking lot of Miller's, as if there was going to be an answer lying around somewhere.

"Would he have taken off? Any place he ever mention wanting to go see?" I asked.

She was frowning again. I had loved seeing her smile earlier. I wanted that back. But we had to get through this shit first.

"Maybe. But where would he have gotten the money to go anywhere? He spends everything he has at Miller's. But he always talks about wanting to go to Florida. I just don't think the Bug could make it there or that he'd have the money to pay for gas to get it there. And when he got there, he'd not have the money to stay anywhere."

He wasn't in Florida. Not even close.

"Let me make a call," I told her, taking out my phone and distancing myself.

I knew I was running out of time, and I had to speed this up. I'd yet to hear from my father today, but it was coming. They would have told him about last night and my reaction. He wouldn't be happy about it. He saw Royal as a pawn in his plan. Nothing more. I wasn't to mess with the pawn or the plan.

I pretended to talk to someone on the phone as I held it to my ear. I already had my story lined up and ready. I'd just had to walk her into this opening.

Slipping the phone back in my pocket, I walked over to her. "Would you rather stay here and wait for him to return or find him now?" I asked her.

"Find him now."

Yeah, I'd known that.

"If the police get involved, they'll find out he is driving with a suspended license. We don't need that. I have a guy who is going to put out a watch for the car description and license plate from here to Florida. Once he has a lead, he will let me know. I can get us a private plane, and we can get to him fast."

She stared at me. "Private plane," she said.

I nodded, knowing I wasn't about to use the family's plane. I'd already found one that had no connection to us, and I'd paid in cash, using a bogus name. My dad wasn't going to have any crumbs to follow me. I had been cleaning up as I went.

She ran her hand over her head. "Wow. Okay. Um, but Grams …"

"Grams can stay at Haven House. She has a room there whenever she needs it. I wanted to be sure she had somewhere to nap and to feel secure. As if she belonged."

"You hadn't mentioned that," she said.

"I should have. I apologize."

She sighed. "Don't apologize. You think of everything. I should have known. I guess then we can go to the house and wait. Do you have somewhere you need to be? Am I keeping you from anything?"

I shook my head. "I wanted to spend the day with you."

She scrunched her nose. "Not what you were expecting, huh?"

I reached out and took her hand, tugging her close to me. "I'm with you. That's what I came for. What we do doesn't matter."

She let out a groan and rested her forehead on my chest. "When you say things like that, I want to strip you naked and climb on top of you."

Fuck. I slid a hand around to her ass and pulled her against me.

"Let's go back to your house, and I will say whatever words that will get you to do exactly what you just described."

Her laughter was muffled against my chest.

Briefly, I had moments when I questioned what I was doing. Preparing to defy my father. Defy the family. Something I'd never have guessed I, of all people, would do. All for a girl I barely knew and someone I wasn't entirely sure who was innocent.

Then, she'd remind me why I was willing to do it. Why I was going to do it.

Her hands slid up and fisted in my shirt, as if she needed me to simply stand. The warmth from her body, the sweet scent of her skin, the way she fit against me, as if she had been made for this spot specifically it was all part of the weakness she had created in me.

The darker side of me that had begun to take shape the more I was with her shifted and stretched, reminding me of all I would do in order to keep her safe. Keep her with me.

The call from my father came, and I silenced it. We weren't to Royal's house yet. Turning left instead of right, I headed to the private airstrip.

"Where are we going?" she asked.

"Just got a hit on your father. The car didn't quite make it to Florida. It was left on the side of the road by a rest stop. But the cameras saw him getting into a semi that was headed south. Currently in Miami. That's its stop and where your father will have to get out. We are flying down there."

"He is in Miami?! What was he thinking? Just taking off and leaving our car. How did he think I was going to get Grams to the doctor appointments? Who was going to stay with her when I had to go to class or make money?"

She sounded furious, but the hurt was so thickly laced in her voice that it twisted me up inside. I didn't like her to be hurt.

"I'll arrange to get your car back," I told her.

She was silent for several minutes.

"Still want to spend time with me? All this work and hassle it's causing you … I can't be worth that." Her words were just above a whisper as she stared out the window.

I hated that she thought so little of herself. That wasn't an act. No one could fake the pain in her eyes.

I didn't care what the Family said about her. I didn't give a fuck what she'd done. Whatever role she had played in the Dancastles' shit, she'd done what she had to. She wasn't going to be used for information or put in harm's way. Not by me. Not by my dad. Not by anyone.

TWENTY-THREE

"Put the tip in."

ROYAL

"You need a distraction," Amory said as he sat across from me in one of the plush leather seats in the private jet he'd hired to go get my father.

My bottom lip was sore from all the chewing I'd done to it. I was nervous that my dad would get away before we found him after Amory had pulled so many strings to find him and get us there. Then, when we found him, I was worried about all the awful things he'd say to me. Maybe I should leave him there. He didn't want to be stuck with us. He'd taken off without a word.

Amory unbuckled and stood up, holding out his hand to me. "Come on."

I unfastened my seat belt, then slid my hand into his as he helped me from my seat.

"What are we doing?" I asked, looking around the small but luxurious cabin.

"Going to explore," he replied.

"Explore what?"

A wicked glint in his eye did wonders for distracting me. Keeping my hand clasped in his, he walked back to the door I assumed was a restroom. He opened it and then pulled me along behind him.

It wasn't a restroom. It was a bedroom. A king-size bed sat in the middle of the small area. There wasn't much else here, except a built-in armoire and another door, which had to lead to a bathroom.

Amory let go of my hand and grabbed my waist, then picked me up and tossed me onto the bed.

I let out a squeal as my bottom bounced on the firm mattress.

He closed the door behind him, making the room appear even smaller, but being in here with Amory also felt cozy. I watched him crawl toward me, and then he maneuvered himself until his body was caging me in as he stared down at me.

"Distracted?" he asked.

I nodded.

"Good."

He lowered his head, and his lips brushed over mine once. I opened to him instantly and was rewarded with the swirl of his tongue. I wanted him closer. Reaching up, I wrapped my arms around his neck and tugged him down. His knee moved between my legs, and his hard body came down until he barely touched me.

"I went to sleep, thinking about this mouth," he said as he licked at my bottom lip.

The husky sound of his voice excited me more, and I rocked against his thigh that rested too close to my ache. The friction felt good, so I scooted closer to it and rubbed some more.

His hands were on the waist of my shorts, and then his mouth left mine. "You want to rub that sweet pussy on me, then you're gonna do it right."

I lifted my hips, and he jerked down my shorts, then tossed them to the side. I heard his boots hit the ground while he began to work on the zipper of his jeans. I didn't think we were ready for sex. At least, I didn't know if I was. I already had strong feelings for him that had come on too fast. Sex was going to escalate it even more.

I was going to tell him that when his jeans were pushed down, and the outline of his erection through the white boxer briefs he was wearing came into view. I'd had that in my mouth last night. Deep in my throat.

With his jeans discarded, his hand went to his briefs, and he paused. "I want to feel your wet pussy against my cock. That's all."

I swallowed hard and nodded.

He quickly got them off, then jerked his shirt over his head, leaving him naked. I'd known he would be beautiful, but I hadn't truly been prepared for just how beautiful. The desire to kiss and lick every spot on him was making it hard for me to think of the reasons why we should slow down.

His fingers began to unbutton my blouse, and I let him. He'd seen the bruises already, and I wanted to feel my naked skin against his. Even if we didn't have sex, I could still enjoy how he felt.

I sat up enough so he could pull my top away, and then I unfastened my bra and tugged it down my arms, leaving me bare. Our heavy breathing could be heard over the roar of the plane's engine.

Amory ran his palms over my nipples, then squeezed my breasts.

"I love your tits." The tone of his voice was different. Deeper but also slightly sinister.

He ran a hand down my stomach as his eyes followed the path. I kept mine on his face, not sure if I should be turned on or alarmed by the change in him. Perhaps I was both.

His fingers slid inside my panties, and I opened my legs wider, drawing out a chuckle from him, although he didn't take his attention from what he was doing. When he slid over my slick mound, a rumble in his chest caused me to tremble.

There was a darker side to Amory Blaine. One that I should probably be wary of, but I found myself clinging to it. Begging him to show me all of it. All of him.

"Fuuuck, that pussy is dripping."

A cry fell from my lips as he sank a finger between my folds, rubbing just over my clit before he found my opening. If he filled me with his finger, I was going to want more.

Two fingers thrust into me, and I arched my back, moaning.

"Damn, that's tight, baby." His voice no longer sounded anything like him. "Needy cunt is squeezing my fingers. You sure you don't want me to fuck this pretty little hole? I'll beg, whatever you want."

His mouth was slightly parted as he jerked the crotch of my panties over to look at what he was doing.

"No wonder you tasted like a peach. This juicy pussy looks like a fucking peach. Jesus, that's perfect."

His eyes lifted to mine, and then he moved back and lowered his head.

I held my breath, not taking my eyes off him.

"If I can't sink my dick into it, I'm gonna eat it."

Oh God. Yes.

Some strange sound that was close to pleading came from me.

Amory ran the tip of his tongue along the center of my slit, and I almost came off the bed. The hand he didn't have between my legs grabbed my right thigh, and he pressed his face so hard up against me that I wasn't sure he could breathe. The growls he began to make vibrated through me, and I started to shake.

I wanted more. I wanted to feel him.

"Just the tip," I gasped. "Put the tip in."

I wasn't sure if that was any different for me emotionally or if it would keep me from getting any more attached to him, but I had to feel him there. I wanted to see his face as he entered me. Even if it was just a little.

He lifted his heady gaze to my face as he licked his lips. My juices glistened around his mouth.

"You want me to just put the head of my cock in your cunt?"

I nodded. "Please."

His nostrils flared, and he took one more taste of me before moving up my body. My gaze fell to his hand as he gripped his large, veiny penis. The swollen red, almost-purple tip moved closer, and I let out a small whimper just before he ran it over my clit, then lower, until it was just there. Right outside. Our gazes lifted at the same time, and our eyes met.

He barely eased inside me as a hiss came from between his teeth, and his neck flexed.

It was there. Just stretching the entrance. I couldn't remember a time that I'd had sex that was better than this.

I rocked slightly, needing to feel it move inside me.

"Don't," Amory growled, sounding almost more animal than man.

Somehow, that made me even more frantic.

"I just want to," I panted, rocking faster.

I wanted this. Oh, God, I wanted this.

Amory pressed his hand to my stomach, stopping me from moving. "Don't," he warned me, his eyes almost black.

The dangerous gleam in them only urged me on, and I wiggled under his hold.

"If you don't stop, I'm going to fuck you." He snarled out his words as he glared down at me with a mix of hunger and rage.

It was exhilarating.

I pulled my knees up and opened my legs wider. "Yes," I moaned.

All reason was gone. I just wanted him.

"Condom." He said the word like a curse.

"I get the shot," panted. "I've been tested, I promise. Please." I was desperate. Losing my mind with need.

His eyes flickered as a wicked change came over him. The depravity in it almost threw me into an orgasm all on its own. I didn't recognize this person I was right now. But I knew that he was going to show me something I'd never had, and I wanted it. I wanted it so bad.

He slowly sank in deeper, his eyes going from where we were connected back to my face. "This? You want more?"

I shook my head, and he stopped.

"All! I want it all," I told him.

A roar tore from his chest as he slammed down into me. The burn from the stretch his size caused was the only thing that kept me from orgasming on the spot. My eyes watered, and I gasped through the pain.

"Fuck!" he swore when his eyes moved back to my face. "Tight. It's real tight. It hurts, doesn't it?"

I nodded. "Yes, but it's easing."

He smirked. "Then, I need to fix that."

He withdrew just until the tip was the only thing inside me before he plunged back into me. This time, he didn't pause, but grabbed my hip with one hand, holding me down while pumping into me even harder.

"I want you to feel where I've been," he panted. "Know who took this tight little cunt and stretched it."

He bent down and licked at one of my nipples, then bit it. "You make me fucking crazy. First, it was those eyes and lips. Now, this tiny little hole. Letting me break it."

The tingle built until I was desperate. His dirty words were pushing me into a frenzied delirium. That, and the rough way he was handling me and the possessive way he was looking at me. Like I was his and he'd kill anyone who tried to take me away.

"Oh God," I cried as I felt the teasing pulse.

"That's it. Let me feel that pussy come."

I clawed at the covers beneath me as the crest hit, and euphoria seized me, holding me there while Amory shouted and jerked. The warmth of his release shot out, spraying across my stomach and breasts.

He stared down at his cum covering my body, as if the sight held him transfixed. When he finally lifted his gaze to meet mine, there was a worshipful expression as he looked at me. As if he'd found something he hadn't expected but cherished it. That couldn't be what he was thinking, but I felt … special. He made me feel that way.

TWENTY-FOUR

"That was my first lie."

ROYAL

This wasn't Florida.

I stood on the stairs of the plane as a coat was placed over my shoulders. Glancing down at it, I realized it was cold.

Where were we? How long had I been asleep, wrapped up in Amory's arms?

"Go on down," he said behind me.

I did as he'd told me to, only because I was sure there was an explanation. Maybe my dad had gotten in another semi and headed north. I'd been asleep and not known when he got the message. He came up behind me and placed his hand on my back, then pressed me forward as he started walking us toward a Hummer. Mountains surrounded us, and there was no airport or even a building. Just a long landing strip.

What was going on? Why would my dad come … here—wherever here was—and where had this Hummer come from?

Amory opened the passenger door and then picked me up to place me inside.

I stared at him questioningly. Was he going to tell me where we were?

He closed the door, then headed around the front to the driver's side.

I'd woken up with a blissful warmth radiating through me. I had never woken up in anyone's arms. It was an experience I hadn't wanted to leave so soon. That moment was fading fast.

In its place was a creeping dread—or perhaps *foreboding* was a better description. The seconds that ticked by without Amory explaining to me what was going on, the more it crept in.

Had something happened to my dad? Did Amory not want to tell me?

The second he closed the door, I blurted out, "What is going on?"

He started the engine, barely glancing at me, but didn't say anything. This was bad. He didn't want to tell me.

My hands fisted in my lap. Was it Grams? No, we wouldn't be here. Wherever here was.

The Hummer began to drive away from the plane, but the road that appeared wasn't paved. It was a rocky dirt path. That was all I could see up ahead. Just the wild open. I'd never been to Alaska, but this was how I pictured it. This couldn't be Alaska though. My father wouldn't be here.

"Amory, why are we here? Where is here? Where is my dad?"

He glanced over at me again. "I can't tell you where we are."

What?

"Why?" I asked.

There seemed to be no logical reason why he couldn't tell me our location.

"Because it's safer this way."

Safer?

"Okay, I'm going to need you to make sense. This entire situation is confusing. Where is my dad?"

"I know you're confused, and I'm sorry about that. This is just how it has to be. I will answer all your questions as soon as we get to the cabin."

What cabin? Was I dreaming? Still asleep on the plane, curled up with his arms around me? That was what I hoped was happening. I wanted to be back there, where things had made sense.

"Where is my dad, Amory?!" I demanded.

"I don't know," he replied.

"You don't know? How do you not know? We were going to Miami, and from the looks of things, we are nowhere near Miami—or even Florida for that matter."

The corner of his lips tugged up slightly, as if he wanted to smile. There was no humor here. Nothing to smile about.

"I never knew."

Not what I had expected him to say. I stared at him, waiting for him to say he was kidding or something.

"Amory, you're starting to scare me."

He reached over and placed his hand over one of my fisted ones. "You never have to be scared of me. I'd never let anything or anyone hurt you."

The fierceness in the way he'd said it would have been sexy if I wasn't on the verge of a panic attack. I had to calm down and think. This was Amory. The guy who had sent his grandmother to stay with mine. Gotten my Grams into a facility meant for the wealthy for free. He sent us food. Had my Vespa fixed. Bailed my dad out of jail. He hadn't done all that for some master plan.

"If that is the case, then why can't you tell me where we are and why?"

His thumb brushed over my hand in a caress. "I will. Just a little farther. I'll tell you everything."

Okay, fine. He wanted us to get to our location. I could wait. He would make all of this make sense. I was being dramatic. That was all.

Opening my hand, I let him thread his fingers through mine. This was good. I needed this. My tension eased, and I looked out the window at the wild outdoors we seemed to be driving through.

Was this Colorado? Wyoming? It was farther north than Tennessee. It had to be. It was cold. Much colder than a Southern October.

My mind played through several scenarios as we drove, taking a handful of turns on more dirt roads. He didn't say anything, and I decided that maybe silence was best. There was something he needed to tell me, and I wanted to demand he tell me now.

Finally, we slowed, and he veered down a narrow path as branches brushed against the sides of the Hummer.

Where in the heck was he taking me?

My thoughts went back to all the criminal televisions shows I'd seen in the past, and I tensed up. No. Amory wasn't going to murder me in the woods.

We came out of the trees, and a small A-frame cabin sat in the middle of a clearing. I looked around, and there was nothing anywhere else in sight. Just the building. Amory pulled up to it and cut off the engine.

"We're here," he told me.

I looked at him, and he flashed me a smile that reminded me he wasn't a serial killer.

"I'll come around and get you out. It's high," he told me before climbing out of the Hummer.

I reached for the door handle and opened it. Amory was there, and I let him take me by the waist and set me down.

He bent his head and inhaled the side of my neck, then straightened and released me. "Let's go inside."

He headed toward the door and pulled out a key from his pocket to unlock it. I stood back and watched as he opened it up, then stepped inside, as if he needed to inspect it. When he turned around, he motioned for me to come in.

The smell of cinnamon and vanilla met my nose as I moved past Amory's body and into the open area. Shiny hardwood floors that looked new were covered by large, shaggy beige area rugs. To the right was a massive fireplace with a brown leather sofa facing it and two dark red recliners on either side. To the left was a kitchen and dining area, and in the center was a spiral staircase, leading upstairs to a loft. It wasn't much square footage, but everything in it was high-end. Even the appliances.

"Where are we, Amory?" I asked him again.

"Let's start with that—my name. That was my first lie. My name is Sebastian Shephard."

• TWENTY-FIVE

"You've had my attention from day one."

SEBASTIAN

Her face paled as she stood there, staring at me. It was as if she didn't recognize me.

"It's still me, Royal. Just another name. My name," I assured her.

She shook her head, and her eyes looked around the room wildly, as if she was looking for an escape.

"You see, Amor—*Sebastian*, that's the problem. You lied to me about your name, and I woke up on a plane nowhere near where you had told me you were taking me. Now, we are in a cabin, in the wilderness, in some remote location with no other living soul for miles."

I took a step toward her, and she took one back, holding up both her hands to stop me. I hadn't wanted this. Especially after she opened her legs to me on the flight and rocked my fucking world. But I was done lying to her—at least about the things I could be honest about. The next time I sank my cock into her, I wanted to hear my name come from those plump pink lips. Not some fucking fictional character in a novel.

"I lied because I had to. If I had told you my name, it would have gotten back to Merce—or worse, you'd have googled me. Neither of those things would have been good."

She let out a sharp laugh that held no humor at all. "And that is supposed to make me feel better?"

I shrugged. "No. It's just the truth."

"How do you know Merce?"

"Our families are connected within many of the same circles."

"So, your family is into politics?"

I shook my head. "No. My family is the Mafia."

Her eyes went wide, and I realized I probably should have said that in a different way.

"Mafia."

I nodded.

"This is getting worse," she whispered. "And if I'd googled you, it would have told me that?"

I laughed and shook my head. "No. It would have told you my family owns a large thoroughbred ranch and we are known for our champions. The Southern Mafia isn't something that is advertised. To many, it is a rumor, and to those with enough power, it is just a part of life."

She crossed her arms over her chest and stared toward one of the front windows. "The Dancastles know who you are then because they have power."

"Yes."

She shifted her gaze back to meet mine. "Sebastian, why am I here?"

"Because Merce Dancastle and his father are funneling a laced drug that the Feds are going to step in and handle if we don't shut it down. We keep that kind of thing out of our area, and it keeps the Feds out of our shit. They turn a blind eye, so to speak. Edward Dancastle is fucking with the wrong people. Merce got your father somewhat involved by having him do some drops for him. Because of that and you dating him, you are now on their radar."

Her mouth fell slightly open, and her already-pale skin seemed to lose the little color it had left.

"What?" she asked. "What, my dad? Me?"

She shook her head, and those eyes told me all I needed to know. She didn't know anything about the drugs.

"Your father left with money he had gotten from the Dancastles to disappear. He left you and your Grams alone with no protection. I had to get you both safe. No one is getting near you, and no one is taking you from me."

Not the complete truth, but it was close enough. If it hadn't been for Dancastle, I'd have never met her. I wouldn't have witnessed the way her father treated her, and he'd not be in our underground right now.

"Whose radar am I on? The Feds? Merce's father?" She looked like she was going to be sick.

I took a step toward her, and she shook her head, backing up again. Fuck, I wish she'd stop that. I wanted to hold her. Reassure her. Get some color back in her pretty face.

"Both," I told her, which wasn't true.

She was on my father's radar, but seeing as she wouldn't come near me, I didn't think telling her I'd brought her here so he wouldn't take her away from me would help the situation.

"I need to go back. I can tell them I didn't know. The Feds. Running makes me look guilty."

"No. They already know about your hustles. You've been investigated thoroughly. You claiming to be innocent means little, I'm afraid, and if Merce Dancastle has to, he'll throw you under the goddamn bus. Then, I'll have to kill him."

Her eyes narrowed slightly. "Kill him?"

"Yes."

Her hands fell to her sides, and she moved farther away from me. "See, that right there. I don't feel safe with you anymore. You're someone I don't know. Kill isn't a threat sane people just toss around."

My patience with this was done. I didn't like hearing her say shit like she didn't know me, and I sure as hell didn't like her saying she didn't feel safe. I stalked toward her as she spun around, wide-eyed, looking terrified.

Fuck! That wasn't what I'd wanted to see.

She backed up until she hit the railing on the stairs, and I caged her in, grabbing the railing on each side of her.

The pulse point on her neck beat frantically, and her body trembled, but I knew it wasn't from arousal. She was scared. I was the last person on earth she ever had to fear. Why couldn't she see that? I'd lied about my name, but I'd told her the truth—or most of it—just now.

"What I am and what I do—it's nothing for you to ever feel threatened by. I will never let anyone hurt you. That's why we are here. I'm going to fix this. All of it. Then, you can go home, and you'll be safe."

She licked her lips as she stared up at me. "I don't know you."

I smirked. "You know me, Ace. I'm the same guy with a different name."

She stiffened. "Not the same guy. The guy I thought I knew wasn't in the Mafia. He was a nice guy with too much money to toss around, but I liked him. I trusted him."

I bent my head and pressed a kiss to her cheek. "I am a nice guy. Compared to my older brother, I'm a goddamn saint," I told her, then moved to kiss the other cheek. There was a slight pink flush in them now, and that eased me some. I moved to kiss the corner of her mouth. "I'm nice,

"Yes."

Her hands fell to her sides, and she moved farther away from me. "See, that right there. I don't feel safe with you anymore. You're someone I don't know. Kill isn't a threat sane people just toss around."

My patience with this was done. I didn't like hearing her say shit like she didn't know me, and I sure as hell didn't like her saying she didn't feel safe. I stalked toward her as she spun around, wide-eyed, looking terrified.

Fuck! That wasn't what I'd wanted to see.

She backed up until she hit the railing on the stairs, and I caged her in, grabbing the railing on each side of her.

The pulse point on her neck beat frantically, and her body trembled, but I knew it wasn't from arousal. She was scared. I was the last person on earth she ever had to fear. Why couldn't she see that? I'd lied about my name, but I'd told her the truth—or most of it—just now.

"What I am and what I do—it's nothing for you to ever feel threatened by. I will never let anyone hurt you. That's why we are here. I'm going to fix this. All of it. Then, you can go home, and you'll be safe."

She licked her lips as she stared up at me. "I don't know you."

I smirked. "You know me, Ace. I'm the same guy with a different name."

She stiffened. "Not the same guy. The guy I thought I knew wasn't in the Mafia. He was a nice guy with too much money to toss around, but I liked him. I trusted him."

I bent my head and pressed a kiss to her cheek. "I am a nice guy. Compared to my older brother, I'm a goddamn saint," I told her, then moved to kiss the other cheek. There was a slight pink flush in them now, and that eased me some. I moved to kiss the corner of her mouth. "I'm nice,

I swear it," I whispered, shifting my attention to the other corner.

I wanted her naked and under me in the king-size bed upstairs. I'd wanted to fuck her since the moment I laid eyes on her, but nothing had prepared me for how incredible it would feel. That she would feel. It had been different in ways I hadn't known existed. It had also seemed to meld my rational mind with the savage, unhinged beast pacing inside. I'd become both, and for the first time in my life, I understood Thatcher. I wasn't on his level of psycho, but if pushed, I would snap. I could feel it just under my skin.

I wanted the small shiver I felt as I trailed kisses from her mouth to her neck to be because she was enjoying this. Thinking about what we'd done on the plane and wanting it again. But she was still uncertain of me. I'd have to give her time. This was only highlighting her fear.

"I'm sorry I had to do it this way," I whispered in her ear, then dropped my hands and stepped back.

She swallowed hard, staring at the floor instead of me. "How long do I have to stay here? Can I call and check on Grams? Is there any way we can find out if my father is safe? Alive?"

I'd left both our phones on the plane. She didn't know that yet though. She would as soon as she went to get hers from her pocket. After I'd woken her up, she'd been too dazed to look for her phone before leaving the plane. It had worked to my advantage. Wilder could trace them. I had set both to Airplane Mode, giving me some time.

The man I'd hired to take us here was going to Mexico next to do an illegal drug pickup. I'd told him to take our phones with him and drop them in the first trash can he came to. I couldn't have the others following me. Not until I showing up because he couldn't stay away. Even the one who lost his shit when your father laid a hand on you. You've had my attention from day one. The more I was around you, the more I wanted to be. Until you were all I wanted."

TWENTY-SIX

Leave it to me to go and catch feelings for a man in the freaking Mafia.

ROYAL

How long had he planned this? It couldn't have been a last-minute decision.

The pale pink satin pajama shorts and matching camisole, along with a pair of lacy white panties, which I had found folded up on the bed when I came upstairs, told me he had been prepared. Unless he'd brought other women here and they were my exact same size. Even knowing he'd lied to me about who he was and that he'd basically abducted me, I didn't like the idea of him buying this for some other female.

What did that say about me or my mental health?

The bedroom with a connected bathroom were the only rooms in the loft area. In the bathroom, fluffy, large white towels had been rolled up neatly and placed in a tall basket near the shower and bathtub. Expensive-smelling body wash, shampoo, and conditioner were already in the shower when I took one. The lock on the bathroom door gave me a little peace so I could attempt to relax while standing under the hot spray.

I doubted he'd allow me to sleep on the sofa. He'd do it instead and give me the bed. But if I was going to escape this house and find a way back to Athens and Grams, he couldn't be so close to the door. If he would just tell me where we were, that would help.

Not having a phone was an even bigger obstacle. I could get lost out there. Starve to death. Staying here while knowing nothing about my Grams or dad wasn't an option.

My dad had decided to leave us. Fine. Maybe I wouldn't check on him. But Grams needed me. There were bills to pay. Our house couldn't just sit there, empty.

There were papers I owed people. They'd realize I was missing.

Anya would start getting concerned when I didn't answer my phone. In fact, by this time tomorrow, she would go to the police. Rodney would wonder why I hadn't come into the pool hall. Milo would notice when I didn't respond to his texts about games. If I found some civilization, then I could ask for a police station. They'd have been alerted that I was a missing person.

When I stepped out of the bathroom, dressed in the satin pajamas, the smell of food met me. He was cooking. The kitchen was stocked then. Just like the bathroom had been. Maybe there were protein bars or nuts I could put in a bag and take with me. Or maybe I could find where he'd put the keys to the Hummer. It would wake him when I started it up, but he would be on foot, and I could get ahead of him easily enough.

Leaving him stranded out here bothered me though. I knew it shouldn't. He'd done this to me. This had been his decision. He'd find a way to get out. It wasn't as if I'd be leaving him here to die. Besides, from the smell of basil, oregano, and garlic, it seemed he had plenty of supplies to keep himself fed.

With my mind made up, I headed down the spiral staircase. Sharing a bed with him, even for a little while, would be a struggle. It wasn't that I couldn't control myself because, after today's truths, having sex with him again wasn't happening.

Now, would I be taunted by the memory of it? Yes. That had been a level of nirvana—

NO! Not thinking about it.

What I'd experienced was with Amory. The guy who didn't exist. The one I'd trusted.

Sebastian Shephard was someone else.

His back was to me as he opened the oven and pulled out a pan of sliced French bread with melted butter. A pan of lasagna sat on the counter, and a glass bowl, filled with a salad, was beside it. My stomach rumbled. It seemed I was hungry. Eating had been the last thing on my mind until I walked down here to see this.

When I reached the bottom, Sebastian set the bread beside the other two items and lifted his eyes to meet mine. His gaze slowly made its way down my body, and I wished I could stop the tingle that spread through me and the flutter in my stomach. But he was beautiful and sexy, and he'd given me the best sex I'd ever had in my life.

He was also my abductor, and he did other things. I wasn't sure what exactly. Drugs didn't seem like something he was involved in, but he had no issue with killing a person. Organized crime was still crime.

What did the Mafia in Georgia actually do? And why hadn't I known there was a Mafia in Georgia?

"Did you enjoy your shower? Find everything you need?" he asked, turning around to take plates from the cabinet. He seemed to know where everything was located.

"Yes. It's well stocked. Do you kidnap girls and bring them here often?" I asked airily, as if making idle conversation.

Sebastian's mouth did that cocky grin that also caused his eyes to twinkle. "No. You're the first female I wanted to kidnap."

That look and the sound of his voice when he said it made my nipples harden. Dammit. I should have worn a bra with this. I'd been thinking about escaping, not what I was wearing.

"I suppose you don't have to kidnap your females. They all just run to you. Throwing themselves at your feet."

Although I was being sarcastic, the image irked me. How often did women throw themselves at him? How many had he given an orgasm to, like he had with me?

"I don't know about women throwing themselves at my feet, but, no, I can't say I've ever struggled to get a female's attention if I wanted it."

Including me, I thought sourly.

"Hungry? I didn't make the lasagna, but I did cook it. Hopefully, it tastes as good as it smells."

Not anymore. Talking about other women had taken my appetite. I was annoyed with myself. I wanted to just shut it off. Feel nothing for him. Unfortunately, that wasn't the case. I'd had sex with him, but I couldn't even blame it on that. He'd gotten to me before. Then, he'd snatched the rug out from under me.

"Are you hiding a chef in the basement?" I asked.

He chuckled. "I had several meals prepared and delivered with the other things."

"Seems very thorough and thought out," I replied, walking over to the table made for only two people.

"I wanted you to be comfortable."

It had been a waste of time and resources because I was leaving tonight. He'd have all the comfortable necessities to himself.

There was a pang in my chest. Part of me didn't want to leave him. I wanted to stay. See if the man I thought he was actually existed. But I'd already been stupid and naive with him. I couldn't do that again.

"Are you going to tell me where we are? That would help. It's not comforting to have no idea what state you're even in." If I had that information, it would help.

Sebastian took a plate that he'd filled and walked around the counter toward me. I tore my gaze off him, not wanting to admire the way he moved or how his jeans fit him. How the muscles in his arms flexed. Nope. Not thinking about it.

He stopped close to me. Too close. "Have a seat," he said gently as he put the plate on the table and pulled out a chair.

God, why did he have to smell so good?

I kept my eyes averted as I took the chair from him and sat down. The food once again made my stomach rumble. It had been a while since I'd had anything to eat, and this did look good.

Sebastian's fingers brushed my shoulder as he pulled back my still-slightly-damp locks back. I tensed and held my breath as he traced the neckline of my camisole.

"I know you're angry. But don't hate me. I couldn't take it if you hated me."

The pained sound in his tone was difficult to hear. I wanted to believe he was sincere. I wanted to believe a lot of things. But I'd trusted him too easily once already.

"I don't hate you," I replied. That was the truth. I didn't, and I knew I wouldn't be able to. What I felt for him was in the opposite direction and not at all safe or healthy for me.

His touch left me, and I sucked in some much-needed oxygen as he walked back to the bar. Closing my eyes, I gave myself a mental lecture about letting my silly emotions get the best of me. Grams needed me. I wasn't going to just leave her there, no matter how nice that place was. She'd think I'd abandoned her.

Then, of course, I had to remember Sebastian was dangerous. Beautiful but dark. Those brief glimpses of that sinister side of him lurking just under the surface, I'd seen. It wasn't in my imagination. He was trying to hide it from me, but when we'd had sex, it had been there staring at me through those eyes of his. He'd been unable to mask the marks on his soul. The things he'd seen and done hadn't left him unscathed. They'd become a part of him. I could never trust that.

But he stopped hurting your dad when you begged him to.

I closed my eyes and pushed that away. Even my subconscious was trying to make excuses for him.

I heard his footsteps and opened my eyes back up to pick up my fork. He put his plate down, then took the seat across from me. It was an odd thing—to have so many different emotions clamoring for the top spot. Especially when I seemed to have no control over any of them.

Fear, anxiety, arousal, regret ... so many that to name them would take a focus I didn't have.

"You have to put it in your mouth to eat it," he said. "Staring at it does nothing."

He was teasing me. Trying to lighten the mood. Nothing could do that, but I used my fork to cut a piece of the lasagna, then lifted it to my mouth. I knew he was watching me, but I didn't look at him. If I let myself think too hard about what I was going to do, I'd find a reason not to. Simply because the part of me that wanted this man was fighting for its choice to be heard.

The decision wasn't up for debate.

Since he'd cooked, I insisted that he let me clean and suggested he go take a shower. With him in the shower, I could find his keys so I wasn't searching for them in the middle of the night. The faster I got out the door, the more likely I'd successfully escape.

The moment I heard the water running, I left the task of loading the dishwasher to start looking. I went to the sofa and lifted the cushions, then in and around the table beside the front door.

The coat he'd put on me when I stepped off the plane was my third place to search. The right-side pocket held the key fob. Sighing in relief, I left it there and went back to the kitchen. I knew where it was. All that was left was for me to wait. When he was sound asleep, I'd make my move.

By the time I was wiping down the counter, the water upstairs shut off. He was done. We hadn't discussed sleeping arrangements. It would be easier if I could sleep down here, but that wasn't going to happen. Sebastian wouldn't allow it.

I wouldn't be in bed with him for long. Besides, with him on one side and me on the other, I doubted we'd even touch. No contact would make it easier. When I reached the top step, I glanced over to see he'd left the bathroom door open.

He stood in front of the sink with nothing but a towel wrapped around his waist. The loose curls that gave him that sexy, messy look were wet, leaving a few ringlets near his neckline. A tattoo was on his back left shoulder that I'd not seen before, but then I had always seen his front when he was shirtless. I tried to make it out, but from here, I couldn't tell what it was exactly.

Just as I narrowed my eyes to study it closer, he turned around, and I snapped my gaze up to his face, feeling as if I'd been caught doing something naughty. Perhaps I had been. The sight of that man, damp and bare, was impossible to look away from.

"Please, don't let me stop you. Look all you want."

Cocky jerk. I rolled my eyes. "I was simply trying to make out what your tattoo was. I hadn't noticed it before."

He walked out of the bathroom, still only wearing the towel. I wasn't sure if I wanted to go tug at it so that it fell to the ground or back away and put distance between us. I stayed where I was, not taking my eyes off him. He didn't come toward me, but rather over to a chest with three drawers. Opening the top one, he took out a pair of navy-blue pajama pants and then swung his gaze back to me.

The towel dropped to the floor, and I sucked in a breath. Yes, his body was even more magnificent than I remembered. Snapping my eyes closed, I spun around as my face grew warm.

"You could have warned me," I said with annoyance that was mostly aimed at me for wanting to keep looking.

"You've had my cock in your mouth. You can't get any closer view than that."

"That was before!" I shot back at him.

"Before …" He said the word as if he needed me to elaborate when he knew good and well what I meant.

"Before you kidnapped me, and I knew you were a liar."

His hand touched my waist, and I jumped, startled.

"Come on, Ace. I've admitted all my lies." His voice was husky and entirely too close to my ear.

"That doesn't matter. I didn't come here of my own free will, and you're keeping me here."

He moved his hand up my side and under the hem of my top. I reached up and grabbed his wrist, pulling it back down just before he reached my breast. I was struggling to breathe, and my heart was racing, but I still had my wits.

"Don't. We can share a bed, but don't," I told him.

I expected him to argue, but he didn't. Instead, he dropped his hand. I should be feeling relief, not disappointment.

"Whatever you want," he replied. The gentleness in his tone didn't make this easier. If he'd acted angry or demanding, perhaps I could fight off my attraction to him.

I turned to see him walking over to the bed.

"Do you have a preference on the side you sleep on?" he asked me as he pulled back the covers on the left side.

My gaze was back on his tattoo as it shifted with his movement. From here, it looked like a shattered clock. The shadows made it appear sinister, which seemed strange for what it was. There were pieces of glass scattered around it.

"If you want to see it up close, I won't bite," he said.

I swung my eyes back up to meet his. He wasn't mocking me, nor was he smirking at having caught me ogling him again.

"Is it a broken clock?" I asked, still unsure if that was what I was seeing.

He nodded. "It is."

I was intrigued.

"What does it mean?"

It had to symbolize something. One didn't randomly choose a shattered clock with broken glass for a tattoo.

"It was a reminder at the time that I got it, but over the years, it changed. Became something else. I'm not the same man I was when I had it done."

That didn't answer my question, and while I should be mentally planning my escape, I was fascinated with his tattoo.

"So, what did it mean then, and what does it mean now?" I prodded, wanting to understand him. The part of me that wanted to strip naked and crawl in that bed with him needed some validation, although the answer to my questions could be another reason for me to run out that door the moment I had a chance.

"When I got it, I thought I was in love. I'd proposed to her, and she said no. This was my reminder that time didn't change our fate, and I had no control over it."

He'd been in love once. I wished I hadn't known that. Why had I asked? It felt like someone had reached into my chest and was squeezing my lungs. That shouldn't hurt so much. This man was not for me.

"And now?" My voice cracked slightly, and I winced.

"That you can achieve too much and not really achieve anything of worth. Not to be a fool and an overachiever."

Did that mean he didn't love her now? Was it someone in his youth? He'd proposed, it was unlikely she was his first love or a teenage romance. He was only twenty-nine now. How long ago could it have been? Not long enough. Was he waiting on her still?

I cleared my throat and stood straighter. I would not let him see that I cared about this woman he'd loved so much that he wanted to marry her and got a shattered clock on his body permanently because of her rejection.

"Seems an odd thing to put on yourself. I don't see how a shattered clock represents either of those things." My tone was snarky, and I knew it.

I was jealous. Plain and simple.

I was running away from this man, but clearly, I cared about who his heart had belonged to.

"You've never read *The Great Gatsby*, I take it?" he replied as I reached the right side of the bed to jerk back the covers with more force than necessary.

"Of course I've read *The Great Gatsby*," I replied sharply.

Then, I paused and let that sink in. The broken clock. My heart felt heavy now, and my throat tightened. Did he mean to tell me that he had loved some woman the way Jay Gatsby did Daisy? That was hard to hear. I should have kept my mouth shut.

"I see," I said tightly, climbing into the bed with my back to him.

I pulled the covers up to my chin and stared at the wall. Sebastian had a Daisy in his life. I'd never stood a chance. No woman could replace a Daisy. God, what was wrong with me? I was about to freaking cry over someone I had already decided I had to get away from. Someone I couldn't trust.

I felt the weight of the bed shift as he sat down on the other side.

What kind of woman had had his love and not wanted it? Had she known about his life and not been able to accept it either? Had he lost her because he was in the Mafia? It was the only thing I could think of that would make any female tell him no. Had he gotten down on one knee? Told her he loved her? That he couldn't live without her?

I placed a hand on my chest and took a steady breath. Whew, this was not pleasant at all. I didn't like it or how it felt. Jealousy had never been an emotion I was familiar with, but I realized it was a powerful one. Sheer envy for some woman I had never met was eating at me.

"Is she married?" I blurted out when I thought about Daisy Buchanan.

For him to have paralleled their story so much that he tattooed the clock on his body, then how similar were they?

"Who?" he asked.

I rolled my eyes, still looking at the wall. "The woman you are in love with. Daisy was married."

He chuckled. "You're taking that too literally, and, yes, she is married now. She wasn't at the time. If I were still in love with Wilder's wife, he'd put a bullet between my eyes. Family or no family, he'd not think twice."

Who was Wilder? Had she married his brother?

Unable to help myself, I turned over and looked at him. "She married your family? Is Wilder your brother?" I asked, horrified.

Sebastian appeared amused for someone whose family had married the woman he'd loved. Why I suddenly went from envying her to hating her, I had no explanation for, but honestly, she sounded like a bitch.

"No, Wilder is not my brother. He is in the family though. The Mafia in the South is also called the family. His grandfather joined the family in the '50s. Mine, however, goes back to the beginning, over a hundred years ago."

So, she'd married another Mafia member. Then that wasn't the reason she'd rejected his proposal.

"How do you handle that?" I asked, finding myself worried about his feelings. "Seeing her with him. Do you even speak to him?"

Sebastian chuckled, but I didn't understand why he was finding humor in this.

"Ace," he said, reaching out and tucking some loose hair behind my ear, "it was years ago, and in Wilder's defense, he loved her first. She loved him, and she never stopped. What I felt for Oakley wasn't love. It was respect and affection, but not love. When she turned me down, I didn't fall apart. I moved on rather quickly, not once looking back. This tattoo isn't me mirroring Jay Gatsby. I love books, significant words that I read on paper. That clock he broke meant something different to me back then than it does now. Everyone has their own interpretation of a story. It's not literal. I don't have a Daisy. I never did."

He loved books. Why did that reminder make it even harder for me to paint him in a villainous light? It shouldn't. He had lied to me and abducted me. His reasons why didn't matter. He'd still done it.

I turned back over to face the wall. "Good night," I told him, wanting to get on with my plan.

The longer I had to think about it, the more I feared I would change my mind. I had to be smarter than that. Even if it was now clear to me that my feelings for Sebastian were much stronger than I'd realized.

Leave it to me to go and catch feelings for a man in the freaking Mafia.

TWENTY-SEVEN

*"I didn't bring you all the way up here
for a bear or wolf to get you."*

SEBASTIAN

I'd been waiting for this, hoping I was wrong, but knowing she wasn't one to be handled. She used her charm and savvy to get by in life, not ever coming against someone who could see right through her. The bed barely moved as she eased herself out of it slowly. It had taken her three hours to either work up the nerve to do it or she was just making sure I was in a dead sleep.

When she had been jealous of the reason behind my tattoo, there had been a moment when I thought I might be able to crack this shell she'd put around her since we'd arrived.

But she'd turned over and told me good night instead.

The barest whisper of her feet as she moved across the floor and to the stairs made me smile. If I wasn't me—someone who had been raised to track, always be one step ahead, use the element of surprise—then she might have just pulled this off.

When she had sent me up to take a shower and insisted that she clean up the kitchen, I'd known exactly what she was up to. The fact that she didn't leave then was interesting.

She wouldn't have gotten far—although the shower was running, I wasn't in it; I was watching her. Standing back just far enough from the railing that the shadows hid me. When she found the key fob, I thought she'd take off, but she left them in the pocket of my coat and went back to the dishes.

I had gone to take a quick shower at that point.

Standing, I moved over the floor silently and was halfway down the stairs when she opened the door. I leaned forward, resting my elbows on the railing.

"Brown bears and wolves," I said, breaking the silence.

She jumped and let out a small scream.

"When the Hummer runs out of gas less than a mile from here, you'll be stuck there. Walking back here or the twenty-plus miles to the nearest house, you'll likely be mauled by a bear or become a wolf's meal."

She closed the door, and her shoulders fell before she turned around to look at me. It had been a decent plan. One I'd been prepared for. The fuel for the tank was locked away and hidden for when we would need it.

"I thought you were asleep," she said.

"I couldn't let you get killed, Ace. I didn't bring you all the way up here for a bear or wolf to get you."

She walked over to the coat rack and shrugged off my coat that had the key fob inside, then hung it back up.

The woman I'd paid to stock this place, including that little pink satin number on Royal's body, needed a bonus.

"I don't want to be here!" she snapped angrily, turning back to me.

I continued down the rest of the stairs and headed toward her. She wanted to be here. She just didn't want to admit it. Stubborn, brave, strong-willed little beauty.

"What's so wrong with here? You have food, heat, a comfortable bed, good company."

The exasperated look on her face made me grin.

"One could argue about the *good company* part."

I took another step toward her, expecting her to back up but she didn't.

"You think so? Am I really that bad?"

She crossed her arms over her chest and glared at me. "Not everyone is charmed by your ridiculously handsome face."

I could work with *ridiculously handsome face*. I took another step toward her. "And here I thought, it was my talent with carrying on an intelligent conversation. Next, are you going to say something about my body and make me feel like nothing more than eye candy?"

She narrowed her eyes as she studied me, she couldn't tell if I was teasing her or not. When I was mere inches from her, I cupped the side of her face. I loved touching her. Seeing her skin flush even if she didn't want it to.

"I told you not to touch me," she said, trying to sound like she didn't enjoy it.

"That's hard for me to do. Especially when I have you all alone, in a remote cabin, dressed in pink satin. I keep thinking about how you tasted. Melted sugar, drizzled over a ripe peach. How sliding into you bare was the most incredible thing I'd ever experienced."

My gaze dropped to her mouth. It was slightly open, and she was panting softly.

Just a little more.

I leaned down to press a kiss beside her ear. "I can take off your bottoms and bury my face between your legs while you orgasm over and over until you pass out," I whispered, my tone husky, thinking about having her like that. Right now.

"I'd never hurt you," I assured her, running my knuckles down the swell of her full tits that pressed against the satin top. "I just want to have you, take care of you, taste you, fuck you." My hand slid over her ass, and I squeezed it, pulling her closer to me.

She let out a small cry, and those blue eyes stared up at me, glazed over with need. That was my girl. Right there. I picked her up, and she wrapped her legs around my waist while I strode purposefully toward the stairs.

Upstairs. Naked. All that golden hair spread out on the pillows. Mine.

"Sebastian." She said my name, and I didn't pause.

"Yes?"

"I'm scared."

Fuck. I'd thought we had moved past that.

"The only thing you have to be scared of is that I won't let you out of this bed. The things I've imagined doing to you …" I paused as we reached the top, then looked her in the eyes. "Please don't be scared of me, Royal. I'm begging you. I can't stand the idea of you fearing me."

She pulled her bottom lip into her mouth, then let it go. I had plans for those lips and that mouth.

"That's not what I mean. I … I feel too much with you already. You make me have these very strong reactions. I've never been jealous before but …" She paused and looked away from me. "I'm afraid the more we do this, the closer we get, the longer we are here … I think I could get addicted to you, very attached. I don't trust myself with that."

A smirk pulled on my lips and continued until we reached the bed and I set her down.

"Would it be such a bad thing?" I asked, thinking it sounded fucking perfect to me.

"Yes. It could be. I don't know. You make me act crazy. What if … what if I become some clingy psycho you can't get rid of when you tire of me?"

I threw back my head and let out a bark of laughter.

Her hand slapped at my chest. "That's not funny!"

Oh, but it was. It was hilarious.

I ran the tip of my tongue over her bottom lip. Fuck, I wanted to suck on that.

"Tell me, is it my cock you're worried about getting addicted to and going fatal attraction on me, or is it my mouth and what it does to your sweet cunt?"

She used both hands to shove at my chest. "I am serious."

As much fun as this was, I was ready to get her naked. I slid a knuckle under her chin, tilting her head back slightly so she was looking me directly in the eyes.

"It would be hot," I told her. "It turns me on that your much younger cunt is taking my dick. That I am sinking into a sexy, barely legal pussy and she wants it as much as I do. Is that twisted? Yeah, probably. But I don't care.

"You've shown me sides of myself that I didn't know I had. To get to have you, I am willing to do things I never imagined I'd do. So, yeah, baby, you just go and get addicted. Be clingy. Act psycho." I kissed her lips as I stuck a hand between her thighs. "Because there is nothing on earth I want more than to make you happy. And if my dick can do that, then that's just fucking magical."

Shoving the crotch of her pajama bottoms and panties aside, I pressed the tip of my middle finger inside to find her soaked. Knowing I had done this to her, that she was creaming her panties because of me?

Yeah, bring on the crazy, baby.

I could handle it all and take care of my girl properly.

Her hands grabbed my biceps as she whimpered, opening her legs wider.

"Let's get these off," I said, removing my hand to grab the shorts and panties to extract them from her body.

She scooted back, bending her knees and letting her legs fall open fully.

Jesus Christ.

"Take the top off," I ordered as I discarded my bottoms.

"I need you in me," she said as she stared up at me pleadingly.

"You told me you had been tested, but not once asked if I had been. Yet here you are, opening up so sweet for me again."

"Because you said you wouldn't hurt me," she panted.

"And I won't," I assured her. "I was going to lick that swollen little clit first and fuck you with my tongue."

She shook her head. "I can't wait. Please, Sebastian."

My name coming from her lips for the first time when we were like this was a new trigger I hadn't been prepared for. Grabbing my cock, I stroked it as I stared down at her glistening wet folds, open for me.

"Turn over and stick your ass in the air," I told her, knowing if I had to look at her face, I'd not last long. Seeing her pleasure was something that set me off too quick.

She closed her legs and rolled onto her stomach, then pulled her knees under her. She slid them apart, giving me not only a clear view of one hole, but two. I wanted both of them. But right now, my girl needed her pussy filled.

Placing a knee on the bed, I moved in behind her, enjoying the soft skin on her hips, then ran my palms over her ass. "Fuck, I want to spank this ass," I growled, squeezing it.

"Yes!" she moaned and shook it at me as an invitation.

With that one move, any control I'd held on to was gone.

My hand landed with a loud smack, causing the round bottom to jiggle. She cried out and taunted me again, shaking it.

Smack, smack, smack. I continued as she begged for more.

The seventh time I did it, she threw her head back and began to jerk as liquid sprayed out from between her legs.

I froze, watching her body shudder. *Holy fuck.*

The inside of her thighs was dripping all the way down to her knees, and there was a large wet spot on the covers beneath us. A deranged sound tore from me as I grabbed her hips and slammed into her.

"FUUUCK!"

"AH!" she screamed beneath me.

The gushing sound it made as I began to move in and out of the hot, tight hole was going to make me come just as quickly as her mouth on my cock had. Goddamn, I'd seen this happen on porn before, but never in real life. Until now, I'd thought it was fake. The squirters I'd fucked never did anything like that.

"Sebastian!" My name tore from her lips again.

Mine. Mine. Mine. That one word repeated in my head like a chant as I thrust into her over and over.

She tensed beneath me, and then her body jerked again as she made a low keening sound. Then, another hard spray shot all over my dick, almost pushing me out of her cunt.

"Sebastian! Oh God, Sebastian." She was clawing at the sheets, her hands reaching in front of her.

The wet slap of our bodies drew my eyes down to where I was taking her. Seeing her last ejaculation all over my lower stomach and coating my cock as it sank into her caused my balls to draw up tight as I shouted out, continuing to pump into her while shooting my load inside her.

I couldn't pull out even if I wanted to. The possessive beast inside my chest had me locking her in a vise grip as satisfaction ripped through me.

TWENTY-EIGHT

"Now, be a good girl and keep me warm."

ROYAL

I fell limply to the bed when Sebastian's hands released me. His body moved over me, and then he lay down on my right side before pulling me into his arms. Lying there, with my head over his heart, I heard the steady rhythm beating faster than normal. He caressed my arms with his fingertips as we both breathed heavily.

I was aware of the wet area that started just below my knee, and I knew I'd done that. Although I'd never done it before. I also realized the warmth trickling out of me between my legs was Sebastian's cum. He hadn't pulled out this time. Although he had known I was on the shot, he had still pulled out the first time. I guessed he no longer felt the need for extra precaution.

Closing my eyes, I couldn't even be upset that I hadn't escaped. I was floating on a cloud, sated, at the pinnacle of all sexual experiences. If this was how sex was supposed to be, then no wonder I'd never gotten off without doing it myself.

"Is it always like this for you?" I asked, wondering if Merce had just been really bad at it or if Sebastian was exceptional.

"Fuck no," he replied. "That was …" He paused, then let out a soft chuckle. "Damn, baby, I don't know what that was. But that fear you had about being clingy and addicted to me? Well, you might need to be worried about me tying your ass to my bed and fucking you fifty times a day."

A giggle bubbled out of me, and I tilted my head back to look up at him. "I don't know if you noticed, but I made a mess. Or at least I do with you. That would be a lot of cleanup."

He grinned. "I'll change the sheets happily. With a motherfucking smile on my face. As many times as I need to."

I was relieved he wasn't freaked out by it because I had been. After I'd stopped orgasming, I'd started to worry, and then he began fucking me like a man possessed, and I'd forgotten about caring.

"I've never done that before," I admitted.

"Hmm. Seems you've got a kink. You loved getting your ass spanked, so much so that you squirted like a water hose. I'll have to remember to put you over my knee often."

I'd done it twice though. Not just when he'd spanked me.

I drew a pattern on his chest as I thought about it. "I think I liked you … I don't know … taking me like that. You were hard and demanding. And it was deep."

"Keep talking like that, and I'll have your ass in the air again," he said in a warning tone.

Smiling, I lifted myself up, resting on the crook of my arm to look down at him.

"I think I like it rough. Like when you treated me as if you were crazed or out of control. Like you couldn't get deep enough inside me or fuck me hard enough. That triggers me."

He lifted his hand to wrap one of my strands of hair around it. "Ace, I'm not kidding. My cock is already getting hard. If you don't want a round two just yet, stop using that pretty little mouth to talk dirty."

I licked my lips. "But I think I like dirty. With you."

Sebastian's eyes flared as he moved his hand further into my hair and fisted it. "You need to be careful. There's some dark, possessive shit in me that you bring out, and telling me you want it dirty is gonna have me taking you before you're ready."

I'd read many books on Greek mythology, and in this moment, Sebastian reminded me of what Zeus was supposed to look like. Perfectly sculpted, beautiful, with a sharp, masculine jaw, and the brightness in his dark eyes, as if they might burst into flames at any moment.

I lifted myself up and straddled him as he lay on his back, his eyes following my every move. Wrapping my hands around his hard length, it gave me a powerful thrill seeing the way my touch affected him.

Moving up, I lined his swollen head with my entrance and ran it back and forth, teasing myself with what I wanted.

"Fuck," he whispered.

I looked up at him to see he was watching me rub myself with his cock.

Tilting my hips, I sank down on it and placed both palms flat on his sculpted abs.

"YES!" I cried at the same time he let out a low, deep groan of pleasure.

I began to move up and down slowly.

"You want to ride it?" he said to me, squeezing my left breast. "Then, fucking ride it. I'm a thoroughbred, Ace. Not a pony."

I bit my bottom lip as I grinned and picked up my pace, having to lean forward more to do so.

As my breasts swung back and forth close to his face, Sebastian lifted his head to lick and suck on one of my nipples.

When his palm slapped my butt, I hadn't expected it, but like before, it excited me.

"More," I begged.

He did as I'd asked in a slow speed at first, but as I began to moan louder, his slaps became faster.

"Damn, my girl likes being spanked." The excitement in his voice as he ran his face over one of my boobs made my inner walls clench. That had happened before.

"It stings. I like it," I panted. "I tried to leave," I reminded him as his eyes locked with mine. "I deserve to be punished."

The next hit was much harder, and I pulled up just as I felt the jolt shoot through me and the release gush from my body.

"Jesus, fuck, that's it. Fuuuck, that's hot." Sebastian's words felt far away.

I was thrown on my back, and my eyes flew open to see Sebastian grabbing my legs and bending them back, exposing me completely before sinking into me.

"That's it. Such a good pussy. Take that dick." His voice was raspy as he got more and more frantic.

His eyes met mine. He was close. I loved watching him like this. Knowing it was me doing this to him.

"So fucking beautiful." His body tensed as he said the words, and the veins on his neck stood out. "GAH!"

The shout came just as the first burst of heat released inside me.

Either it was his face or the way his cum felt as he ejaculated—or both—but I screamed his name as another climax took me with him.

The wall of warmth behind me felt amazing when I began to wake. The room was cold, but I scooted back further against the heat, and the muscular, corded arm that was wrapped around me tightened. His hand slid up and cupped one of my breasts.

A pleased grunt was followed by one of his legs also covering me and bringing me even closer. "This is the way to wake up," he said in a husky voice, then bent his head to bury his face in my neck. "If this is a fucking dream, don't wake me up."

I laughed, reaching up to hold on to his arm. "Not a dream," I told him. "I have a rather tender ass to prove it."

"Mmm," he replied, then slid his hand from my boob to my bottom to rub it. "I'll put some cream on it. I gotta take care of this thing. It's my magic button."

Grinning, I turned onto my back slightly so I could look at him. "Magic button?"

He nodded.

With his hooded eyes, stubbled jaw, and messy hair, he was the most erotic thing I'd seen in my life.

"I spank this ass, and your cunt sprays me like a porn star."

I tried to pull away from him. "Don't compare me to that!"

He pulled me back tighter. "No need to get feisty, Ace. That's every boy's dream from the moment he sees his first porn. Now, be a good girl and keep me warm."

How any woman could resist this man, I had no idea. To think, he'd wanted to marry someone, and she hadn't wanted him.

"I'd like to see this Wilder guy," I said aloud.

Sebastian leaned up to look down at me with a small frown between his brows. "Why?"

I shrugged. "I am just struggling with the fact that some woman didn't fall victim to your charms."

His lips quirked, and he bent his head to nuzzle my cleavage. "You don't get to meet him. In fact, you aren't going in public again. Nowhere that other men can take you from me."

Although there was a teasing quality in his tone, I also felt like he meant it—or at least the part about someone taking me from him. Was he insecure? It seemed impossible for someone like him to have any reason to feel insecure. I was the one who had to worry about other women. We wouldn't be locked away in this cabin alone forever. The real world was coming, and when it did, would he have had his fill of me?

"And if you get tired of me?" The words weren't meant to be said aloud, but my mouth had a mind of its own.

He stilled, then looked at me. The way he studied me was as if he was trying to decide if I was making a joke. Maybe I should play it off as one. Not become the needy, clingy young girl I had been worried about. He might like it with sex, but in the light of day, he was a grown man. He had a life. One that I knew nothing about.

Sebastian kept his eyes on me but continued to kiss a path down my stomach.

"What are you doing?" I asked as he spread my thighs open.

"I'm going to show you how unlikely it is that I'll ever tire of you."

I opened my mouth to argue that this didn't have anything to do with it, but then his tongue touched me, and I let my head fall back on the pillow with a moan. Never mind. He could show me all he wanted to.

TWENTY-NINE

"I don't expect perfection, just don't hurt anyone for me, okay?"

SEBASTIAN

Looking up from the book I had been reading, I watched Royal walk down the stairs while drying her hair with a towel. I'd had to find something to distract me so I wouldn't go get in the shower with her. She hadn't complained, but her cunt had to be sore. I'd fucked her hard four times in the past twelve hours.

When she reached the bottom stair, her eyes met mine, and then they dropped to the book I was holding. "Talk about porn."

I held up my book. "Nothing about *To Kill a Mockingbird* could be considered porn."

She grinned as she sauntered over to me. The sweatsuit she was wearing did nothing to ease my need for her. It didn't matter what she was wearing. Royal Shelton was a constant smolder. Her appeal never faded. She was always there, making me ache to touch her. Keep her close.

"I meant the sight of you sitting there, all six foot three inches of sexy man candy, with a book in your hand. That's my kind of porn."

I dropped my gaze back to the book. "In that case, let me read some more."

Her laughter made my chest feel light as she sank down beside me on the sofa, curling her feet beneath her. "I used the cream you'd set out for my bottom," she told me.

The reminder of her perfect, round red ass made my cock twitch.

Down, boy. You've had plenty.

"I'd have done it, but then I'd have ended up fucking you again," I told her, closing the book and putting it on the table beside me.

"You say that like it's a bad thing."

I laid my head back and closed my eyes tightly. "It will be if I fuck us both to death."

"I think you might be a tad bit dramatic, but I digress." She finished with her hair, folded the towel neatly, and then set it down before standing back up. "Got to brush it."

I watched her, wishing I could see her naked red ass with my handprints on it. "Bring me the brush. Let me do it."

She stopped and glanced back over her shoulder. "You want to brush my hair?"

I nodded.

Her lips curled up at the corners. "Okay."

I wondered if anyone had ever brushed her hair. How much had she done for herself as a child? Her Grams seemed nice, but I didn't know the woman she had been when she was in her right mind.

Had she done things for Royal that mothers did? Fuck knew her father hadn't.

She didn't talk about her mom. I knew more about the woman than she did. I wondered if she wanted to meet her. See her. Have any relationship with her. Not that the bitch deserved it for leaving her with Vinson Shelton.

Royal came back, holding the brush, with a sway to her hips. "Since we aren't naked and crazed, can we talk about how long you think we are going to be here? And maybe you could tell me where we are."

She held the brush out to me, and I grabbed a pillow and put it on the floor between my feet. Royal looked at it, then grinned before sitting down and crossing her legs with her back to me.

I slowly ran the bristles through her damp locks. If she was going to trust me again, then I had to trust her. After last night, I wanted to believe she wouldn't try and leave.

"I think, under the circumstances, about a week," I told her. Although I wanted it to be longer than that.

I also knew that no amount of covering my tracks was going to stop my father from finding me. It might take them longer than usual because I knew how they found people, but in the end, Wilder was the genius who could trace just about anyone. He just needed a crumb, and he'd find one.

"Do we have enough food for a week?"

"Yeah. Enough for two."

"I'll be a missing person. Probably already am."

I enjoyed watching the brush glide through the silky strands.

"Missing people don't send texts, telling those they are close to that they're going to look for their dad and not take their phone, for fear he might track it. That they have a burner and will contact them in a week, if not sooner, but not to worry. That they're fine and they have someone with them."

She spun around and looked up at me, wide-eyed. "You sent that?"

"I'm thorough," I replied.

Plus, my brother had abducted his girlfriend without thinking anything through, and that had been a mess to clean up. I learned from his mistakes.

"Is the *where are we* thing still something you won't tell me?"

I wanted to trust her. I'd never wanted anything more than to know she wouldn't leave me. That she was as fucking obsessed with me as I was her.

"Alaska," I told her.

She didn't seem shocked. "I thought so. Especially when you said the brown bears and wolves."

I finished with her hair and laid the brush down. So much she still didn't know. I wanted her to know it all, but I couldn't trust she wouldn't turn against me. If I could get her to fall in love with me, then maybe I could be completely honest.

"Done already?" she asked. "I was enjoying it. That felt good."

Smirking, I picked the brush back up and placed a hand on her shoulder when she started to get up.

"If it feels good, then I'll keep doing it."

She eased back down and made an appreciative little sound.

"Does Haven House know my Grams is gonna be there for at least a week?"

"Yes," I assured her, "they do."

"Thought so," she said with a sigh. "Sebastian?"

"Yeah, Ace?"

"Why were you at Railhouse that night we met?"

"There was a man who owed us money. His loan was due, and he was late. We were waiting on him. The morons you were hustling at pool worked for him. When we met with them outside, I also took the liberty of getting what they owed you."

She was quiet for a moment. "Why?"

"Why get your money?"

"Yes. Why did you care if they paid me or not?"

That one was easy.

"Because from the moment I'd walked in, you'd had my full attention. I was fascinated with you. I loved watching you laugh, and damn if you didn't have the prettiest blue eyes I'd ever seen."

She turned to look at me, and I stopped brushing.

"Really?"

I grinned. "That can't be so hard for you to believe, Ace. You've looked in a mirror."

She lifted one shoulder in a half shrug. "You're different though, you're, well, older and sexy and rich. I would think you had gorgeous women at your beck and call."

I let my gaze drift over her features. Each one so achingly perfect. "Yeah, I guess I do. But they don't have your fire. They don't entertain me, and they never surprise me. It's not just about beauty—that doesn't last—and honestly, it fades quick when they start to talk. But with you, every word that came out of your mouth had me transfixed. I couldn't get enough."

She licked her lips and ducked her head, hiding the smile on her lips.

"Thank you," she said just above a whisper.

"Why are you thanking me, Ace?"

When she lifted her eyes back to meet mine, the emotion in them struck a chord deep in my soul.

"For making me feel like I'm worth something. That ... that I deserve to be wanted for more than just how I look."

I set the brush down and held out my hand to her. "Come here."

She stood, and I took her hand to pull her onto my lap.

"Baby, you've got a face and body that can stop fucking traffic. But that wasn't why I watched you that night. It was the intelligence shining in those eyes of yours. You were crafty and cunning and damn adorable, all at the same time. I couldn't look away. Anyone who doesn't see all that, who doesn't cherish the beauty of the wildly ingenious, loyal, determined woman that you are, doesn't deserve to know you. I'll also happily ki—uh, cause pain to the bastards who don't treat you the way you deserve."

Her eyes were watery as she looked from my chest to my face. A small smile tugged on her lips. "That was the sweetest, nicest thing anyone had ever said to me … and then you had to threaten to maim and torture."

I ran my hand up her back. "Eh, no one is perfect."

She let out a small giggle, then a full-blown laugh before laying her head back on my shoulder. "I don't expect perfection, just don't hurt anyone for me, okay?"

A little too late for that, but at least I hadn't killed her father.

• THIRTY •

"What is it you need, baby?"

ROYAL

Every day that passed with just me and Sebastian in that cabin, I lost a little more hold on my good sense, and my self-preservation had gone to hell. It was impossible not to fall for a man who said all the things I'd always needed to hear. Slowly, he was healing the damage my father had caused me, growing up. Giving me the belief in myself that I was worth being loved. That I was someone to be proud of, not hidden away and embarrassed, like the way Merce had made me feel.

When Sebastian watched me across the room, even if I wasn't looking at him, I'd feel it, and my heart would start to race. Stopping myself from going to him and curling up in his lap was something I'd just given up on. He didn't seem to mind me doing it; in fact, he seemed to enjoy it as much as I did.

He'd begun reading to me while I sat in his lap. Listening to his deep Southern drawl was my new favorite pastime. Scratch that. It was my second favorite. Sex with Sebastian was my first. That was something else I couldn't get enough of, and thankfully, he seemed to be as needy for me as I was for him.

Our days went by much quicker than I'd expected, and by the fourth day, I was starting to dread the end, although I knew it had to come. I stood at the window, looking out over the vast land outside, while Sebastian brought wood onto the small, covered porch from a shed that was out back. He'd said the thick, dense clouds meant the first snow was coming. He doubted it would be bad, but the electricity often went out, and there was only so much fuel for the generator. He hadn't considered it could snow.

The idea of getting snowed in so we could stay longer was appealing, but then there was Grams. If it wasn't for my worry about her, I'd not ever want to leave. Her memory might be going, but she would remember me and wonder where I had gone. Where Dad had gone.

Sebastian stopped and reached into his back pocket and pulled out a phone. It wasn't his iPhone, but I hadn't realized he had any phone at all. Why had he not told me?

His eyes swung to the house, and I stood there as his gaze locked with mine. The tense stance of his body and the way his jaw was set were signs he was angry. With me? I hadn't done anything but find out he'd not told me he had a phone.

He started toward the house, and I stepped back away from the window, crossing my arms over my chest, hating this feeling. It wasn't a huge deal, but it was something he hadn't told me, which meant he didn't trust me.

The door swung open, and he scanned the area until he found me. Then, he closed the door behind him, shrugging off his coat and taking off his boots, not looking away from me. I couldn't read his body language, but I knew it wasn't what I had gotten used to this week with him.

When he began stalking toward me, I lifted my chin in the only defiance I could muster. "You have a phone."

He stopped, his brows drawing together. "Did you think I wouldn't have some form of communication? It's a burner phone, and I don't use it much, but I need it to check on things. Like your Grams."

Honestly, at some point in the midst of our sex and reading time and me falling in love with him, I hadn't considered he might need or have a phone. I had been living for the next moment I could be close to him. Just admitting it made me feel pathetic.

"You didn't tell me," I pointed out.

He tilted his head to the side, just an inch. "I assumed you knew. What's wrong? It can't be the phone?"

He reached out to brush my hair back, then cupped my cheek, which he did a lot. It made me feel special. I soaked it up like the emotionally hungry female I hadn't known I was. Not until him.

"Who called you just now?" I asked.

The tic in his jaw worried me. Had he gotten bad news? Was it my dad?

"They're closing in on us," he said. "Not sure how much time we have left."

I grabbed his wrist. "Who? The Feds? Are they going to question me?" I felt the panic roll through my body at the thought of being accused of something I'd had nothing to do with.

"No. Not the Feds. The family," he said almost apologetically.

Okay, what? Why were they looking for us?

"I don't understand."

He nodded. "Yeah, I know."

I watched as he ran his hand over his mussed locks. I'd grown fond of burying my hands in it when his mouth was between my legs.

I needed a clear head. Don't think about his hair and sex.

"They were the main reason I took you," he said, snapping me out of my sexual thoughts.

"The family?"

"Yeah. My father—he's not the boss, but he is in charge of the Georgia branch of the family. I, uh, showed some lack of restraint where you were concerned, and with the Dancastles being linked to you and us having to handle the drug trafficking before the Feds did, that wasn't a distraction he'd allow me to have. He was going to order me to stay away from you." He paused. "And I couldn't do that."

My head was swimming. More information that he'd failed to share with me. What else did I not know? Were the Feds even a threat to me?

"You abducted me because of the Mafia. Your dad. Not because I was in danger."

"No—yes—fuck!"

He looked so torn that I almost went to wrap my arms around him to tell him it didn't matter. But I caught myself. It did matter.

"Which is it?" I demanded.

His eyes met mine. "I don't know how much the Feds know about you, but they do know about your and your father's connection to Merce. The Dancastles will use whoever they have to in order to save their asses. But I could have protected you from either of them without ever leaving Georgia. What I couldn't stop was my father taking you from me, and I … I wasn't going to let that happen."

I stared at him. How was I supposed to feel? He had lied—kind of—again. I was here because he hadn't been willing to stay away from me. He wanted me so much that he'd kidnapped me and run off. From the Mafia. From his father.

It wasn't a sane response, but then again, I was that important to him. I'd not been important to Merce, and we'd been together for eight months. Sebastian had defied the Mafia to keep me. There was a lot of warm, gooey, tingly things happening right now that I knew shouldn't be. The lying thing and he had taken me somewhere without my permission.

He had gone to a whole lot of trouble to get me here. Just to …

"This was all because you didn't want to stay away from me?"

His eyes were dark pools, filled with a lurking danger, I knew I should be wary of, possibly run from. But the pleading and … love—those were what trumped everything else. He hadn't told me he loved me with words, but his actions had said it. Didn't they?

"Yes."

One simple word. No other excuses.

"Was it worth it?" I asked, but I really meant, *Was I worth it?*

"Absolutely."

This was not how healthy relationships were built, but then when had I ever witnessed one to know what it looked like? What I did know was that I needed him. I ached to belong to him. To never have to leave his side.

I closed the space between us and went on my tiptoes, grabbing his face and pressing my mouth to his. There was a franticness churning inside me. Fear of what all would change when we left here. His hands closed around my waist, and he picked me up to carry me to the counter and set me down.

My hands went to his shirt, and I started to unbutton it as our tongues tangled together. My urgency became a form of madness. When I got the last button undone, I shoved his shirt off his wide shoulders, and he helped by pulling it free of his arms and dropping it to the ground.

"What is it you need, baby?" he asked, breaking the kiss to pull the sweater I was wearing over my head. "You need my cock? Is that it?"

I nodded, my hands going to his jeans. Off. I wanted it all off.

"Damn, baby," he groaned. "As much as I want to bend you over that table and fuck you, I'm worried about where this is coming from."

I opened his jeans and looked up at him. "What do you mean? I always want you inside me."

He lifted one side of my hips to tug my leggings down, along with my panties, then the other side.

"Yeah, but not normally when we are having a serious conversation," he said, reaching down to take my bottoms down my legs.

"Sebastian, I want you to fuck me. Hard. I want to feel your cum inside me."

His eyes heated as I talked.

"Take off your jeans and fuck me like you're punishing me."

"Fuck," he hissed and shoved his jeans down, then stepped out of them and his boxers. "Come here." His tone was dark and demanding.

He picked me up and put me back on the ground. "Bend over the goddamn table," he said with a gentle shove in that direction.

I had to go up on my tiptoes as I did it, and I spread my legs open the way he liked.

His hand ran over where he had spanked me last night. "I left too many marks. I was too rough." His tone softened.

Not now. I wasn't ready for the sweet. I needed to bind him to me. Try to hold on to what we had here.

"I was bad and deserved it," I told him. "You did what you had to."

His eyes went from my bottom to meet mine.

"You drive me fucking crazy. You know that?" The growl in his voice made me shiver.

"And you make me dripping wet."

"Pretty mouth talking dirty," he said with a shake of his head as he grabbed my hips and sank into me with one firm thrust.

"OH GOD! SEBASTIAN! YES!"

"Fuck, I love this cunt."

The table beneath me shook as he took me savagely. His hands slid around and covered my breasts just enough so that he could feel them bounce. He kissed my shoulder and the center of my back. Even while our bodies slammed forcefully against each other, he was trying to make me feel as if it were more.

"Sebastian." His name tore from my lips on a cry as the emotion built along with the promise of release.

"Is this what you needed, baby?" he asked, still leaving kisses along my spine. "Is that deep enough?"

"Yes," I panted, meeting his thrusts.

"God, I want to bite that ass. Seeing it jiggle."

"Oh!"

His hands left my chest to run over my bottom. "Mine," he said just above a whisper.

I sucked in a breath as he continued to caress my tender flesh.

"Mine." There was a growl when he said it this time.

The world exploded for me, and I pushed back one more time, shaking.

Sebastian's arms wrapped around my waist as he sank into me. "MINE," he snarled, and then his body jerked as he released into me.

It was always at this moment when I felt the closest to him. When we were both vulnerable and locked together.

He had become so important to me in such a short time. I was sure I could forgive him for almost anything.

• THIRTY-ONE •

"All right, little brother. You've gone and gotten territorial."

SEBASTIAN

Holding Royal in my lap felt different tonight. Before, I'd enjoyed it. I'd fucking loved it. Craved it. The urgency to pull her tighter to me, lock her in my arms, find a way to keep her with me was gnawing at me now.

I'd called her mine. I had said it out loud.

And she'd orgasmed.

My arms flexed around her.

I'd thought we had a week, if not more. I should have known they'd find us sooner than that. The person who had called my burner from an unknown number didn't say a word. To those who didn't know better, they'd think it was a wrong number or spam. But I knew. They'd found me. Even if I destroyed the phone, the location had been locked, and it was too late.

"Are you hungry?" I asked Royal.

"Not really," she replied.

After I had taken her over the table, we had eaten sandwiches, then showered together. She asked to come down here and sit. For a while, I'd read to her, but then I had wanted to hold her in silence.

"What are you thinking about?" I asked her, pressing a kiss to her head.

She traced a pattern on my hand, not looking up at me. "What will happen next?"

"You'll stay with me."

Her head tilted back, and our eyes met. "I can't do that. I have Grams to think about."

Haven House was fifteen minutes from Athens and seventeen minutes from Shephard Ranch. I knew her Grams would be better there than at home with Royal, but pushing that on her would be a mistake. She felt responsible for her grandmother and their home. Even if that was something that should have never been placed on her shoulders.

She sat up, her eyes going to the window, and a smile spread across her face. "It's snowing!" she exclaimed before leaving me to rush to the door.

I was behind her immediately to stop her from opening it. I didn't want to deprive her of the joy she seemed to be getting from the snow that had started to fall, but they were coming. I had considered loading her in the Hummer and leaving to some other location today, but I hadn't had time to set it up properly. I wasn't going to take her somewhere without knowing it would be comfortable for her. Not when she was in danger.

"Don't open it," I told her, and she turned to frown at me.

Then, understanding lit her eyes, and she dropped her hand from the doorknob.

"Won't the snow make it hard for them to get to us?"

I'd like to think so. I fucking hoped a damn blizzard came, but I doubted we would be that lucky. It was just October.

"Depends on how close they were when I got the call."

"Oh," she replied, no longer looking happy. "I thought the snow meant we had more time."

I started to say something when the faint sound of a boot stepping onto the porch stopped me.

"Go to the bathroom. Close the door," I whispered in her ear.

Her eyes went wide, and she shook her head.

I grabbed her hand and moved her back, placing her behind me. "Now, Royal," I hissed.

"I'm not leaving you," she replied in a quiet yet firm tone.

Damn stubborn girl.

"Baby, please," I begged, but it was too late for all that.

The doorknob turned, and although it was locked, I knew it was coming open anyway. The loud sound of it being kicked in made Royal grab me as a small scream escaped her. I reached back and placed a hand on her to reassure her that she was safe.

My brother came strolling inside as if he hadn't just broken down the goddamn door. His gaze slowly scanned the place as he took a cigarette from his pocket and stuck it between his teeth, then reached for his lighter.

"Not bad. Cozy. I like it," he said, then lit the cigarette before finally looking at me.

No one was barreling in behind him, but the grip Royal had on my shirt tightened.

"I'd be impressed if I wasn't fucking annoyed," he said, then took a pull from the habit in his mouth before taking it out. "Had to leave Capri. You know how much I hate that."

"Where are the others?" I asked him as I watched him step over the door and move farther into the cabin.

"They're a little behind," he said, sticking the cigarette back in his mouth. "Figured I'd get here first. Help you sort things out."

I looked outside, not sure how behind they were. "I don't need help sorting out anything."

Thatcher glanced briefly at Royal standing behind me. "Looks like you do. The question is, Romeo, is this one different? Or is that sensitive heart of yours doing shit that can get you killed for someone who isn't worth it?"

Royal released my shirt and came around me, her eyes looking up at me, panicking. "Killed?" she asked.

I gently grabbed her by the shoulders. "No one is going to kill me. He's a dick. Don't listen to the things he says."

She was on the verge of fucking tears. I didn't care how damn psycho my brother was; this time, I wasn't backing down from him. He didn't get to come in here and scare her like this.

"Our father might not kill you since you're Mom's favorite, but Blaise Hughes isn't happy. In fact, the boss wants you brought directly to him. You broke orders, little brother. Took information we needed and ran."

Dammit! He needed to shut up. She was about to lose it.

"Thatcher," I warned him, "don't."

The corner of his mouth twitched, and he took another pull before taking the cigarette from his mouth. "If she can't handle something like that, then she's not gonna last long in this world of ours."

I moved her beside me and took a step in his direction. "Shut your goddamn mouth!" I snarled.

"Sebastian," Royal called.

"Jesus, Thatch. You weren't supposed to come in here and pick a fight," Wilder said, and I swung my glare from my brother to him as he walked in, surveying the door on the ground. "Was this necessary?"

Thatcher raised the cigarette back to his mouth and held it between his teeth. "It was locked."

Wilder gave my brother an exasperated look. "So, you smashed it in? You couldn't knock?" He waved a hand at me. "It's Sebastian. Not the drug cartel."

Thatcher smirked, but said nothing.

"Where are the others?" I asked Wilder.

He shot my brother another look before answering, "They won't get here until tomorrow. Weather grounded the plane. We left before alerting them that I'd found your location. It was either that or let Thatch come alone, and I wasn't doing that."

Royal moved closer to my side. I needed to know how much trouble I was in and where things stood with the Dancastle situation, but asking with her already on the verge of a damn panic attack wasn't an option.

I turned to look down at her. "Ace, go upstairs. Stay there. I'm going to step outside and talk to them. I won't be long."

She shook her head, her eyes shifting to Thatcher. "No, I don't trust him." Then, she glanced at Wilder. "Who is that?"

I tucked her hair behind her ear, wishing we were alone. I could make her forget all of this if we were.

"That's Wilder. And Thatcher isn't going to hurt me. I know comes off as demented, but he's my brother."

A frown puckered her brow, and she turned to look at Wilder. "That is Wilder?" she asked, a touch of disbelief in her tone.

I had forgotten for a moment that I'd told her about him. The night she'd seen my tattoo. She had been jealous.

Wilder looked from her to me questioningly.

"I don't get it," she said, then shook her head and turned back to look up at me.

I wanted to laugh out loud, but I didn't. Now was not the time. But, damn, the urge to toss her over my shoulder and go upstairs with her was strong. To hell with these two. I'd close the damn bathroom door and fuck her in there. Until she was screaming my name.

"Since no one else is gonna ask, what the fuck is it she doesn't get?" Thatcher drawled.

I lifted my eyes to look at him, then shifted them to Wilder, unable not to grin. Hell, I wasn't grinning; I was smirking.

"Oakley's choice in men."

Wilder's eyes narrowed, and Thatcher let out a bark of laughter so unlike him that it startled me. My lips stretched wider into a smile as I turned to see my brother actually amused.

"I think he found his Juliet. No fucking wonder he was breaking bones and acting like we were related."

The humor of the moment was sucked out of the room as I shook my head at him. He needed to stop. Now. She couldn't know about that.

His dark eyes still glinted with amusement, but he seemed to understand my silent warning.

"Then, she is worth it to you? Because when we leave here, we have to take you directly to Ocala," Wilder told me.

He didn't elaborate, and I was thankful for that. Royal didn't know what that meant. She had no idea who Blaise Hughes was or the power he held.

I nodded my head. "But she stays with me."

Wilder shook his head. "You can't take her there."

"I'm not leaving her!" I growled, already moving her behind me.

Thatcher let out a low whistle. "All right, little brother. You've gone and gotten territorial. We got it. But she can't go there. You know that. You're already in deep enough shit. What about if we take her to Maeme? No one will get near her there. Not even dear old Dad."

The idea of leaving her, not being there to protect her, made me want to tear down the fucking walls around us. My eyes shifted from the two of them. Royal wrapped herself around my arm, reminding me that she was watching me. If I acted like a crazed maniac, it would scare her.

"He's right. You know he is. Let Thatcher take her to Maeme, and I'll go with you to Ocala."

"I'm going to Ocala," Thatcher told him.

Wilder looked at my brother. "That's not a good idea."

Thatcher took the cigarette from his mouth as his eyes shifted into that lethal gleam that never ended well. "If Sebastian has to go to Ocala, I'm going with him."

Wilder cut his eyes to me, and I saw the uncertainty there. We both knew Thatcher held very little regard for life. He was too detached to react to things normally.

"Thatch, he's got to answer for taking her and running. He broke orders."

Thatcher tilted his head to the side as the room chilled from more than the open door and cold night.

"If the boss wants to see him then he gets a visited from me too." His words were spoken slowly, laced with a threat that no one wanted to push with Thatcher.

I could see Wilder back down as he turned to me.

"He'll have Presley there," Wilder said. "I doubt Levi is even in the house. Don't expect to have blood there to back you up."

Thatcher let out a sinister cackle. Wilder tensed, and the concern in his eyes made it clear that he didn't think this was going to end well.

• THIRTY-TWO •

"The family is just that—family."

ROYAL

The moment the plane leveled out, Sebastian reached over and unbuckled me, then took my hand to pull me over into his lap. The private jet that had been at the airstrip as soon as the snow stopped was larger and more luxurious than the one we'd taken to get here.

I'd hoped we would be snowed in, even if it meant Sebastian's brother would be in the cabin too. Something was not right about him. Sure, he had the same sexy, dark good looks as Sebastian, but there was a sinister way about him. He frightened me, but he seemed protective of Sebastian. *That* I was thankful for.

"You okay?" Sebastian whispered in my ear as he slid his fingers through mine to hold my hand.

I wasn't, but from what I'd gathered from the other two men, he was in trouble because of me. I didn't want to add to his stress. I'd been the cause of enough of it for him.

"Yes," I lied.

The corner of his mouth lifted, but his eyes held a darkness. "For such a talented hustler, Ace, you are a bad liar."

I rolled my eyes, and he tightened his hold on me.

"You're going to be fine. Nothing will happen to you. Except Maeme might feed you too much, but other than that, you're good."

They sure seemed to have a lot of faith in the safety of his grandmother's house. I didn't understand that. Why did they think she'd agree to keep me and not let his dad in? Was she not their dad's mother? Was she their mother's mom? It didn't matter. I wasn't worried about my safety.

"What about you?" I asked as my chest clenched tightly.

They hadn't said much, but I'd picked up that wherever it was Sebastian had to go, it wasn't good.

"Are y'all gonna sit over there and whisper the entire fucking flight?" Thatcher drawled from across the cabin of the plane.

Sebastian's stare hardened as he glared at his brother. "Does it bother you?"

Thatcher picked up a glass of what I assumed was whiskey. "It's verging on nauseating."

"Leave them alone," Wilder told him. "Don't act like you're not worse with Capri."

That was the second time I'd heard Capri mentioned. Was there a female who was actually close to that man? It would be like befriending the Devil. What would a woman who could do that be like?

"I gave you as long as I could. He should thank me for the five days that he got," Thatcher said.

"You gave me five days? What? You think you could have found me sooner?" Sebastian asked with a touch of amusement in his tone, as if that wasn't a possibility.

The corner of Thatcher's lips tugged up just barely as he drank from his glass. "You can't hide from me. Never could."

Sebastian's brows drew together in a frown. "I used no connections to the family. I paid in cash. I covered every fucking base I could to make sure it wasn't easy to find us. I'm still trying to wrap my head around how the hell Wilder figured out my burner phone number. I even bought that in cash myself. It wasn't one of ours."

Thatcher shrugged, looking smug.

"He put a fucking AirTag in the sole of one of your boots," Wilder said. "Didn't tell me about it until this morning. After you bought the burner phone and left, he went inside the place, held a knife to the man's throat, and got the info he needed to trace it."

Sebastian straightened as he narrowed his eyes at his brother. "You what?!"

Thatcher flicked his eyes in my direction, and I sank in closer to Sebastian. The man disturbed me.

"I saw a familiar glint in your eyes when you … walked out of that room, little brother. One that I knew too well. I expected something like this. To protect you from rash decisions, I had to do something."

Even though Thatcher seemed detached and, well, frightening, he did care about Sebastian. At least, it sounded as if he did. There were moments though when I'd seen a bone-chilling look in his eyes that made it hard to believe he cared about anything.

"How did you know which shoes I'd wear?" Sebastian shot back at him, sounding annoyed. "Did you see that in my fucking glint too?"

A faint chuckle came from the man as he continued to sip from his glass.

"I'd check the soles of all your shoes," Wilder replied with a shrug.

Thatcher glanced back at the other man. "And here I thought we were friends."

Wilder cut his eyes at Sebastian and gave him an amused smirk as he shook his head at the comment, as if Thatcher had no friends and they all knew it.

Sebastian held my face in his hands as he gazed down at me with a look that made my knees weak and my heart race. Knowing he was about to walk away and leave me here to go face some man in Florida that Thatcher felt he needed protection from terrified me. I held on to his forearms as I tried to tell him without words all the things I wanted to say and couldn't.

That I loved him. I wanted him to stay with me. Not leave.

"I'll be back as soon as I can," he assured me. "Maeme will keep you occupied, and no one can get to you here. I swear it. Trust me, Ace. I can't stand seeing the fear in those pretty eyes."

He thought I was scared for me. I wasn't worried about my safety. Not anymore. It was him I wanted to wrap up and hide away. He'd obviously made a grave error when he took me and ran.

"You promise you will come back? The way they were talking on the plane ..." I stopped, unable to verbalize it. My throat constricted as my eyes burned.

The thought that something could happen to him ... I couldn't bear that.

He bent his head and pressed a kiss to the corner of my lips. "I swear," he said softly, then went to the other side and did the same. "I'll be fine. Besides, Thatcher is going to be with me."

I wouldn't lie; that did give me a touch of comfort. I might never want to be in the same room as his brother again in this lifetime, but he had one redeeming quality—he loved his brother. It was the only slightly human thing I'd seen in his eyes.

"Wilder said something about a man named Presley and seemed concerned," I said, needing reassurance that whoever that was wouldn't hurt Sebastian.

He nodded. "Yeah, well, Gage Presley isn't someone people want to cross. He's an unhinged son of a bitch. But Thatch is a psychopath. It's an even playing field with the two, I'd wager."

That was the only thing easing my mind.

I'd wanted to go, too, but Sebastian had said I wasn't allowed. Everything had changed for me in the past five days, but it'd felt like more time had passed. Being alone in the cabin had given us time to get to know each other. Everything I'd learned about Sebastian only made me fall more in love with him. I had found even the bad things weren't really so bad, or perhaps my feelings for him just outweighed the rest.

Thatcher walked out of the door behind us and tilted his head toward the driveway, but said nothing as he passed.

He'd bolted from the vehicle the moment we arrived, and I'd not seen him since. I'd assumed he had to go to the bathroom, but he'd been gone too long for that.

"We have to go, Sebastian," a deep voice called from the black Escalade.

It was the man who had picked us up at the airport. His name was King, and he was the main reason my concern had gone to full-blown fear. He was worried. The hard lines and grim expression he'd held the entire ride here made me realize this was a bigger deal than they'd let on.

Sebastian's nostrils flared, and his jaw clenched. "I've got to go," he told me, then pulled me in close for a kiss.

I slid my hands up his chest and clung to the warmth of his body. He groaned as he slowly pulled back, giving me one last look before letting me go and turning to walk away. I stood there, watching him leave down the driveway. The tall, attractive man who stood at the open driver's side shifted his gaze from me to Sebastian before getting inside. King was older than him. He seemed to be closer to Thatcher's and Wilder's age. They were all there in the vehicle with him.

A hand touched my upper arm and squeezed gently. "Come on in. I've got some cupcakes made, and we are gonna open us a bottle of wine," Maeme told me.

I managed a nod but waited until Sebastian glanced back at me before getting inside the back of the SUV with Wilder. Turning, I let Maeme lead me into the house.

It was a lovely home. The type you'd see on a *Southern Living* magazine cover. It fit her. This was exactly the kind of place I'd have expected the classy older woman to live in. My Grams would love it—at least, she would have before. Now, well, it would just depend on the day.

When I stepped inside the house, the inviting scent of vanilla met my nose. It smelled of baking and comfort. A petite blonde woman walked into the foyer, wearing a pink gingham apron. She gave me a soft smile, seeming to understand what I was feeling, although I'd never met her before.

"I thought perhaps brownies would be good too," she said, glancing at Maeme. "They should be done in twenty minutes."

"Brownies are always good," she agreed. "Royal, this is Capri," she informed me. "Capri, this is Royal."

The name caused me to gasp slightly, and I studied her more closely now. She reminded me of a magical pixie or perhaps a Disney princess. This could not be the same woman who was connected to Thatcher. I'd expected tattoos and piercings. Perhaps the same darkness in her eyes. Not ... her.

She stepped forward, looking uncertain but holding a sweet smile. My reaction to her was probably coming off as rude, I realized. Trying to gather myself from the surprise, I returned her smile.

"I'm sorry. I ..." How did I say this? *You're not what I expected? Thatcher is unbalanced, and you look ... breakable?* "You aren't what I was expecting," I said apologetically.

A soft tinkling laugh followed my explanation as her eyes danced with amusement. "Because of Thatcher," she replied.

I nodded. No use in lying about it.

Maeme patted my back. "It befuddled us all. But she's his own bright light in all that darkness he carries. Now, come on then. Let's go eat our weight in sugary goodness and drink until our nerves are eased. Shall we?"

The older woman headed toward the doorway where Capri had appeared.

"It'll be okay," she said.

I looked at the other woman, still reeling from the fact that someone who seemed so doll like and sweet could be in a relationship with Thatcher Shephard.

"Thatcher won't let anything happen to Sebastian," she told me. "If anything, it's me who needs to be worried. He can be ... unpredictable?" She said the last word as if it was a question, not a statement.

"So, you're dating Thatcher?" I asked.

She pressed her lips together, and then a small giggle escaped. "Yes. But I guess it's more than that. We live together."

Wow. She lived with that man.

"He is intense," I said, lacking a better word.

"That's one way to put it," she agreed, grinning at me. "Come on. Maeme will be rounding to come wrangle us again if we don't get in there."

I nodded, then followed her down a wide hallway with pictures of a boy, growing into a young man, covering the walls. He looked very much like King. How odd. Why did she only have photos of King? Was he related to Sebastian too?

"Are these pictures of King?" I asked.

Capri glanced back at me over her shoulder. "Yes. King is her grandson."

Confused, I frowned, trying to work that out in my head.

"You thought she was Sebastian's grandmother," Capri said. "Yeah, that is confusing at first. But Maeme is a Salazar. King's father is her only son. But she's the matriarch around here. You'll learn that there might not be a blood relation between the Shephards, Jones, Salazars, and Kingstons, but the connection they have is much stronger. It's a deep bond that goes back decades. The family is just that—family. Much thicker than any blood I've ever seen."

• THIRTY-THREE

"That's because you don't have a brother."

SEBASTIAN

When Blaise Hughes's eyes lifted from something he had been looking at on his desk, there was a chilling threat in his demeanor that I'd never had directed at me. The green of his eyes seemed to have darkened to match that of his mood.

My father hadn't come. He hadn't even called to speak to me. This was something he didn't want to face. Now that I was here in this room, I understood why.

Gage Presley stood to his right while Huck Kingston was on his left. Huck was Storm's first cousin, but Storm hadn't been sent here with us. In the back-right corner behind me stood Kye Levine, and in the opposite corner was Trev Hughes, Blaise's younger brother.

Wilder had been right. Although my cousin Levi was one of Blaise Hughes's closest friends, he wasn't here. The slight chance that blood relations might play any role on loyalty had been removed. It also didn't escape me that although Gage Presley was in attendance, Blaise had felt the need to have three more of his men surrounding us. All because of my brother.

"Out of Stellan's two sons," Blaise began, leaning back in his chair, "I have to say, you aren't the one I thought would ever disobey an order."

Before Royal, I'd have thought the same.

Gage's hand moved so quickly that I didn't even see it until his Glock was pointed at my brother. My heart slammed against my chest as I turned to see what the hell he had done. We'd just gotten here.

Thatcher held up a cigarette in his hand. "Jesus, Presley. I need a fucking smoke," he drawled with an amused twitch of his lips.

"Then say you're getting a motherfucking cigarette from your pocket before you go reaching back there again," Gage warned him.

"Put the gun away," Blaise said, his jaw firmly set, as if he were dealing with wayward children who bordered on annoying him.

Gage kept his eyes on my brother as he lowered his gun and tucked it back into its holster.

"Are we all aware that I'm gonna need to get my lighter now, or should I make an announcement?" Thatcher asked.

Huck took a step forward, his narrowed eyes directed at my brother, not finding his humor at all funny. Blaise's hand shot up to stop his lead enforcer, but his focus remained on me.

"You're a Shephard," Blaise said. "And that is the only reason you're standing in my office right now instead of being strung up underground. I've beaten and tortured men who did far less than what you've done."

I'd already known this, and the entire trip here, I'd mentally prepared myself for what he might do to me. I hadn't been able to think about it when Royal was with me. She'd pick up on my mood. But once I'd walked away from her, I'd let the reality of what I'd done sink in.

Blaise stood up. "Because of the loyalty that your last name demands, seeing as how Jediah Hughes began this with Charles Shephard by his side, I'm giving you a reprieve." He paused, and his steely gaze locked on me. "But only once. Loyalty is two-sided, Sebastian. You need to remember that."

Wilder let out a sigh beside me, as if this had been his verdict, not mine. I wasn't sure if he had been more worried about me or what Thatcher might have done if Blaise had ordered a punishment my brother wouldn't accept.

A war within the family had never happened. Once, thirty years ago, there had been a disturbance, but Boyd Eagen had been shot between the eyes, along with his two brothers who had sided with him. Blaise's father, Garrett Hughes, hadn't given them a chance to defend their actions, and the Louisiana branch of the family—where the men had come from—didn't react to it. That was the only time in the history of the family there'd been a possible uprising within the ranks.

"Weaknesses get you killed. If you're going to have one, make sure she's worth it," Blaise said. He shifted his gaze over my shoulder toward his brother and nodded at him, then returned his focus to me. "Knowing that I would rip out my own heart and hand it over before I allowed one hair on my wife's head to be harmed, I understand that weakness. However, she's loyal. She's worthy of my devotion and willingness to die for her."

Trev walked up to the desk and handed Blaise an iPad. Blaise took it, and his younger brother returned to his corner of the office.

"You see, every female who becomes a weakness to this family is tested." He glanced back at Gage. "Even after she proves her willingness to give her life to protect me for the sake of my wife and child, I test her. Make sure she is ready to devote her life to not only the man she loves, but also the family he belongs to."

I wanted to speak, assure him that Royal was, but I couldn't. He was talking about love, and we hadn't said that word to each other. At least not out loud. I'd wanted to, even when I knew this infatuation I had for her was more than some passionate word that was used too lightly and too often.

"Ten minutes before you walked into my office," Blaise said, tapping the screen, "I sat and watched this live feed." He held the iPad out to me.

Reaching out for the device, I felt a tightness in my chest. I didn't know what he was going to show me, but a foreboding settled over me. The cool metal touched my fingertips, and I wanted to jerk my hand back, as if it had bitten me. Whatever it was, I knew I didn't want to see it.

My eyes reluctantly dropped to the screen, and my hands tightened at the sight of Merce Dancastle stepping out of a car. He was in the middle of a road; the area around him was dark, and although it could be any country road, I recognized it. I'd driven down it a million times throughout my life.

What was he doing in front of Maeme's house?

I glanced up at Blaise as panic gripped me. This had happened already?

"Look at it," Blaise demanded.

I dropped my eyes back to the iPad.

Royal stepped onto the road and stood there, speaking to Merce. She didn't look like she wanted to be there.

Couldn't he see the way she was shaken up? The fear on her face? Where the fuck was Maeme? Why was Royal outside, near the road, this late? She should be in bed.

I couldn't hear what they were saying. The surveillance feed that far out only showed the picture. Royal was using her hands, talking animatedly, as if she were yelling at him.

Then, she paused. Her hands fell to her sides, and she just stared at him.

What had he said to her?

I could feel my heart slamming against my chest as the iPad trembled in my hands from the fury building inside me.

Merce was on my land. He'd had the fucking balls to come after her there. Where I had promised her she would be safe.

She began walking toward his car, and I froze. Dread pooled in my gut as I stared in horror at her opening the passenger door and climbing inside. The car drove away.

She'd gotten in it, and it had driven off. She'd left. With Merce Dancastle.

I shook my head. There had to be an explanation. She wouldn't have gone to him like that.

"Something is wrong. I don't know what he said to her, but she wouldn't do that. Wilder"—I swung my gaze from the screen to him—"get the sound from this. There has to be a way to do that. She's in danger with that motherfucker. He lied to her, and now, he has her!" My voice was getting louder, I realized, verging on a shout.

The iPad was snatched from my hands, and I turned to my brother, who put it back on Blaise's desk.

"She wouldn't just go outside that late alone. Out to the road," I told Blaise. "I know her. She's scared. She was fucking terrified when I left. For me. If we can get the sound, it'll tell us what happened. How that happened."

"I know how it happened," Blaise replied, cutting me off. "I set her up. She failed."

What the hell did that mean?

I had to get out of here. I had to get to Athens. Find her. I considered running, but I doubted I'd make it to the door without getting shot.

"She didn't fail! She was lied to. He threatened her. I don't know. But there is a reason!" The franticness in my voice didn't come close to matching the clawing inside my chest.

He'd taken her. She'd been taken from me.

"Her father is why she left," Blaise said.

If blood could freeze in the veins, mine just did. I'd assumed he was dead by now.

"I used him. Gave him an out. We'd gotten all we needed out of him. You'd taken one of our key players and run off with her. I could either have the job finished or use him one last time. He did exactly as instructed, and he got to live. The bastard had no problem agreeing to set up his daughter in exchange for his life."

The pounding in my skull was getting louder. Every time I inhaled, my lungs burned like they were going to explode. I didn't want to know what he'd done, but I had to. It was the only way I could save her. If something happened to her, I'd not see another day because they'd put a bullet in my head, but not before I took down everyone who had played a part in this.

"Where is she?" My voice sounded like a strangled growl.

I noticed movement in my peripheral vision, but all I could focus on was Blaise and what he was going to tell me.

"Let's not cause any more drama than there already is," my brother suggested.

I didn't know what was happening around me, nor did I give a fuck.

Blaise held his hand up in Gage's direction, as if to stop him from doing something.

"Royal was given a phone tonight. A replacement for the one you had disposed of. The same number as before. She was told it was so you could reach her if needed before she went to bed.

"Her father called her on that phone and told her the truth. Where he had been, what we—you—had done to him, and said he was going home. He asked her if she wanted to go with him. That he could get her if she did."

Blaise paused, giving me a pointed look.

"That's why she was out at the road. What Merce told her? I don't know. But Vinson was to get Merce Dancastle to be the one waiting on her.

"If she'd walked out there just to see if her father was okay, but not to leave with him, she would have passed. Of course, not going out there at all and staying inside to wait on your return was what I'd hoped for. The fact is, she not only went out there, but her father wasn't there, and she left with Merce Dancastle—who we are now positive is involved in the laced drugs, although his father isn't aware of it.

"Vinson told us she knew about the drugs and Merce's involvement. He said she helped with it, did some drops herself. However, there is no proof, and it's just his word, which means nothing.

"But she did leave Maeme's to go to her father when he called."

There were no words that came to me to defend her. I stood there, saying nothing.

I didn't believe she'd just left me. I had been so sure that she felt something strong. The way she looked at me, there was love shining in her eyes. The sweet way she'd curl up in my lap and her hand would touch my chest. Her soft, contented sighs when I held her.

Was the truth about what had happened to her father — hearing his word without listening to mine—really all it had taken for her to leave me? To just walk away without a word? There had to be something else. I could not accept that the woman who had become the most important person in my life would turn on me so easily.

"Are we done here?" Thatcher asked, sounding so casual. As if the world hadn't just been snatched out from under my feet.

Blaise shifted his gaze to my brother, then to King and Wilder. "The next time you're given an order, obey it. There won't be any more forgiveness for the sake of your lineage."

I couldn't speak. My throat was closed up. I nodded my head once.

"King," Blaise said before we turned to leave.

"Yes, boss?"

"Tell Stellan that unless he's ready to hand the reins to his oldest son, then he will do his job instead of handing it off to Thatcher. Sebastian is under Stellan's authority. It should have been him who accompanied Sebastian today."

King nodded. "Yes, sir."

An amused hum came from my brother's direction. "I do believe my father intends to outlive me to ensure that I never hold that power."

"Your father knows he doesn't get to make that decision. When I'm ready, I'll make the call."

Thatcher put his cigarette out in the ashtray on the table beside him. "You really think that's wise? Come now, Blaise. We've known each other all our lives. I'm"—he paused, then smirked—"the psycho."

The corner of Blaise's lips quirked. "You're an effective weapon with the ability to hide a vulnerability. And I'm not talking about Capri who you can keep safe. The one I am referring to is one you can't keep out of harm's way. In fact, you surprised me today." Blaise sat back in his chair. "We share that flaw except mine isn't a secret. I can't hide mine the way you do."

There was silence for a moment as we all stood there.

"Am I the only one who is lost as fuck?" Gage asked, breaking the silence.

"Then, you should know why it was me who came instead of my father," Thatcher replied.

"Because he would have stood back, no matter what my decision was," Blaise offered.

"Exactly," was Thatcher's response.

"If it wasn't a blatant disregard for my position, I might respect you for it," Blaise said.

Thatcher glanced back at Trev Hughes, then looked at Blaise. "You're right. You can't mask it well at all, boss."

Blaise threw his head back and laughed out loud then waved his hand toward the door. "You can go."

I followed King out of the office as my mind began to spin through every excuse there could be as to why Royal had left with Merce. I needed to hear her voice. Know she was okay.

It wasn't until we were all inside the Escalade that any of us spoke.

King started the ignition, then glanced through the rearview mirror at Thatcher, who had climbed in the back with me. "I do not want to be the one to tell Stellan that shit."

"What? That Blaise wants me to take his place sooner than my father planned or that Blaise is pissed that it was me who came and not him? Both I'd like to be present for."

King shook his head and chuckled. "I wasn't going to say it, but I didn't know what the hell Blaise was talking about in there with your vulnerability."

Thatcher rolled down the window and reached into his pocket for a cigarette. "That's because you don't have a brother," he replied, not glancing my way as he lit up and took a long pull.

I hadn't been confused. I'd known what Blaise was talking about before he made his own comparison with Trev. The fact Thatcher came today ready to protect me hadn't shocked me. He might be a lunatic but he was also my brother.

"It's better you know now," Wilder said, and I shifted my gaze to him. He turned in his seat to look at me. "Before your feelings for her deepened."

I swallowed against the bile in my throat. "She has a reason. I just have to talk to her."

Wilder glanced at King, and I knew they were going to tell me it was a bad idea. That I'd gotten lucky today and I didn't need to test Blaise. They just didn't understand that it was too late. She already owned me.

· THIRTY-FOUR ·

My soul was backing out. Deciding it'd had all it could take.

ROYAL

I stood in the middle of the living room of the guesthouse that Merce had brought me and Grams to. Sebastian's name lit up the screen as the phone rang, and I wanted to throw it against the wall, scream at the top of my lungs, and answer it, all at the same time.

I'd do the latter if everything that Merce had told me weren't perfect puzzle pieces to the things I hadn't understood. The pictures my father had sent me of his battered face and the casts on both his arms also made it impossible for me to cling to the hope that he and Merce had lied to me.

"I have to paint today," Grams said as she walked through the living room, looking around for something.

She'd been so happy to see me, and then she began showing me around as if Haven House were her new house and everyone there were guests. When I had told her it was time to go, she balked at me and said that was impossible. She had a party to host. Thankfully, she forgot about her party and asked me if I knew where little Vin had run off to. I had gotten her to leave by telling her we needed to go pick him up from school.

The front door opened, and my head snapped up from my phone to see Merce walk inside with a bag of food he'd said he was going to get.

He held it up. "As promised. There should be enough until I get back tomorrow. I have an event tonight and can't stay long."

Good. The more I looked at him, the sicker I felt. Of all people for me to have to rely on.

Dad had sent him to get me, and I refused to leave with him. Until he told me that if we didn't go get my Grams, then the mafia would use her to draw me and my dad out. Dad had escaped because Merce had sent some people in to help him. But Dad had to hide out too. We couldn't even go home.

I nodded my head, but said nothing more.

Merce glanced at my Grams, who was still searching for her art class. She made him uncomfortable. Just like when we had been dating.

"Uh, okay," he said, then pushed back open the door. "I'll be back in the morning."

He hurried out, as if I might ask him to stay. The lock clicked in place.

What had I done? This was all my fault. I'd believed Sebastian. Even after he abducted me and told me he was in the Mafia, I trusted him. All because … all because I'd fallen in love with him.

I placed a hand on my stomach when I thought of how Dad had said Sebastian had broken his arms. What kind of sick person could do that? Well, I mean, I could imagine Thatcher doing it, even if his girlfriend had been so sweet and nice to me.

NO! They were all criminals. All of them. Even Maeme.

I had been fooled just to get to Merce and my father.

Sebastian had helped me look for my dad. He'd taken me places, gone with me to look for my father, and he was the one who had taken my dad. God, had I really been so blind?

My phone began to ring again, and anger burned in my chest at his name taunting me. He kept calling. What was he going to say? My father had escaped. Was he supposed to use me now to find my dad, just like he'd come to the pool hall to find me? To charm me and make me think he was interested in me just to get information?

I hit Accept and put the phone to my ear.

"Nothing you say—*nothing*—will ever make what all you lied to me about, everything you did to my family, and how you used me okay," I sneered into the line. "I hate you. Leave me alone. You took my life away from me."

I ended the call and threw the phone on the ground, then covered my face to hide my tears. Grams wouldn't understand.

"Oh dear, you dropped your phone," she said, shuffling over toward me.

She'd fall if she bent over and tried to pick it up.

"I got it, Grams. It's fine. Come to the kitchen. I'll fix you something to eat."

"All right! I'll go get the fine china," she replied happily.

Right now, I wished I could live in that world of hers. Free of the pain that felt as if it was going to eat me alive. Taking all the horror of my reality with it. Leaving me a shell with no remorse.

My phone didn't ring again that evening. No more calls came through. Long after Grams was asleep, I lay there, staring at the ceiling, battling every memory of Sebastian that haunted me. None of it had been real. That hurt more than anything. Even more than the fact that he'd tortured my dad. If nothing else, that was proof my soul was black.

When my dad had told me what had happened to him and where he had been, I'd almost defended Sebastian's actions. Telling myself that he loved me so much that he couldn't handle anyone hurting me. I had truly believed it too.

But that hadn't been the case. Sebastian and the rest of his mafia family hadn't believed my dad was telling the truth, and they broke his bones, sliced his face, broke his ribs, broke his nose, busted out two of his teeth, all because they were trying to get him to talk. Tell them about the Dancastles and some drugs.

It was then that my heart had shattered, and the truth of my reality had set in.

Sebastian Shephard had never loved me. I didn't even know if he liked me. All that sex that I had thought was incredible because of our feelings for each other and our connection—it had been a lie. He'd just fucked a lot of women, and he knew exactly how to use my body to manipulate me into believing his lies. The girl who had never had a man's love. I was the poster child for daddy issues, and he'd seen it and used it against me.

Then, to get rid of me, he and the others had an elaborate tale that he was in trouble and going to face the boss. He had never been in any danger. They'd probably all gotten drunk and laughed at my naivety. How easy it had been for Sebastian to dupe me.

Never again. I would never again trust a soul with my heart.

I tucked the covers under my chin as hot tears rolled down my face. The irony of it all was, even though it hadn't been real to him. It had been to me. He had ruined me. No man would ever compare to what I'd thought we had. That might possibly be the saddest part of this all. I was a broken, pathetic, lost little girl who had handed over her heart on a silver platter.

It was almost noon, and Merce hadn't stopped by with any food, although I had warmed up last night's meal and fed Grams breakfast. I had no appetite, so I could get one more meal out of it for her before I started to get worried. But Merce would come back. He wasn't an early riser. Morning to him was often early afternoon for most.

My phone rang, and I tensed as I glanced down at it, but then I saw my dad's name. I was thankful that Merce had helped him get another phone with his old number. I would need to do the same as soon as I could leave. I didn't want anything that Sebastian and his Mafia lords could trace. Right now though, this was all I had.

"Dad," I said in greeting.

"Royal," he replied, sounding chipper for a man who was as beaten up as he was. "Seems I am in the clear. The Mafia called me and informed me that they no longer needed me. We are free to return home as long as we keep our distance from the Dancastles. I didn't tell them you were with Merce, but they knew. The man I spoke with said you and Grams had until today to get back to our house in order to clear your name. If you stayed with Merce, then they would believe you were helping him."

I sank down onto the sofa behind me. "They aren't mad you escaped?" I asked, no longer believing anything those men said. As much as I wanted to go home, this could be a trap.

"No. Seems I didn't escape. They were done with me and let me go free. The people Merce sent were just my ride."

Frowning, I stared at the wall. That didn't make sense. "Your ride? I thought you were tied up and hung from the ceiling?"

"Yeah, I was all right. But they let me down and untied me. Anyway, it's all over. Merce ain't answering, and I want free of them dirty politicians. Got us in enough trouble already. Has he been there this morning? Reckon you can get an Uber?"

I shook my head, still not sure this was all as up-and-up as he thought it was.

"Where are you?" I asked.

"Back at home, and I can't do a thing with two broken arms. I need you to get on back here."

"Dad, how did you get home?" I demanded.

He could very likely be sitting bait for Sebastian and those men. Nothing they said was the truth.

"They sent someone to fetch me. Brought me here."

"WHO?!" I shouted. Merce had said dad was in the hospital and he'd take me to see him today. Who had taken him from there?

"No reason to break my damn eardrum too," he snapped. "The Mafia. Sent a guy after they called. That's what they did. Now, get an Uber and pick up some food on the way. Ain't nothin' here."

"Dad," I said as calmly as I could. "Last night, you called me, then sent me pictures of your injuries, detailing what all the Mafia had done to you. You called Sebastian by his name, not Amory. You knew who they were, and they'd almost killed you. Now, you are telling me, less than twenty-four hours later, that you believe that they are done with us? You left the hospital with these men. The ones who hurt you with no fear of them hurting you again? This does not make sense!"

It wasn't that I didn't want to go home. It was that I was terrified to trust anyone. And this time, I had Grams to protect.

He sighed heavily into the phone. "Last night, I didn't know they'd let me go. I thought they were gonna come lookin' for me. I thought they'd get to me in the hospital. Kill me this time. But they didn't! They came and got me and brought me home. If they was gonna kill me they would have taken me back to the damn room and finished the job."

I pressed my forefinger and thumb against my temples and rubbed. He wasn't thinking this all through.

"What about me? Did you think of that? I ran off too. Sebastian called me several times yesterday, and I ignored it. What if this is a way to draw me out?"

"It ain't. They said that Sebastian was done with you. He got what he needed. You left and saved them the trouble of having to get rid of you. The man even told me to tell you, uh, somethin' about, *That's the best you can be, little girl—a beautiful little fool.* Or was it, *That's the best thing a girl can* … or … fuck, I can't remember. He said to pass that along, and I did. Whatever. Just get home."

"*That's the best thing a girl can be in this world—a beautiful little fool,*" I whispered, remembering the line from *The Great Gatsby*.

And I'd thought Sebastian couldn't hurt me anymore. He was right. I was a fool.

"Yeah! That sounds about right," he agreed.

I ended the call as Grams walked by, talking about her lemon Bundt cake she'd made for the neighbors. A numbness slowly seeped through me. Nothing seemed important as if I could just sit here and stare at the wall. Let the world pass me by. Forget everything and just exist. Perhaps this was self-preservation, or my soul was backing out. Deciding it'd had all it could take.

THIRTY-FIVE

I'd been fooled by the world's prettiest blue eyes and most magical cunt in the goddamn world.

SEBASTIAN

The door to my set of rooms swung open, and Thatcher strolled inside. His gaze dropped to the bottle of whiskey in my hand, then back to me before he tossed something at me.

A new iPhone dropped in my lap. I didn't reach to pick it up. Instead, I took another drink from the bottle.

Over the past three weeks, I'd found if I drank steadily all day, then I could stay in that balance of not giving a shit. So far, so good.

"Don't smash that one," Thatcher told me. "That's the third phone in three weeks, and I'm done with replacing it."

I shrugged. "Then, stop doing it." Seemed like a reasonable suggestion.

"You need a goddamn phone. Just because you're working on a visit to rehab soon doesn't mean you aren't required to be on call at all times."

I laughed. Yeah, I would be real good at a job. Just point, and I'd shoot.

"How much longer is this shit gonna last?" he asked me.

I tilted my head and pretended to consider this. "I dunno. Perhaps if I keep it up, I'll need shock therapy, and it will fry my brain. Tell me, does that take away memories?"

He gave me an annoyed glance, then headed back for the door. "Sober up. Breeders' Cup is in two days, and with me there, you need to be in your right head here."

"Ah, yes. The Breeders' Cup. How could I forget? I'm surprised you aren't there with Capri now. Didn't she already leave?"

"I had planned to leave with her, but I've got you trying to kill your liver," he replied. "Get sober, or I'll hold your ass in a cold shower and pour coffee down your fucking throat until you are."

I glared at the door after he was gone. Sobering up meant feeling. I didn't want to do that. Every time I tried, it was too much. I couldn't deal with it.

She'd been at Merce's. The tracker on her phone had put her at Merce's. And she hated me. The traitorous little hustler hated me. She'd made me think she felt something. I had believed it. All of it.

Hell, I had given her three days after leaving Merce's and returning home to come find me. Call me. Fuck! Do something. Show me that she gave a fucking shit. But she never called.

I'd been fooled by the world's prettiest blue eyes and most magical cunt in the goddamn world. Her birthday had come and gone. I'd had such big plans for that day. So much I wanted to experience with her. Places to take her. But she didn't want me.

Picking up my phone, I started to slam it against the fireplace and stopped. Not again. It was time I got a grip. Standing up, I stared at the bottle in my other hand, and then I smashed it, letting what was left of the liquor to spray the floor around me.

Stepping over the broken glass, I headed back to my en suite to take a shower.

THIRTY-SIX

"You aren't the first girl to reject him. But you're the first one to wreck him."

ROYAL

Picking up the last of the dishes, I headed back to the kitchen at the all-night diner I was now working at. I couldn't trust Dad to stay home with Grams, so I waited until she went to bed at night before coming in to work until thirty minutes before she woke up. There weren't as many customers as there were during the day, but we did get truckers, and they were normally good about tipping. Tonight, I'd had three, and I there was almost a hundred dollars tucked away in my pocket.

I missed going to classes. I even missed writing all those papers. But seeing as the police had escorted me off the campus the day I returned, that was no longer an option. They'd been tipped off about me. I didn't have to ask by who. I just couldn't understand why Sebastian would still want to hurt me. He'd done a fantastic job of it already. The embarrassment and humiliation—not to mention the trauma of being handcuffed and escorted off the Howison campus—were things he could have skipped.

Rodney had said he couldn't have me coming in and playing pool anymore. He'd been questioned by the cops about it. Seemed Sebastian had made sure to slice me every way he could. Rodney's dad owned the All-Right All-Night Diner Dive just off the interstate, and he'd gotten me a job here.

"Been a good night so far," Linda, the night cook and extra server when needed, said to me with a smile as I entered the kitchen with the dirty dishes.

There were no busboys on the night shifts, so it was a my job to clean the booths and tables when the customers left.

"Yep. Power-bill paying day for me," I said, thankful I'd made enough tonight that I could finally get it paid.

The bell chimed, and Linda's eyebrows shot up. "Another one, and it's almost three. We are popular tonight."

Yeah. Lucky us.

I headed back out to the dining area, but the dark hair and even darker eyes stopped me. A chill ran over my body, and while my mind was screaming, *RUN*, I was glued to the floor.

The only reason Thatcher Shephard would walk into a place like this was because he was looking for someone. That someone being me.

He surveyed the place. "Swanky," he said sarcastically before turning his eyes back to me.

"What do you want?" I asked, trying to sound like I wasn't terrified, but the fact that my voice was just above a whisper didn't really sell that for me.

My reaction amused him, although he never really smiled. It was in his eyes.

"You're gonna need to be nicer if you want good tips. I know making money on the right side of the law is new to you. But I hear there are more rules and etiquette involved."

Was he making jokes? My hands clenched into fists, and I reminded myself this man wasn't sane. Telling him to go to hell was a bad idea. I was pretty sure that was where he'd already escaped from. Satan needed to come retrieve his wayward son.

He held up both hands. "Too soon," he said. "I get it."

When he took a step toward me, I was finally able to move. I almost fell on my butt though, trying to get away from him.

"Easy there ... what was it my brother called you? Oh, yes. Ace."

I glared at him. I hated that name. I hated that memory. I hated that my heart felt like it was being ripped apart all over again at the reminder of what I'd never had.

"Please leave. I've not done anything to you. Or him. Neither has my dad. Just go away."

Thatcher pulled out a stool and sat down on it. "We need to have a chat first," he said.

I glanced back at the kitchen to see if Linda was heading this way. I didn't want to be alone with him, but Linda had three grandkids and a bad hip she needed replaced. She didn't need Thatcher doing anything to her.

"What is it?" I snapped.

There was almost a smirk on his lips, but it faded before it formed. He pulled out a cigarette from his pocket and stuck it between his lips.

"You can't smoke in here," I told him pointing at the sign on the door.

He quirked one eyebrow as he lit the cigarette. "What? Are they afraid it will sully their greasy plastic coated establishment?"

I glared at him saying nothing as he took a long pull. There was no reason to argue with him. He was going to smoke it no matter what the sign or I said.

"I have two questions," he told me. "Answer them truthfully, and I'll walk away. Lie to me and well, it's often a poor choice. I don't like liars."

"I don't like them either," I agreed biting back what I wanted to shout at him. That it was his brother who was the liar. They all were. The whole entire mafia.

Thatcher studied me. His eyes were as frightening as I remembered. That cold, demented glint seemed to always be there.

He stood back up, and I immediately wondered if I could outrun him.

"Interesting," he said.

I began to plan my escape route mentally while he stood there smoking.

"I just need one question answered now," he told me. "What did Merce Dancastle say to you to get you into his car?"

He knew I had gotten in Merce's car. How? Maeme and Capri had been asleep for hours when I snuck out.

"He told me that my Grams was in danger. My father had escaped your dungeon and that y'all would get my Grams next as punishment."

Thatcher inhaled more smoke then replied, "I see."

No, he didn't see anything. None of them did, nor did they care.

"I doubt it." The sarcasm dripping from my tone was a mistake. I hadn't meant to speak my thoughts. It had just come out.

Thatcher's glare held me there. Frozen as the evil just beneath his surface swirled with the constant threat that he may snap at any moment.

"Sebastian waited for you," he said taking the cigarette from his mouth. He looked down at the lit end. "He was fucking convinced you'd call, text, even show up. He swore that you'd explain why you left. He was so damn sure you had a reason for leaving him." Thatcher's emotionless gaze hardened. "You aren't the first girl to reject him. But you're the first one to wreck him."

"Don't!" I warned, no longer caring how dangerous this man was. I would not listen to this. Any of it. "DO not try and make me believe he cared. It wasn't real for him!" I stopped to swallow and take a deep breath. Pain and rage were now battling for first place inside my chest.

"Whatever this is or whatever game you are now playing, just tell me what it is you want from me. Because I know I was a pawn in your plan. I know I was used. And Sebastian made sure I'd never have the faith to trust anyone ever again."

Thatcher scowled, and it was effective at shutting me up. I took a step back.

"I'm not here to convince you that you're wrong. Although you are. I came to find out if you were worthy of Sebastian." He paused. "And honestly, I think he deserves better. You don't seem to know him at all."

Clenching my teeth, I stared back at him. "How could I know him! Everything he said to me was a lie."

Thatcher tilted his head and narrowed his eyes. "Does that help you sleep at night? Believing he *wronged you*?"

I wanted to scream at him to leave but I couldn't be sure he wouldn't kill me and Linda before he did.

"He was willing to face the boss of the Southern Mafia, and take whatever punishment he received, knowing death could be a possibility. All because he was afraid you were going to be taken from him. That, little girl, was never part of our plan. He ignored orders for you." He pointed at his chest. "I was there when he saw the video feed of you getting into Merce's car. I saw the look in his eyes."

I sucked in a breath, wanting to close my ears and scream at him to stop. I couldn't listen to this. I couldn't survive any hope that the man I'd loved was real. That even a small portion of what we'd had in the cabin meant something to him.

"He broke my dad's arms!" I shouted.

Thatcher gave me a disgusted look, as if my words made him ill. "Did you ever think to ask why? Or was the fact that he did it enough for you?" He shook his head. "You're not worthy of him."

I stood there, watching as Thatcher headed for the door. He was leaving.

"Why?" I called out. "Why did he do it?"

Thatcher stopped, not turning around to look at me, and for a moment, I thought he was going to leave without replying.

"When your dad called you a slut, Sebastian broke his nose. When your dad called you a liar about his handprints on your arms, Sebastian broke his arms. When your dad said you knew about the drugs and were involved because you were fucking Merce"—Thatcher looked back at me—"Sebastian wrapped his hands around his throat to shut him up. He could have killed him. But he didn't."

I sucked in a breath. "My dad gets drunk. He calls me names. He doesn't mean it."

"So, you'll defend the man who was meant to protect and take care of you, but has never done that once in your life, but not the man who loved you so goddamn much that he was willing to do anything to keep you safe regardless of his own life."

He shook his head, then walked out the door.

What Sebastian had done wasn't right. I stood there, telling myself that his actions weren't sane or normal.

But …

Thatcher had said Sebastian loved me.

I pressed a hand to my chest at the sharp pang, and my eyes swung back to the door before I broke out into a run. I heard Linda call my name, but I didn't top to answer her. I sprinted outside into the almost-empty parking lot.

A black truck was backing up, but it stopped. I didn't know if he saw me or not—the windows were tinted. I ran toward it. I needed to know.

The window rolled down, and the orange glow from the cigarette in his mouth was the only light.

There were so many questions racing through my head, but only one mattered.

"Does he really love me?" I blurted out.

"He did," Thatcher said with his cigarette clenched in his teeth. "Reckon only you can find out if he still does."

"How?"

He shrugged. "Go see him. Look him in the eyes. Tell him your side of the story and listen to his, like you should have done three weeks ago."

"How do I know he will see me?" I threw up my arms in frustration. "He has gone out of his way to make sure that I'm barely scraping by to pay the bills."

Thatcher took his cigarette out of his mouth. "There you go, assuming shit again. Blaming him for something when you have no goddamn proof. Was he the only one who could have ratted your ass out? If you think Sebastian would have done that to you, then I'm right and you don't fucking deserve him."

He started to roll up the window.

"WAIT! Please. I need to see him to know. Where can I do that?"

Thatcher reached for something, then bent his head slightly before looking back at me and tossing a wadded-up piece of paper out the window. I missed it and turned to run go get it. Once I picked it up, I looked back to see the black truck pulling out and driving away.

Opening up the paper, I smoothed it out. An address, this Saturday's date, and a time were scribbled on the page. Nothing more.

THIRTY-SEVEN

She was jealous. That was good.

SEBASTIAN

This was the first Breeders' Cup I had missed in years. The last time, it had been because I was sick with the flu.

Fall sat in my lap as I stared up at the screen. Hughes Farm had a horse in the next race, but I couldn't bring myself to give a damn.

Since she'd arrived, Fall had been trying to get me to fuck her. The top she'd been wearing was long gone, and she had taken my hand and put it between her legs to show me she was bare under her short skirt.

I played with her cunt to make her happy, but my head wasn't in it. I was too sober. Her hair was too thin, her tits too hard, and she smelled like perfume. Determined to get my attention, she threw her leg over mine to straddle me, leaning closer to rub her nipples in my face.

"You know how much I love fucking with an audience," she told me, then ran the tip of her tongue over her red lips.

I considered it. Maybe if I got the blonde who was with Teller right now and had two at one time. But the image in my head didn't spur my interest either.

"Uh, Sebastian," Wells called out.

I reached up to roll one of Fall's nipples between my fingers, although they weren't the right color either.

"What?" I asked, glancing at him.

He pointed the bottle of beer in his hand toward the door. "I'm gonna guess she's here to see you."

Shifting in my seat so I could see the door, I froze the moment my eyes locked on blue eyes that I couldn't even drink out of my dreams at night.

"Oh, wow," Fall said, rubbing her cunt against my jeans. "She's hot. I'll eat her pussy. You'd like to watch that, wouldn't you?"

Royal stood there, her eyes shifting from me to Fall. The pain in her expression almost had me dumping Fall onto the floor and jumping up, but then I remembered. What she'd done. How she'd left me. Her lies.

She straightened her shoulders, and she lifted her chin slightly as she began walking toward me.

Fucking hell. What was she doing here?

I'd been sober going on forty-two hours now, and she was about to screw it up. Her hips swayed in the jeans she was wearing, and there was a sliver of her smooth, flat stomach showing beneath her long-sleeved crop top. I wouldn't let her see me react to her. She wasn't going to get to know what this did to me. Seeing her. Remembering the girl curled in my lap in the cabin while I read to her. The dirty words coming from that sweet mouth.

NO! She wasn't fucking sweet. She'd played me.

"Sebastian." My name coming from her mouth was torture.

"Don't recall putting you on the guest list," I replied, hating that everything in me wanted to touch her. Hold her. Beg her to tell me why. That she had a reason.

She glanced nervously at Fall, although she was trying to act as if a topless woman wasn't straddling my lap, struggling with holding the fake smile in place.

"Oh, yeah. I, uh … well …" Her eyes did a quick survey of the room. "I didn't know it was a party. I came to talk."

She stopped as Fall placed her hands on my shoulders and let out a moan while she rocked over my cock, which wasn't anywhere near hard enough for the sounds she was making.

There it was again. The slight glimpse of hurt before Royal dropped her eyes to the floor and shook her head.

"Never mind. This isn't …" She stopped whatever she was going to say, then spun around and headed back to the door she'd entered.

"That's a shame. Feels like she was doing it for you. This is the hardest you've been since I got here," Fall purred, too close to my ear.

Grabbing her waist, I lifted her off me, setting her on the floor, and stalked after Royal. She had no fucking right, walking into my stables uninvited after what she'd done. She didn't get to come in here and fuck with my head and just leave. Jerking the door open, I exited the lounge and headed after her perfect, round ass.

"You come on my property, interrupt me getting fucked, and then walk out!" I shouted.

She stopped, but she didn't turn around.

"You came to say something, Royal. Fucking say it. God knows I'm gonna need a bottle of whiskey either way once you leave. So, at least make it worth it."

The searing pain in my chest was almost debilitating. Just having her this close. Knowing that in a few long strides I could touch her. I'd thought she'd already done all the damage to me she could possibly do.

I was wrong.

"I'm sorry. This was a mistake," she replied with a waver in her voice.

"I think you made it clear already what a mistake I was. Did you have to show up and make me look at you again to drive it home?" I asked, taking another step toward her. "It wasn't necessary."

Her shoulders rose and fell as she took a deep breath.

Why was she doing this to me? Did she get off on causing me agony? Was that it? Making me want to rip open my chest and get my fucking heart, soul, whatever it was that she had claimed so thoroughly out of me so I could breathe again.

"I came because …" she said, then turned around to look at me. The trail of tears down her cheeks didn't match the defiant gleam in her eyes. "I came because I thought maybe … maybe it hadn't been fake. Maybe I was wrong and you felt something for me, no matter how small. But I can see you are fine. I …" She shook her head and wiped at her cheeks. "I need to get to work."

She started to turn back around.

Not bolting after her and demanding she say more was almost impossible. But I knew to survive this—to survive her once again—I couldn't be that fool.

"You left me. You got in Merce Dancastle's car and then went to his property." I tossed out that fact, and she stilled.

Even now, looking at her, I wasn't so sure I didn't want to tell her I'd forgive it all. If she'd just let me hold her one more time. How fucking weak was I?

"You lied to me. Helped me look for my father when you knew exactly where he was. You'd broken his nose and arms. You said there were no more lies between us, but there was. What did you expect me to do? Stay and let you explain that?

How was I supposed to trust you?" Her tone wasn't accusatory as she spoke. It wasn't even angry.

Her eyes searched my face, looking for something. What, I didn't know. If I could fucking lie to her right now and deny all that, I would. But I couldn't.

"Yeah, I did. And looking back, I'd do it again. The way he talked about you … I had no control over my actions. Rage. I was full of fucking rage."

She blinked and wiped at a tear that had escaped.

"I waited," I told her. "I was so sure you had a reason for leaving me. That you'd come back and explain. That I'd get something from you that would make you running away make sense."

She threw her hands up in the air. "My father told me what you'd done to him. He said he had to come get me, that I was being used. I went out to talk to him and see it for myself, but Merce showed up. He said you were going to take my Grams and use her as leverage to get my dad back because he'd escaped. YES! I believed them. Both of them. What they told me filled in holes in the things that had happened!"

I shook my head. "See, that's where we are different. Because I stood in the mafia boss's office. A man who could have me killed and no one would do a damn thing about it. And I watched you get in that fucker's car. And although my chest was being cracked the fuck open as you betrayed me, all I could do was defend you. To survive it, I had to believe there was a reason and that you …" I paused, not sure if I could give her this power. To know how I felt. How deeply it went for me.

"I had a rea—"

"That you loved me! I thought you loved me, Royal. You fooled me. I fell for the hustle. I was the fool who saw a pair of pretty blue eyes and lost his goddamn head."

"I did—I DO love you! And it was me who was the fool that got played. You made sure to send word that I was a fool with that stupid quote from *The Great Gatsby*! I got it. It shattered me!" she shouted as tears streamed down her face.

I watched as she gasped for air and wrapped her arms around her chest. Then, she spun around and began to hurry toward the exit.

I broke into a run after her, grabbing her arms and pushing her back against the wall. She couldn't scream those words at me, then fucking walk away. My chest rose and fell hard as I stared down at her. Hating how that face of hers haunted me. How just the thought of her was a daily torment.

"That quote was about me," I said, my voice thick with emotion. "I said to tell you, *It should have said that the worst thing a girl could do in this world was to use her beauty to make a man her little fool.*"

She closed her eyes and inhaled through her nose. Her bottom lip quivered.

I wanted to believe her. I didn't give a fuck what test she'd failed. I'd forgive her anything if she loved me.

"They tested you," I told her. "I didn't know about it. But it's what they do. Your father did as instructed, and you failed."

Her long, wet, spiky lashes outlined her eyes, as she stared up at me. I'd give anything to live the rest of my life in that cabin with her. No one else. Just us.

"Sebastian," Fall's voice called, and I tensed.

That was not what I needed right now. When I turned to look back at her, she placed a hand on her hip.

"When are you going to come back and finish getting me off? You left me with a wet pussy."

Fucking hell.

"I need to go," Royal said as her hands shoved at my chest to get me to move.

I stepped closer, holding her so that she couldn't slip free. My cock found life the moment it touched her body.

"Change of plans. Go find Wells or Teller," I called out, turning my gaze back to Royal.

"You sure you want to do that? The sight of her has your cock so hard; it might bruise my stomach." Royal's tone was icy.

She was jealous. That was good.

"The only time my cock has gotten hard in three weeks is the moment I set eyes on you," I told her.

She licked her lips, and her breathing quickened. "I find that difficult to believe, considering she was straddling you like a cowgirl with her tits in your face when I walked in."

The corner of my lips quirked. "Careful, Ace. You sound jealous."

Her eyebrows shot up. "I told you I love you. Did you think I wouldn't mind watching you with another woman?"

There was a fucking disaster between us. One we had barely started to work through. But I didn't care about any of it. Not if she loved me. I'd accept it all. I'd forgive her for stabbing me in the back if that was the case.

"You love me?" I asked, brushing my thumb over her lips.

"Yes."

"You left me, Ace. You shredded me. Tore my heart out of my chest."

"I didn't know," she said, her hand sliding over my right pec.

Her touch was like the sweetest balm in the world. I closed my eyes and let out a hum of pleasure before looking at her again.

"I thought you were using me."

I bent my head until my lips hovered over hers. "I was. I was using your perfect cunt to reach fucking nirvana every chance I got."

A breathy giggle bubbled out of her, and I slid a hand down to cup her ass, pulling her tighter against me.

"My orders were to use you for information. Make you trust me. Feel something for me. Whatever it took," I admitted to her. "But I don't think I ever got the chance. You became my obsession long before you trusted me."

Her gaze dropped to my mouth, then lifted back to look me in the eyes. "Is that it then? I'm your obsession? It's not love?"

A grin tugged at my lips. "Some might define this as love. But that's a basic word. Entirely overused. What I feel for you is more expansive than that." I brushed a kiss over her lips. "There was no beauty in my life until you. I set out to charm you, and instead, I ended up being completely enchanted."

Royal pressed her lips to mine gently. Every horrible second that I'd endured the past three weeks melted away. She was here, in my arms. Her sweet taste reminding me just how addictive she was. Why my damn soul had shriveled up to die without her.

"I don't want to ever lose you again," she said against my lips. "We tell each other everything. No more secrets."

I pulled back, knowing if I didn't, I'd not remember what I needed to tell her if she kept rubbing against me like that.

"In that case, I need to tell you that I know where your mother lives, her husband's name, where they work, and the fact that you have a ten-year-old half brother."

Her eyes went wide as she stood there, staring up at me. Talking about the woman who had left her while I had her soft and sweet in my arms was the last thing I had wanted to do, but I couldn't chance keeping something like this and her finding out. Losing her was a nightmare I never wanted to relive.

"Why? How?" she asked, confusion in her eyes.

I sighed. "Another thing you should know about the family. We can and do get all backgrounds and details of everyone we deal with. Knowledge is power. I hate that woman for leaving you with that bastard, but if you want to see her, I want you to know I have the information you need."

She dropped her gaze and stayed silent for a moment. I wanted her lips on mine again. Her body pressing against me. Not this torn, confused expression. I fucking hated upsetting her.

Finally, she lifted her eyes to mine. "Not right now. But maybe one day."

I nodded. "You say the word, and I'll make it happen."

She slid her arms around my neck. "I took you from your party."

"You did. But I have no complaints."

"You sure? Looked like you were having fun when I walked in."

I chuckled. "There's my jealous girl."

"Do you want to go back in there? That was a horse race on the screen I saw. Is it one of yours?"

"It is," I told her, pressing a kiss to her neck, then inhaling. God, I'd missed that smell. "And nothing on this earth is going to get me to let go of you. Fuck the damn races."

She laughed softly and arched her neck for me to reach more. "I could go in there with you. I'll sit in your lap. Replace the other girl."

I paused and pulled back to look at her. "Ace, there is no fucking way in hell you're going to take off your top and show these tits to anyone else."

She grinned at me, and I realized she was teasing me. She wasn't serious.

"Is there somewhere we can go so I can sit in your lap, naked?"

I reached down and grabbed her hand in mine, then started toward the stairs.

"I take it, there is?" she said, having to jog to keep up with my long, determined strides.

"I have a bedroom upstairs," I told her, stopping at the bottom step and picking her up so I could get up there faster.

The door opened across from us.

Wells stepped out, shirtless. His gaze went from Royal to me, and then he grinned. "Thank fuck!" he said, then turned around to the room full of people. "I think we just got Sebastian back!" he shouted to the room.

I smirked and headed the rest of the way up the stairs, taking them two at a time with her in my arms. I was getting a second chance, and this time, I'd make sure she never had a reason to doubt me again.

In the darkness of our world, when you found your light, you didn't fucking let it go.

THIRTY-EIGHT

Bring it on, Boss.

ROYAL

I paused outside the restaurant in Little Rock, Arkansas. Sebastian's hand squeezed mine. He was with me. I could do this. Face her. The woman who'd left me at six months old, never looking back. No calls. Not even a birthday card. Nothing.

I hadn't decided to do this because I wanted to know her. It was more of a need for closure. One I'd never had the chance to have. Sebastian hadn't questioned it when I told him that I wanted to meet her. He asked me how, where, when and handled it all. He'd even made the contact with her. I just … I just couldn't do that.

Some hurts were too deep. This was one that had been a part of me all my life. It was like finally looking under the bed to confront the monster hiding there—or at least, that was how I was looking at it.

My dad was currently in prison. When Blaise Hughes had handed over Merce to the Feds and all the proof they needed that he was the one behind the distribution of the laced drugs, Merce had listed everyone who had been involved. Merce's father had been innocent in it all, but his reelection was going to take a hit. The family seemed happy about that and already knew who they intended to take his place. Although I was sure it was Merce who told the college about my sitting in on classes and writing papers for money, along with the illegal gambling ring and the pool hall he hadn't tried to lie and include me in his drug trafficking. He did hand over my dad but there had been plenty proof of his involvement.

Grams was happily back in Haven House with her own suite. I visited her daily. I never had to worry about her well-being when I wasn't there anymore.

"If you change your mind, we leave. Your choice, Ace," Sebastian said beside me.

He'd been wonderful through all this.

I took a deep breath. "I'm ready. This is a door I need to close."

He pressed a kiss to my temple. "Then, let's do this," he agreed.

Let's. Us. I was part of an *us*. I wasn't alone anymore.

He stepped up and opened the door to the restaurant, not letting my hand go. I walked inside, and he stayed close to my side. The warmth from his body was reassuring. I'd not relied on anyone since my Grams had started losing her memory. Now, I wondered how I had ever managed.

After I had told Sebastian I wanted to do this, I had also asked to see the picture he had of her. He had a couple. She had aged well, but she was no longer the younger woman in the only photo I'd seen of her.

Sebastian led me toward the far back right of the dining room, telling the server we were meeting someone when she asked if we would like a table.

I recognized Jill's face from the photos as she stood up slowly. Her eyes were locked on me, and the emotion in her expression almost sent me turning and running out. She didn't get to look at me like that. Like she cared. Like she … she felt something.

Sebastian's hand tightened on mine again, as if he knew what I was thinking. If I left, he'd not question it and handle everything. But he had gone to all this trouble, and I was here. There was no turning back.

When we reached the table, no words came to me. What did I say to her? Why hadn't I thought this out more? Planned this moment in my head?

"Jill," Sebastian said in greeting. "I'm Sebastian Shephard. We spoke on the phone." He turned to me then. "And this is Royal."

The woman who had given birth to me stared at me anxiously. "You're beautiful," she said as a smile broke across her face.

Did I say thank you for that? No. That seemed stupid.

Finally, I pulled myself together and decided to treat her like I would any stranger.

"It's nice to meet you, Jill," I replied.

Sebastian pulled out a seat for me, and I took it as Jill sat back in hers.

"I was surprised when I got the call from, er, Sebastian," she said with a small nod in his direction. "I've wanted to reach out to you, but I was scared that you'd reject me or that I'd cause drama in your life."

Was she serious? Cause drama in my life?

I tensed, and Sebastian released my hand to lay his on my thigh. His calm reassurance helped.

"You lived with my dad. Do you truly think you could have made it any more difficult?" The question came out harsh, but I'd meant it to. She was the monster under my bed after all.

She tensed, and a pained look flashed in her eyes. "I guess … well, I hoped that Maude would make sure you had a good life."

"She did," I replied. "Grams is the best mom a girl could have. But she started forgetting things my senior year of high school. She has full-blown dementia now."

Jill's eyes widened. "Oh no," she whispered. "I didn't know. I'm so sorry. She was the only reason I thought I could stay there. But I was young and selfish. And Vinson made it difficult. I found out later—years later, in fact—that I'd been suffering from postpartum depression. I hadn't known that was a thing or anything about it when I had you. But when I had Alvie, my son, I had a very bad case of it. The doctor diagnosed me and gave me medications to help. I knew then that was what had been wrong with me after you were born. I think … at least, I want to believe that if I had known that, I'd have stayed or taken you with me. No. I know I would have taken you with me. I was just scared that I couldn't be a good mother. It was the postpartum doing that to me. I felt the same way with Alvie."

I sat there, knowing I should respond—or at least that she was waiting for me to. She had a reason for why she had left me. Somehow, that helped. A weight eased inside me that I hadn't realized was there.

"Grams was great. Really. Dad didn't make life easy for her, but she handled him just fine until she couldn't anymore. By then, I was old enough to step in and take over."

The server appeared at our table, and I turned to look at Sebastian.

"What can I get y'all to drink?" she asked as she barely glanced at Jill and me. Her main focus was Sebastian. It was something I had gotten used to with him.

He looked down at me. The concern in his eyes, the understanding, made me want to curl up against him and let him handle all my problems. I wouldn't ever do that, but it was so tempting.

"Lemonade?" he asked me.

I nodded. "Yes, please."

He motioned for Jill to order. The server asked him if she could get anything else for him, and he asked for bread to be brought to the table as he looked at me. When she walked off, I wanted to grin because she was clearly not happy that she hadn't held his attention.

"Can I ask how you two met?"

I turned my gaze back to Jill. There was a soft smile on her face as she watched us.

"I witnessed her hustle two men at a game of pool one night while having a drink. Couldn't take my eyes off her. Then, she made me work for it. Took me stalking her to get her to agree to a date," Sebastian replied with a smirk on his gorgeous face.

Jill's eyebrows shot up, and I wanted to laugh at his summary of how we had begun.

"That's not exactly how it happened," I told her, biting back a laugh.

He slid his hand over my back and leaned closer to me. "Yes, it is. I'm not embarrassed by my instant obsession."

Jill chuckled. "Well, I can understand why he did it. I'm sure you've had boys falling at your feet since puberty. Now, tell me about this *hustling men at pool* thing."

I shrugged. "My best friend, Anya's, soon-to-be brother-in-law owns a pool hall. He used to let me go there, and I'd make some money."

"Hustling men at pool, you mean," she urged.

I nodded. "Yep."

"She's quite the entrepreneur," Sebastian told her. "I've convinced her to come work on my family's ranch with me though. I don't much care for other men flirting with her."

The server returned with our drinks and a basket of bread. Sebastian told her to give us a few more minutes to decide on food and sent her on her way.

Jill picked up her water and took a sip. Other than telling me about the postpartum depression, she hadn't mentioned her son. My half brother. I was curious. I wasn't sure I wanted to meet him yet, but I found I'd like to know about the only sibling I had.

"I'll admit," Jill informed him, "after we spoke on the phone, I googled you. I wanted to know who this man was, calling me about my daughter. It was impressive. The Shephard Ranch, that is. You've won a lot of horse races."

Sebastian took a drink before responding, "Yes. We've been in the business for decades."

She turned her gaze back to me. "And you're not in college."

I wanted to laugh—and not the amused kind either. "No. I'm not. With Grams's dementia and Dad drinking away all our money, it wasn't something that worked for me. Even with the scholarships I received, I couldn't move off and leave Grams."

She winced. If that made her wince, she had no idea about the other ugly truths in my life.

"You had scholarships?" she asked.

"Several. She's fucking brilliant."

I glanced up at Sebastian. The pride in his eyes made my heart flutter. I wasn't brilliant, but the fact that he thought so made me happy.

"I hate that you weren't able to take one of those. That's unfair to you. I'd hoped that Vinson would change with fatherhood. It seems that's not the case."

"He's in prison for drug trafficking," I informed her.

She paled slightly, and I could see she hadn't known that either. I guessed, when she had been googling, she hadn't googled him.

"Oh my God," she breathed. "Where is Maude?"

"She's in a luxury facility that caters to those with dementia and Alzheimer's. The best doctors and nurses on hand daily. Activities to help with her memory or at least make the last years of her life easier. She's only fifteen minutes from where we live, and I see her every day."

Jill's gaze shifted to Sebastian. "And you are the one paying for that?" she asked.

"My family owns the building it is in. I was able to get her in there at an affordable price."

"That's very kind of you."

Sebastian turned to look at me. "It's not kindness. I'd find a way to walk on water if that was what Royal needed me to do."

I loved this man.

"When you called me to set this up, I assumed you were more than casual. This is love then. I mean, I could tell that the moment you walked in the door and I saw you together. I just ... " She paused, and I could tell she was nervous. Unsure. "I had planned on asking you to come stay with us. I have a guest bedroom, and I wanted to get to spend time with you—"

"No," Sebastian interrupted her.

She swung her eyes to him.

"She's staying with me. If she wants to get to know you, that's fine. But"—his jaw clenched as he looked at me—"she's aware I don't respond well when I don't have her close."

Maybe I should get mad at him for taking control and making my decisions for me. But I didn't want to go live in her house. I was grown now. I wasn't a child anymore. She was Jill. The woman who had given birth to me. My mother was Grams. I wasn't looking for a replacement.

"I didn't mean to step on toes," she said.

I shook my head. "You didn't. But I didn't come here today to make that connection. I needed to see you. It was closure for me. I, uh ... I'm not ready for more. Not now. Perhaps in time. I would like to know about Alvie though."

I could see my words had hurt her, but they were the truth. I wasn't ready to just forget that she'd left me and never come back twenty-one years ago. I had forgiven her, I realized. But if she wanted more, it would take me time to move forward with that.

She began to tell me about Alvie, and I listened, asking questions with Sebastian beside me. He stayed quiet, his hand on my thigh. The meal went smoothly, and I found myself relaxed and enjoying the conversation. I knew when I left here today, not only would the monster under my bed be gone for good, but the mark she'd left me with wouldn't haunt me anymore.

There was only one person I couldn't live without in my life. Sebastian was my future. He had become the center of my world. I knew that one day soon I'd be tested again and I looked forward to it. I was going to ace the test with flying colors. *Bring it on, Boss.*

• ABOUT ABBI •

Abbi Glines is a #1 New York Times, USA Today, Wall Street Journal, and International bestselling author of the Rosemary Beach, Sea Breeze, Smoke Series, Vincent Boys, Boys South of the Mason Dixon, and The Field Party Series. She is also author to the Sweet Trilogy and the Black Souls Trilogy. She believes in ghosts and has a habit of asking people if their house is haunted before she goes in it. Her house was built in 1820 and she finally has her own haunted house but they're friendly spirits. She drinks afternoon tea because she wants

Printed in Dunstable, United Kingdom